PUFFI

THE WEATHER WITCH

Clee Manor is all that survives of a village that mysteriously disappeared 400 years ago. Kerry and Joe go there to stay with their Great-Aunt Eleanor, but it's the last place they really want to spend the summer. They even have their hair done in weird styles in the hope that their rather dotty relative will send them back to London.

But they are direct descendants of Megwyn Nashe and from the moment they set foot in the Manor, they begin to realize that they are to play an important part in unravelling the mystery of the village's fate. However, it is only when Kerry and Joe discover the village and come face to face with the Weather Witch herself that they comprehend the enormity of their task and the awesome power they must overcome.

By the author of *The Thought Domain*, this is a marvellously original and exciting novel that is sure to win many fans.

Paul Stewart was born in London. He studied at Lancaster University and completed an MA in Creative Writing under Malcolm Bradbury at the University of East Anglia. He is married and lives in Brighton where he teaches English as a foreign language. This is his second novel.

Also by Paul Stewart

THE THOUGHT DOMAIN

THE
WEATHER
WITCH

Paul Stewart

Illustrated by Jon Riley

PUFFIN BOOKS

PUFFIN BOOKS

Published by the Penguin Group
Penguin Books Ltd, 27 Wrights Lane, London W8 5TZ, England
Penguin Books USA Inc., 375 Hudson Street, New York, New York 10014, USA
Penguin Books Australia Ltd, Ringwood, Victoria, Australia
Penguin Books Canada Ltd, 10 Alcorn Avenue, Toronto, Ontario, Canada M4V 3B2
Penguin Books (NZ) Ltd, 182–190 Wairau Road, Auckland 10, New Zealand

Penguin Books Ltd, Registered Offices: Harmondsworth, Middlesex, England

First published by Viking Kestrel 1989
Published in Puffin Books 1991
3 5 7 9 10 8 6 4

Text copyright © Paul Stewart, 1989
Illustrations copyright © Jon Riley, 1989
All rights reserved

Lines from 'I Know an Old Lady' by Rose Bonne
(music by Alan Mills) reproduced by kind permission
of Southern Music Publishing Co. Ltd
© Copyright 1952 by Peer International (Canada) Limited
© Copyright 1960 by Peer International (Canada) Limited

Printed in England by Clays Ltd, St Ives plc

Except in the United States of America, this book is sold subject
to the condition that it shall not, by way of trade or otherwise, be lent,
re-sold, hired out, or otherwise circulated without the publisher's
prior consent in any form of binding or cover other than that in
which it is published and without a similar condition including this
condition being imposed on the subsequent purchaser

To Jeanne

ONE

'But I don't want to go,' shouted Joe.

'Neither do I,' echoed Kerry.

'And why should we go anyway?' Joe persisted. 'It's not fair.'

'No, it's not fair,' repeated Kerry tearfully.

Their mother looked at them calmly. Her mind was completely made up, and no amount of wheedling, whining or wangling would make her change it again at this late stage. She looked at the obstinate little faces of her son and daughter: why couldn't they see that she was doing it for their own good? She had tried to explain the whole situation as well as possible, but they wouldn't listen. And if they weren't prepared to listen to reason . . .

Susan suddenly found herself shouting out two of those awful sentences which parents use the whole time to put an end to any further dissent: sentences she had sworn she would never use. She knew she wasn't being fair and winced as she heard those same words that, as a child, used to drive *her* mad – coming out of her own mouth! 'You're going away because *I* say so, and I don't want to hear anything else about what is and isn't fair. A lot of things in this world aren't fair. And that's that.'

Kerry looked at Joe and shrugged. She, at least, could tell that her mother was not going to give up on this occasion.

'Couldn't I just stay one more week?' said Joe quietly.

'Aunt Eleanor is expecting you tomorrow evening,' said his mother more evenly now. 'She hasn't got a phone, so I can't alter the arrangements.'

'She hasn't even got a phone!' said Joe, in exasperation, raising his eyes to the ceiling. He too knew that he had been beaten.

'Now, I want the pair of you to go upstairs and get all the stuff you want to take with you ready. Leave it out in piles on the bed and I'll come and help you pack. All right?'

The two children turned round and sullenly made their way up the stairs.

'All right?' she repeated.

'All right!' muttered Joe and Kerry together.

As she heard their doors slam shut Susan Chapman let out a deep sigh. Why couldn't they see that it was just as awful for her having to send them away for the summer holidays?

She looked at the headlines of the local paper again. No, she simply couldn't afford to take the risk. The danger was all too real. CHILDREN IN DRUGS SHOCK! It wasn't even as if she could dismiss the reports as sensationalism: it was happening all around her. Once they'd got over their initial reticence, even colleagues at work had confirmed her worst fears about the access kids had to drugs. Every one of them had a story to tell. The article in the paper outlined how easy it had become for children to get hold of cheap heroin – 'chasing the dragon', the reporter had called it. But it didn't stop there, did it? Glue, lighter fuel, speed, crack: the sheer number of dangers open to a bored teenager made Susan's head reel.

And who was it everyone blamed if a child did fall prey to the stuff? Certainly not the child. Nor the growers or importers, nor the suppliers or even the dealers. No, it was always the parents who had failed. Well, maybe she was over-reacting. Maybe there was no need for alarm. But this was one mother who was not going to allow her children to become just another statistic.

Ideally, she would have liked to take the time off work to be with them for the holiday. But since Mick had walked out there was no way that she could afford such a long break. She sat down in the chair and looked over at the photograph on the television. They were all there, smiling inanely into the camera. They'd still been a real family then. It was difficult not to let yourself become bitter, she thought.

'Mum, where're my trunks?' Joe shouted down.

'Where you last put them,' she called back automatically.

'Oh, Mum!' she heard Joe calling out, irritated by her unhelpful response.

'Damn,' she thought to herself. 'I'm becoming a real old misery.'

'Check at the back of the airing cupboard, love,' she called out. 'If they're not there, I'll come up and have a look with you.'

Still, she thought, if the children had to go somewhere, they could do a lot worse than visiting Aunt Eleanor. She thought back fondly to her own childhood holidays spent in the rambling old house on the lake. Eleanor was her father's sister and so was Joe and Kerry's great-aunt.

It was funny to think of her as old. By comparison with Susan's parents, Eleanor had always seemed so young and adventurous. When she was a teenager, Susan had felt precociously old and wise, and it had been Aunt Eleanor who had stood up for her choice of boyfriends, supported her decision to decorate her hair with flowers and bells and reminded her parents what a mess their generation had made of things. And now Aunt Eleanor was coming to the rescue again, coming, this time, to help *her* children, who now seemed to be suffering from all the problems that Susan's generation had caused in the first place. It seemed as though you couldn't win.

'They're not there, Mum,' called Joe.

'OK,' she said. 'I'm coming.'

'Don't you think you're a bit old for Mr Simpkins?' asked Susan.

'But he always goes where I go,' said Kerry miserably. Susan didn't press the point. She'd noticed that since Mick had walked out, Kerry had taken to sleeping with her old teddy bear all over again.

She looked at her daughter: twelve years old and sometimes she seemed so old already. She'd already caught Kerry experimenting with make-up. In fact, she applied it a lot more professionally than her mother. And there were already knowing sniggers and winks whenever the subject of boyfriends came

3

up. They didn't stay young for very long, did they? And yet here Kerry was insisting on taking her comfortingly tatty old bear with her.

'OK,' said Susan, as she pushed Mr Simpkins into one of the side pockets of the rucksack.

'And you, Joe, are you nearly finished?'

'Almost,' said Joe.

'What's that you've got there?' she asked, seeing him slip something red down the side of the bag.

'Nothing,' he said guiltily.

'What do you mean, "nothing"? I saw something,' she said. 'Show me.'

Joe pulled out the object from his bag and handed it to his mother.

'A Swiss Army knife,' she said. 'Where did you get that from?'

'Dad gave it to me,' he said.

'What, at the weekend?' she asked, interested in their meeting despite herself.

'Yes,' said Joe.

'It's very nice,' she said, pulling open a small blade and a cork-screw.

'Isn't it!' said Joe more enthusiastically now that he could see his mother wasn't going to take it away from him.

'It's got eighteen different blades, and they all do something useful,' he explained. 'And a bottle opener and a corkscrew. And it's even got a little torch thing here . . . Look. It's really great.'

'Well, just make sure you don't cut yourself on it,' she said, 'those blades are sharp. What did Daddy get you, Kerry?'

'New headphones for my Walkman,' said Kerry taking them out of her rucksack to show her mother.

'Lovely, darling,' she said. 'Why didn't you show me before?'

'Dad said not to,' said Joe. 'He didn't know if you'd like it.'

Susan pursed her lips and kept quiet. Of course she didn't like it. He'd walked out, gone off with another woman; she wanted to provide everything for her children now. But the presents were nice. Joe seemed to be quite boisterous enough without being given knives – he was still sporting the remnants of a black eye he refused to talk about – but then presumably he'd asked for one, and it was good of Mick not to have bought Kerry something stereotypically feminine like make-up.

'Of course I like it when Dad buys you presents,' she said finally. 'Promise you won't hide them from me again.'

They both nodded.

'OK, now what's the time?'

'20.53,' said Kerry, reading her digital display.

'Right, well, you can watch *The Dan Dole Show*, and then I think you ought to get a good night's sleep. We've got an early start tomorrow.'

Everything went slightly wrong the following morning. There were no great disasters, but bit by bit the time they had saved by getting up extra early was eaten away. Having to scrape the burned toast took some of the time. Trying to find the telephone directory to ring for a taxi took a little bit more. Kerry seemed to need longer than ever in the bathroom, and Joe spent a good half-hour looking for one of his trainers. And once they were finally all ready and waiting for the taxi to take them to the train station, inevitably it didn't arrive.

'Come on, come on,' said Susan irritably, looking up and down the street for the missing mini-cab. 'Whenever you really need one they don't come,' she said to no one in particular.

Another five minutes passed. She couldn't be late for the office again. They had made enough concessions to her over the last few months, what with the break-up of her marriage and all, and that morning an important client was due: she simply could not let them down.

'Right,' she said. 'I cannot wait any longer. We'll have to go by Tube. Kerry, Joe, pick up your bags, and don't forget your jackets. We're off.'

The rush hour was in full swing — just what she had wanted to avoid — and all three of them had to stand on the train. She glanced at her watch a couple of times. They should just make it. The train was due to leave at 9.03 and as long as she was at work by ten, everything would be fine.

At Baker Street the train seemed to develop a fault in the doors. They would close for a moment; the train would jolt but refuse to move an inch. And then the doors would open again. Four, five times it happened.

'What's the matter with the doors, Mum?' asked Kerry.

'I haven't got a clue,' she snapped. 'I just wish they'd get a move-on.'

She could feel herself becoming increasingly tense, and even when the train did finally get back under way she was convinced that the kids would miss their train, that she'd be late for work, lose the deal and be sacked. And then they'd all end up living off Aunt Eleanor's charity.

The worst happened, of course. They got to Paddington Station with barely five minutes to spare. The sheer volume of commuters made it impossible to hurry down the endless tunnels. And as they emerged into the departure hall the one announcement they hadn't wanted to hear was echoing round the whole station.

'The train leaving from Platform 6 is the 9.03 service to Cardiff, calling at . . .'

'Dammit!' shouted Susan.

'Are we too late, Mum?' asked Kerry.

'Well, you're certainly the quick one this morning,' snapped her mother sarcastically. She realized immediately what she had said and looked down at her daughter's face as it threatened to dissolve into tears. Sometimes she forgot that she was still just a kid — with feelings.

'I'm sorry, angel,' said Susan. 'I've just got a lot on my mind.'

'You don't have to wait,' said Joe.

'But . . .'

'The tickets are still valid,' he said, 'and the next train leaves in an hour.'

'But . . .'

'It's all right. Honest. There's no point you hanging around.'

Susan thought about it. He was right, of course. There was nothing much she could do anyway. And yet she didn't like the idea of leaving them standing around a station on their own. On the other hand, it would mean she could still make the meeting.

'You're sure you know where to change?' she said.

'Reading.'

'You'll have to find out the new time of the connecting train,' she said.

'I know that,' said Joe impatiently. 'This isn't the first time I've travelled on a train.'

'True,' said Susan. 'Well, I'll take you along to the waiting room and you can read your comics and things there.'

'Mum,' said Joe seriously, 'stop fussing.'

'Now, you're going to be meeting Aunt Eleanor a bit late, so apologize nicely to her. And comb your hair before you get off the train,' she said to Joe. 'Kerry, I'm leaving it up to you to make sure that you both look nice when you arrive.'

Joe sniggered.

'What's the matter with you, young man?' asked Susan.

'Nothing, Mum,' he said. 'I'll give my hair a comb if I can.'

Kerry giggled as well.

'Good grief, it's like talking to a couple of half-wits sometimes,' she said. 'Look, I really must be going. I'll write to you this evening.'

'We'll write too,' said Kerry.

'And be good!'

'We will,' said Kerry.

'Bye-bye then,' said Susan.

'See you,' her two children replied.

*

Joe got up from the bench and watched his mother rush off into the crowds of people and disappear down an escalator which led back to the Tube line.

'I thought she'd never go!' he said.

'It worked out even better than we thought,' said Kerry, with a grin. 'Did you bring the dye?'

''Course I did,' said Joe. 'I thought that was what she'd seen last night when she asked me about the knife.' He reached into the side of his bag and pulled out a couple of sachets of Crazy Color.

'Here you go: Shocking Pink and True Blue. All yours.'

'Did you notice a hairdresser's as we came in?' asked Kerry.

'I did,' said Joe. 'Or rather I saw a barber's, but there may be a problem. I don't know if they'll allow you in. The entrance seemed to be down with the Gents.'

'Oh, what?' said Kerry. 'Well, why don't you nip down and see?'

'OK, then. You wait here a minute.'

It was an old-style barber's shop with big leather chairs and green marbled lino on the floor. An assortment of magazines were strewn across the low table near the low benches where people waited for their turn. Apart from the barber himself – a middle-aged man wearing a maroon nylon coat – the place was completely empty.

'Morning,' he said.

'Hello,' said Joe.

'Haircut, is it?' said the barber, in a strong Welsh accent.

'Yes,' said Joe, 'but not just for me. Can you do a girl's hair as well?'

He looked round. 'Well, it's a bit of a problem, isn't it?' he said.

'Oh, go on,' said Joe. 'There's nobody about and it's really important.'

The man looked at Joe's earnest face for one of those never-ending moments.

'OK,' he said, finally. 'Go up and get her then.'

'Thanks a lot,' said Joe, rushing out of the shop and up the stairs.

'He's said it's OK,' he said to his sister. 'Come on.'

'You can do mine as well?' said Kerry to the barber as she walked in through the door.

'I can do it *too*. I don't know whether I can do it as well,' he said, and winked at Joe. 'I think we'll be all right though, as long as you don't want a perm, and I doubt whether you do.'

'No, I don't,' said Kerry, 'but I do want to put these colours in.'

'Dyes, is it?' said the barber.

'Oh, they're just temporary,' said Kerry. 'They come out in a couple of washes. But I need to have it done and I can't do it on the train.'

'Well,' said the barber. 'As I'm not exactly rushed off my feet at the moment, I suppose I can.'

Joe breathed a sigh of relief.

'Come on, then, young lady,' he said. 'Sit yourself up here and I'll see what I can do. You want it cutting as well, I take it.'

'Oh, yes,' said Kerry. 'Erm . . . I want this bit left, and this bit made sort of spiky and the side bits really short, like that. And then the blue bit here. And the pink bit there.'

'Uh huh,' said the barber. 'Going to a fancy-dress party, are you?'

'Sort of,' said Kerry.

Joe flicked through an old copy of the *TV Times* as the barber set to work, the sound of the scissors interrupted only by Kerry's continual instructions.

'Just a little bit more off there, but you can leave that.'

'Right,' said the barber finally. 'If madam is happy with that, I think we can move on. Head forward, over the sink. That's it. Now you want the blue here, right? And the pink like this?'

9

'Yes,' said Kerry. 'Yeah, that's fine.'

He knotted up the two bunches of hair and wrapped a blue towel around her head.

'Right, well, we can leave you for a few minutes while we see to your . . . boyfriend?'

'Brother,' said Kerry, pulling a face.

'Brother, is it?' said the barber. 'Come on then, son. Now what can I do for you?'

Joe looked at himself in the mirror. It was true what all his aunts and uncles said: he did look like his dad – and it was that fact that had decided him how to annoy Great-Aunt Eleanor the most. He'd seen loads of photos of Mick when he was about seventeen or eighteen looking a real yob. Mick Chapman, football fan: terror of the terraces. 'Good grief, you looked awful then,' his mum had said to him as they had gone through their old photo albums.

Awful! thought Joe to himself. Perfect.

He looked up at the list of prices above the mirror. It was still an option, and the cheapest one at that.

'A skinhead,' said Joe.

'A skinhead, is it?' said the barber. 'What number?'

'Number?' repeated Joe.

'Different lengths, you see,' he explained.

'I dunno,' said Joe. 'Very short. And I want a couple of lines on each side cut like a parting, but going right down the back to the bottom.'

A couple of the black kids in his class had had the razored partings put in and Joe thought they looked really good. With luck, Great-Aunt Eleanor would think otherwise.

'Parallel with each other, you mean?' said the barber.

'Yep,' said Joe.

'You're going to the same party then, are you?' he said.

'Sort of,' answered Joe.

The barber plugged in the clippers and set to work. Joe could hear Kerry sniggering.

'You don't look that great,' he reminded her.

'Keep your head still,' said the barber.

And as the barber systematically passed the clippers over his scalp, Joe watched his head shrink as the thick, wavy, fair hair dropped down on to the nylon coverall.

'That should do you,' said the barber at last, switching off the humming clippers. 'You still want the tramlines?'

'Please,' said Joe.

'Right, well, I can't guarantee they're going to be one hundred per cent equal, but I can only try my best.'

He removed the plastic attachment from the clippers and slowly and carefully started to etch the lines in: beginning on the left, he followed the curve around the ears and down to the nape of Joe's neck.

'Now the right side,' he muttered to himself. 'And . . . presto! Go-faster stripes,' he said, with a laugh.

As Kerry had her hair rinsed through and blow-dried, Joe got the tiny bits of hair out of his ears. It felt funny running his hand over the top – all bristly. And, yes, a further look in the mirror confirmed that he did look like Mick had done – though, to be honest, he didn't think it looked all that bad.

As long as Great-Aunt Eleanor didn't like it!

They got to the train just in time.

'Blimey, that was lucky,' said Joe, collapsing into a seat next to the window, 'we nearly missed that one as well.'

An old woman with a tweed coat and silk scarf eyed them with obvious hostility from the seat opposite. This was exactly the reaction Joe and Kerry had wanted, and they looked at one another and grinned.

'Better get my make-up on,' she said, pulling out her cosmetics case from the secret compartment at the bottom of her rucksack. 'I did promise Mum we'd both look nice when we arrived.'

'Yeah,' said Joe. 'Don't let me forget to comb my hair.'

Kerry stroked her brother's head. 'You feel like Mr Simpkins,' she said.

Joe was dreaming of doing the high jump better than anyone else in the school when Kerry brought him back down to earth by shaking his shoulders.

'It's the next stop,' he heard her saying.

'That was quick,' said Joe.

'You've been asleep since Reading,' she said. 'Really boring.'

Kerry gelled her new spiky and colourful hair into place and took her rucksack down from the rack. Joe grinned at the unfamiliar reflection of himself in the mirror. If everything did go as planned, he'd have his mother's anger to face the following day. But it would be worth it.

As the train slowed down at the station, both children leant out of the window to see anyone who might be their Great-Aunt Eleanor. There were only a few people standing there, but the identity of their relative was never for a moment in doubt.

'Wow!' said Joe, looking at his sister. 'She looks weirder than you!'

Great-Aunt Eleanor was dressed in a baggy floral frock which was being pushed out of its natural shape by a tight cotton jacket made up of mauve and orange patches and tied at the middle with a long chiffon scarf. On her feet she was wearing striped blue-and-red socks and a pair of tennis trainers, quite like Joe's own, he noticed with a touch of irritation. Her head was covered with a straw hat, decorated with a bunch of maroon cherries, and in her hand was an almost matching straw basket. Both basket and hat had seen better days: Sellotape and Blu-tac were keeping the two of them together.

'Oh, dear,' said Kerry, as she saw the blotches of badly applied mascara and blusher. 'And what colour is *her* hair meant to be?' The natural blonde-grey had been henna-ed over, and the resulting mish-mash of rusting colours looked infinitely worse than Kerry's attempts to be unacceptable.

The train lurched to a standstill. Both of them wondered briefly whether it wouldn't be better simply to stay on the train, get off at the following stop and take the next train back to London.

But they both knew that it wasn't on. Joe looked at Kerry and shrugged. 'Here goes nothing,' he said.

Any last remaining hopes that this weird, almost crazy-looking old woman was not related to them disappeared the instant they set foot on the platform. With hair, dress and scarf flapping, she came rushing towards them, arms open wide.

'Kerry and Joe. How wonderful to see you both, my lovelies. Wonderful, wonderful!'

'We're awfully sorry we're late,' said Kerry, as politely as she could manage. 'We missed our train.'

'Just as well you did,' said Great-Aunt Eleanor. 'I couldn't possibly have made it a moment earlier. Perfect timing, in fact. Come on, then, follow me. I parked the car just in front of . . . Oh dear, where did I park it? It doesn't seem to be . . .'

Joe looked at Kerry and shrugged. Great-Aunt Eleanor stood in the middle of the road, apparently waiting for inspiration to come to her as to where she had parked her car. Finally it did come.

'Next to the greengrocer's, of course,' she said and trotted off, presumably assuming that the children were following her.

The car was (for Joe, inevitably) a lemon-yellow Citroën Diane, plastered with political stickers demanding the 'saving' of this, the 'banning' of that and 'no, thanks' to the other.

'Not the most attractive beast in the world,' said Great-Aunt Eleanor, stroking the car, 'but Glub Dub and I get on so well.'

'Glub Dub?' the children mouthed at each other and started sniggering.

As their great-aunt ground the gears into top and hurtled round the corner, Joe couldn't help wondering whether his mother had made the right decision. Sniffing glue was probably less hazardous to your health than Great-Aunt Eleanor's driving!

It wasn't exactly the first time that the two of them had been in the country: Mick had taken them tobogganing on Box Hill a couple of times in the winter, and one year, when they hadn't been to Spain, they'd had a holiday up on the Norfolk Broads. But this was different. Much wilder than anything they'd seen before in England. In the distance there were steep hills scarred with dark-grey outcrops of rock; thin ribbons of water cascaded down over them. The trees were gnarled and wind-twisted with their knobbly roots exposed.

The car swayed and lurched its way along the narrow roads almost, but not quite, scraping its sides along the mossy dry-stone walls at every bend.

'Green, isn't it?' said Kerry, looking out at the lush meadow-land the walls had divided up into a patchwork of tiny fields.

'Good Lord, my dear,' said Great-Aunt Eleanor, 'you sound just like an American tourist!'

Kerry blushed.

'Well,' said Joe, 'it's certainly quite different from London.'

'Not quite so many cows and sheep there, I imagine,' said Great-Aunt Eleanor.

Joe looked at her. Was the old lady taking the mickey? The wink she gave him confirmed his suspicion.

'Oh, there are the odd couple,' he said, playing along.

'What?' said Kerry.

Joe and Great-Aunt Eleanor both laughed. Kerry, feeling somehow betrayed by her brother, looked back out of the window.

'Hey, a rabbit!' she shouted excitedly a moment later.

'You'll see a lot of rabbits around here,' said Great-Aunt Eleanor. 'And weasels, owls, badgers – otters, if you're lucky.'

'Otters,' said Kerry slowly. Ever since she'd seen a wildlife programme about them on television she'd wanted to see one. 'Do they really live around here?' she said.

'Of course they do, my dear,' said Great-Aunt Eleanor. 'They haven't managed to kill off *all* of the animals just yet,' she said, adding under her breath that it was hardly for the want of trying. 'I live next to a lake, you see, and they come down the nearby stream and splash around in the water at the bottom of my garden. Delightful little creatures.'

'I can't wait to see them,' said Kerry.

It was Joe's turn to feel a bit betrayed now. Hadn't they both decided what they wanted to do that summer? The plan was to get back to London, not go on some nature ramble.

'I've got a boat, as well, so if there weren't any near the house, you could go out exploring on the lake. Can you row, Joe?' she asked.

'I've tried it a couple of times,' he said as nonchalantly as he could.

'Those paddle-boats are hardly rowing,' said Kerry patronizingly.

Joe glared at her.

'Well, you can try the real thing here,' said Great-Aunt Eleanor, ignoring Kerry's taunts. 'You look stocky enough — you'll love it.'

He felt his defences slipping again. There was something about the old girl that kept making him drop his guard. *London*, he reminded himself again. And yet, he had to admit to himself, the idea of going out on a lake on his own in a boat did appeal. Perhaps he could try it just once before heading back.

'Almost there,' said Great-Aunt Eleanor.

Joe and Kerry looked outside. Where? they both wondered. There was nothing to be seen: nothing except for more fields, walls and sheep.

Suddenly, pulling the steering-wheel sharply to the left, Eleanor turned down a tiny track they hadn't even noticed before.

'Blimey, I thought we were going to hit the wall,' said Joe.

'Oh, ye of little faith,' said Great-Aunt Eleanor. 'Soon be at our destination and you can both go and have a nice hot bath.'

'It smells funny,' said Kerry.

'Probably the silos,' said Great-Aunt Eleanor. 'Sort of fishy, isn't it? I think it's the sugar-beet that they store for the animals.'

'It's horrible,' said Joe.

'A couple of days here and you won't even notice it,' said Great-Aunt Eleanor.

Joe looked at Kerry. There was something curiously sharp and alert beneath their great-aunt's scatty exterior. She seemed to be quite unrufflable – unlike their parents, who were always getting angry about something or other. Perhaps it was what came of living out in the country. They were crawling downhill now with the car in first gear and, as they rounded a long bend, the view over the wall suddenly opened up.

'Wow!' said Joe, despite himself.

Below them was a wide, silver lake stretching away into the distance. Pines and beech trees surrounded it, and down at the water's edge rushes and irises were growing. Great-Aunt Eleanor's house was, as she had said, next to the lake. It was a large, imposing house with a steep roof and tall, brick chimneys which were twisted round like cough candy. The windows were tiny and made up of leaded diamonds of glass: some had been almost obscured by a tall climbing rose, which was a blaze of yellow petals.

'Welcome to Clee Manor,' said Great-Aunt Eleanor, as the car came to a jolting halt.

'It's beautiful,' said Kerry.

'*I* like it,' said Great-Aunt Eleanor. 'And I hope you will too.'

'And that's yours, is it?' said Joe, pointing to a small wooden rowing-boat tied up at the end of the lakeside jetty.

'It is,' said Great-Aunt Eleanor. 'But while you're here, you must treat it as your own. Here we are then,' she said, opening the solid oak door.

'Don't you lock it, then?' said Kerry.

'Oh, no,' said Great-Aunt Eleanor. 'No need for that sort of thing around here.'

As they stepped over the threshold of the house and into the hallway both Joe and Kerry felt a curious, tingling shudder zipping up and down their spines. They stole a quick glance at each other to check that they had both experienced the same eerie sensation.

'Do you think it's haunted?' whispered Kerry.

'No idea,' said Joe, 'but we're certainly going to find out.'

The likelihood of their returning to London was slowly but surely receding, and yet neither Kerry nor Joe was too upset about it. Both of them found themselves weighing up the pros and cons of the situation. To be honest, the prospect of spending the summer with weird (but nice) Great-Aunt Eleanor in her (possibly ghost-ridden) house on the lake (with the boat) was gradually becoming more and more appealing.

TWO

'Anything else, either of you?' asked Great-Aunt Eleanor.

'No thanks,' said Kerry.

'I'm completely full,' said Joe. Which was true but surprising, as the two of them had looked at the spread of food with initial dismay.

'What is it?' Joe had mouthed at Kerry.

Kerry had merely shrugged.

'Right, then, for starters I thought we could all have a nice bowl of lettuce soup with homemade bread,' Great-Aunt Eleanor had answered from over near the cooker, as though she'd got eyes in the back of her head. 'Followed by,' she continued, 'nut cutlets with vegetables straight from the garden and then, to conclude, a trifle of trifle.' And she laughed at her own little joke, oblivious of the eyebrows the two children were raising behind her.

The soup was almost luminous-green in colour and tasted more of mint than of lettuce. Worse than that, it was cold! A spiral of cream decorated the middle. Despite Joe's initial reaction it really wasn't that bad at all.

'And how are the cutlets?' asked Great-Aunt Eleanor, as Kerry bit into her third.

'Lovely,' they both mumbled.

'I'm afraid I'm not a very good vegetarian,' she confessed. 'I love meat, but I found this wonderful recipe book, and all the dishes in it taste so meaty. So now I can walk around the fields without feeling unduly guilty the whole time *and* enjoy my food.'

'You mean this isn't a beefburger?' said Joe, astounded.

'You see!' she said. 'Hard to believe, isn't it?'

'I presume you didn't want to leave London for the summer holidays, did you?' said Great-Aunt Eleanor, totally out of the blue as they were spooning up the last drops of raspberry juice from their bowls of trifle.

Joe felt his newly exposed ears burning with embarrassment. Kerry coughed, spluttered and finally managed to blurt out that, no, of course they had wanted to come and visit her.

'It's just a bit strange not spending the holidays with my mates,' said Joe, not wanting to sound over-enthusiastic about being there. He hadn't one hundred per cent given up the idea of going back to London – just postponed it a little. At least until he'd tried out the boat.

'Oh, it's quite all right, my dears,' said Great-Aunt Eleanor with irritating understanding. 'I can imagine just what you must be missing. I mean, after all, you hardly *look* like a country lad and lass, do you now? I take it you must look fashionable in the city?' she said.

Kerry looked down at her plate, not knowing whether to laugh, keep a straight face or just admit to what the pair of them had had done at the station barber's. Joe felt his ears, face and chest burning redder than ever and rubbed his hand awkwardly around the bristly back of his neck. If only he hadn't had it cut quite so short.

'Please don't think I'm criticizing,' she said. 'Good grief, if I could grow my strawberries the same colour that you two are, I'd win prizes. You should have seen your mother when she was your age: lank, greasy hair all braided up with beads and bells and Heaven knows what else. Fringe permanently over one eye. Oh, and that awful smell of patchouli oil. Made me feel quite sick.'

Both children were laughing at the thought of their mother looking like one of the hippies they had seen on old newsreels.

'In fact, given the choice, I'd take the way you two look any day. Practical and fun!' she said, looking from Joe to Kerry.

The plan to make themselves look so unacceptable that Great-Aunt Eleanor would stick them on the next train back could hardly have proven less successful. If only they had known about the patchouli oil!

'Now why don't you two explore the house for a bit, while I do the washing-up? By the way, you're only escaping the drying-up this evening as it's your first day here. And I'll tell you all about the house, the lake, the boat, oh, and a horse you might be able to ride and how to get to the nearest village – they have a cinema night on Tuesdays.'

The two children looked at each other.

'No, I suppose that can't sound particularly impressive, can it? Anyway, any questions you have, I'll try and answer.'

'Where shall we start?' said Kerry.

'The cellars,' said Joe, 'and we can work upwards.'

The flights of stairs to the cellars were all in short sections, split up by large landings. The banisters were dark and worn smooth by the hands of generations of people going up and down. At the bottom they had to go through a small door and, having switched on the very welcome light, went down a final, uncarpeted flight.

'I think it's spooky,' said Kerry.

'You would,' said Joe, glad that she had been the one to express her unease first. For the second time since they had entered the house they had felt the shivers up and down their spines.

The cellars were made up of several alcoves which nestled under the arched foundation walls of the house. A few of them had been sectioned off into individual rooms by the addition of slatted partitions with doors in them. There were wine racks and sacks, old barrels and bottles, crates and boxes, all piled up in complete disorder. And everything was covered with a thick layer of dust and cobwebs. Joe thought he heard something scurry across the floor but kept his mouth shut: he didn't want his sister to start making fun of him.

'What was that?' said Kerry in a nervous whisper.

'Your imagination,' said Joe, unfairly.

'Well,' said Kerry, 'I think I've seen enough. You can stay down here as long as you want – on your own.'

'Oh, I think we may as well go and check out the rest of the house,' said Joe as coolly as possible.

As they closed the cellar door they noticed that it was the middle one of three identical doors set into the wall. Rather disappointingly, they found that both of the other two led into walk-in cupboards. The first one was full of shelves of bottled fruits, massive tins of tea and coffee beans, and a year's supply of soap, disinfectant, bleach and the like in boxes on the floor. The second one, in complete contrast, was totally empty.

'Strange,' said Joe.

If the back of the cupboard had been properly closed, they would never have seen the chink of light coming through. Perhaps Great-Aunt Eleanor had done it deliberately, just to keep their interest in the place.

'Try pulling on that hook,' suggested Kerry.

Joe did so, and the whole of the back wall of the cupboard swung open to reveal yet another short flight of stairs. It took them up to a half-level between the ground floor and the first floor. The room there was crammed full of musical instruments. There were two pianos, a harmonium and a drum kit around the walls. In the centre of the room were three chairs with cases lying on them.

'There's a flute in this one,' said Kerry.

'And here's a violin,' said Joe. 'And what's this?'

'An oboe, I think,' said Kerry. 'And look at all the music there,' she said.

Over by the harmonium were stacks and stacks of sheet music, all yellowed and well-thumbed. Kerry picked out a short piece by Schubert, put it on the piano and made an attempt to sight-read the tune.

''Orrible!' said Joe, making a bee-line for the drum kit.

'I wish I hadn't given up,' said Kerry, ignoring her brother and continuing to bash out the tune in fits and starts.

Joe also started to bash something out, thumping the bass

beat with the pedal drum and doing a series of rolls and cymbal crashes with the sticks.

'Uh huh, and that doesn't sound horrible at all,' said Kerry.

'Joe. Kerry. Come along now,' they heard Great-Aunt Eleanor calling. 'I'm in the lounge. Come and have a cup of drinking chocolate.'

'Blast,' said Joe, under his breath. 'I was really getting into that.'

'You've got all the time in the world to play with the drums, Joe,' he heard his aunt calling back. He found her apparent ability to read minds quite unnerving.

'Coming,' they both called back.

Returning to the door they'd come through, they found that it was concealed by a large mirror with a heavy gold frame.

'Clever,' said Joe, tugging at it.

'I wonder how many other secret rooms there are in the house,' said Kerry.

'So you found the music room, I take it,' said Great-Aunt Eleanor. 'How much else did you discover?'

'Not that much,' said Kerry. 'We went down to the cellars.'

'Mm-hmm,' said Great-Aunt Eleanor, nodding. Joe had the feeling that she was sounding them out.

'What's that smell?' said Joe, changing the subject. 'Sort of like burning.'

'Oh, that's nothing,' said Great-Aunt Eleanor. 'I just let the milk boil over. I'm always doing that. I put it on, then forget about it . . .' Her voice trailed off. 'And you didn't see anything else of interest?' she persisted.

'No,' said Joe, who had decided to go back and explore the cellar at the earliest possible opportunity.

'It is a beautiful old house,' said Great-Aunt Eleanor, after a while. 'A beautiful house and *so* full of history. It was built back in 1559, the year Good Queen Bess had her coronation. In fact, I did hear that the foundation stone was laid on exactly the same day — though as that was a Sunday, I'm not too sure about it.'

As she spoke the words, both Kerry and Joe had the distinct impression that the house itself was objecting to her scepticism. It seemed to creak with irritation. Daft as it sounded, ever since they had entered the house they had both felt they were being watched, and the moment Great-Aunt Eleanor had cast aspersions on the authenticity of one of the traditions of the house, whatever was observing them had reacted negatively. Kerry shuddered involuntarily.

'Yes, it gets chilly, doesn't it, even in the middle of summer?' said Great-Aunt Eleanor. 'Where was I?'

'The foundation stone,' said Joe.

'Ah, yes,' said Great-Aunt Eleanor. 'Well, whenever the stone was laid, what is certain is that the family that built it was the most important family in the area.'

'Are any of them still here?' asked Kerry.

'Well, just the one with the same name now,' said Great-Aunt Eleanor with a smile. 'But there are a couple of others who are directly descended.'

Kerry twigged. 'Was it the Nashe family?' she asked.

'It most certainly was,' said Great-Aunt Eleanor.

'That's Mum's maiden name, isn't it?' said Joe.

'Oh, Brain of Britain,' said Kerry scathingly.

'Shut up,' said Joe, irritated with himself for being so slow. 'And you're Eleanor Nashe,' he said to Great-Aunt Eleanor to try and score a point for himself.

'The very same,' she said. 'Don't let your chocolate get cold,' she added.

Kerry and Joe sipped at their mugs as Great-Aunt Eleanor took a deep breath and began her story about the house. Outside the wind was getting up, and the leaves were rustling like a running stream. Some small animal screeched as an owl swooped and sank its talons deep into its back. A couple of wading birds called to each other across the lake. But in the large, dark sitting-room the two children were oblivious to any sounds other than the hushed voice of their great-aunt.

'All I can tell you is all I know,' she said, her bright, animated eyes darting from one to the other. Kerry and Joe stared back at her, mesmerized by her almost supernatural calm. And as they stared, any annoyance they might have felt about being told a stupid fairy-tale drained away.

Great-Aunt Eleanor swept away a strand of her multi-coloured hair with a bony finger and pulled her shawl tighter around her shoulders. Both Kerry and Joe waited, motionless, spellbound, as the old lady prepared to tell her tale. Kerry felt tingles at the nape of her neck that took her back to her primary school when she had been told stories. Friday afternoon meant story-hour, and that had always been her favourite. She suddenly became all self-conscious, a twelve-year-old getting all excited about a fairy-tale like some infant waiting for *Jackanory*, and glanced round at her brother to make sure he wasn't sneering at her interest. But he looked even more enthralled than she did, with his mouth slightly open as he waited for the story to begin.

'Well,' began Great-Aunt Eleanor, 'I can tell that the pair of you are extremely worldly children, and I wouldn't want to insult your intelligence with a load of old nonsense. But,' she said with a sigh, 'as your mother has evidently not told you the tale I told her – a tale which was told to me by my mother and told to her by her mother and so on, back for twenty-one generations – it would seem that it falls to me to repeat the legend before it is lost for ever.'

'Why didn't she tell us?' said Kerry.

'Oh, you know what she's like,' said Joe. 'She probably forgot.'

'Yes, my dears. I'm afraid you're probably right. Either that or she thought it was too silly to bother with.'

Kerry and Joe waited as Great-Aunt Eleanor gazed intently into mid-air.

'Oh, perhaps it *is*,' she said finally.

'Is what?' they both asked together.

'Too silly to bother with,' said Great-Aunt Eleanor.

But by this time the two children had been won over, and there was no way they were going to let their great-aunt get away with not telling her tale.

'Oh, no, come on. Tell us,' said Joe.

'We want to hear the story,' said Kerry.

Great-Aunt Eleanor looked at them and smiled.

'All right,' she said, raising her finger to quieten them down. 'Well, it all started a long, long time ago. I haven't been able to find out exactly when the Nashe family first moved to this area but the earliest record I've found was dated 1313.'

'Coo, that sounds like an unlucky year,' said Joe.

'It does, doesn't it?' said Great-Aunt Eleanor. 'And yet the family were extremely happy, and the village of Cleedale that they established was meant to be the happiest, prettiest, wealthiest place in the whole of Europe. The inhabitants were all the best of whatever they became.'

'What do you mean?' said Kerry.

'Well, there were farmers, of course, and they were the best in the country. Their fruit and vegetables, butter and cheese, pork and beef became the talk of the town in London; in fact, stamped on the side of a barrel or box the word Cleedale became synonymous with high quality. Then there were the sculptors – from their humble beginnings, working on the local church, they became world-renowned, travelling all over Europe. And there were musicians and painters, lace-makers and lute-makers, weavers and tailors. Whatever profession the people of Cleedale took up, they soon rose to the very top.'

'It sounds lovely,' said Kerry.

The house itself seemed to approve of the story being related, and both children felt themselves being bathed in a warm, cosy glow.

'Oh, it was meant to be a little paradise,' said Great-Aunt

Eleanor. 'But, of course, the remarkable success of the village didn't go unnoticed, drawing negative as well as positive reactions from outsiders. They became jealous and started to spread malicious rumours.'

'What sort of rumours?' asked Joe.

'Well, you must remember that people were extremely superstitious in those days,' said Great-Aunt Eleanor ominously. 'The village was, according to all the records, ringed with a field of wild clover. And not just ordinary clover, but the four-leafed variety.'

'That's meant to be lucky, isn't it?' said Kerry.

'Very much so,' said Great-Aunt Eleanor. 'In fact, it was the clover which gave the village its name. "Dale" comes from the old word meaning "valley", and "clee" is the Old Saxon word for "clover". So originally it used to mean "Valley of Clover". But I digress,' she said. 'The thing is that people from outside the village knew all about the ring of clover and the phenomenal luck of the people who lived in Cleedale, and they started to maintain that the villagers were in league with the Devil, that they held pagan rites and sacrifices, and that the whole of the village ought to be razed to the ground.'

'Typical,' said Joe, with an involuntary shudder as an icy draught passed through the room. 'As soon as you've got something that someone else hasn't, they try to make trouble.'

'Precisely,' said Great-Aunt Eleanor quietly.

'So what *did* they do?' said Kerry.

Great-Aunt Eleanor sighed. 'Well, this is the tragic part, I suppose,' she said. 'In retrospect, the best thing the villagers could have done was to try to conceal their excellence, to become a little more modest about their successes. But they did the opposite. The more the outside world criticized them, the more they scorned anyone *not* from Cleedale. The more hideous the rumours that began to circulate were, the more shameless the behaviour of the villagers became. The more people demanded that they learn a little humility, the more brazenly they sang their own praises. In short, the more threatened they felt, the more arrogant they became.'

'But the village wasn't destroyed?' said Kerry.

'No,' said Great-Aunt Eleanor. 'Or at least not then. So many of the men of Cleedale had attained high positions in the royal court that there were always enough influential people around the Queen to speak up for Cleedale and against its enemies. Until 1589, that is,' she said darkly. And once again a cold blast chilled the room.

'Fifteen eighty-nine?' said Joe. 'That's four hundred years ago.'

'Four hundred years and twenty-one generations,' said Great-Aunt Eleanor dreamily.

'What happened then?' said Kerry.

'That was the year in which the beautiful village of Cleedale came to an end,' said Great-Aunt Eleanor.

There was a sudden loud bang as one of the downstairs doors slammed shut angrily. Both Joe and Kerry jumped and then gave a nervous little giggle as they realized what had startled them.

'Just the wind,' said Great-Aunt Eleanor. But neither of the two children was so sure. They both found themselves looking nervously up at the giant, tarnished mirror above the mantelpiece. Both of them had the strangest feeling that someone or something was on the other side of the mirror watching their every move.

'It was a strange time historically,' said Great-Aunt Eleanor. 'Have you done anything about it at school?'

'I think so,' said Joe, racking his brains to remember all he could about the Tudors and Stuarts. 'Henry VIII and his six wives, Bloody Mary, Sir Francis Drake and the Armada, and the Gunpowder Plot against James I,' he rattled off.

Kerry had to admit she was impressed. Her brother always acted like such a lazy slob at school, and yet something had evidently sunk in.

'Yes, that's the type of thing,' said Great-Aunt Eleanor. 'But you know what the reason was for all the twists and turns in the fates and fortunes of the people of Merrie England? Religion. From the time of Henry the people had been instructed by the Crown to become Protestants one day, Catholics the next. And it was finally this, coupled with the villagers' conceited feeling of invulnerability, that brought about the downfall of Cleedale. It found itself right in the middle, trapped in the vice-like grip of the whims of the monarchs. And finally it was crushed out of existence.'

'But why?' said Kerry.

'Well,' said Great-Aunt Eleanor, as the house continued to creak and groan hideously all round them, 'I suppose you could say the people of the village backed the wrong horse. For whatever reason, they thought the Catholics would win. And they were wrong. The village became a famous haven for persecuted priests to hide out in, and when this finally came to light, a furious Queen Elizabeth gave the command for Cleedale to be wiped from the map.'

'So the soldiers came and destroyed the place, did they?' said Joe.

'No,' said Great-Aunt Eleanor, 'and here comes the part of the legend which is the hardest to swallow, where magic or sorcery or the supernatural or divine intervention — call it what you will — took over.'

'Divine intervention,' said Joe scornfully, turning his nose up at the whole idea.

'I'm only telling you the story I was told, young man,' said Great-Aunt Eleanor a little sniffily. 'It's entirely up to you whether you decide to believe it or not.'

Joe looked down at the floor.

'Well, I want to hear it,' said Kerry, 'even if he doesn't.'

'There was an old woman of the village called Megwyn,' she continued matter-of-factly, obviously a bit offended by Joe's show of scepticism. 'Megwyn Nashe: my seventeen-times-great-grandmother. She was supposed to be a witch, and it was

28

she who apparently saved Cleedale from being destroyed. It is said that she used all her power to conjure up a spell so mighty that the village was concealed for ever.'

Great-Aunt Eleanor took a deep breath and leant back in her chair. Both children looked up at her expectantly, but she didn't seem about to continue.

'Where did it go to?' said Kerry finally, fascinated by the idea of a whole village simply disappearing.

'That I can't answer,' said Great-Aunt Eleanor, 'because I don't know. All I do know is that when the soldiers came, they couldn't find anything to destroy except for this house.'

Kerry looked at Joe and shrugged.

'And that's it, is it?' he said, as disappointed as his sister by the abrupt end.

'I'm afraid it is,' said Great-Aunt Eleanor. 'And I know exactly what an anticlimax it is. Remember I heard the same story from my mother. I was just as disappointed at the ending. I spent years trying to find out what had happened to the village, but to no avail.' She smiled at them both encouragingly. 'Perhaps you'll be luckier than I was.'

It had been a very long day for both Kerry and Joe, and they dropped off to sleep the instant their heads sank into the soft pillows. And as they abandoned their conscious thoughts to the night, the house, which had already been making them feel welcome one minute, putting them on edge the next, somehow worked its way into their dreams, revealing a couple more of its secrets.

'It's so soft,' Kerry found herself saying, as she ran her fingers over the silk and satin of the long dress and admired herself in the full-length mirror. 'And the lace is perfect,' she added, tracing round the intricate patterns decorating the sleeves and ruff around the neck.

'They say there is even demand for my lacework in Ghent, the lace-making capital of Europe,' said the little woman who had presented Kerry with her new clothes. 'Fit for a queen,' she said, laughing.

And Kerry left, swishing off to the massive ballroom with its black-and-white tiled floor and sparkling chandeliers. Before her partner could whisk her away for the first dance there was a pounding at the front door, followed by a splintering crash. Some of the guests screamed, and Kerry found herself running, terrified, with the others.

'They'll never take us alive,' swore Joe, fingering his sword. It was made of the finest steel and honed to razor sharpness.

'Keep your voice down,' whispered his companion.

Joe peered around the tiny, triangular room. His eyes had grown accustomed to the dark, but his legs would never get used to being all folded up. He felt them beginning to go to sleep and shifted round awkwardly.

'And stop moving about,' whispered his companion. 'If they find us, we're done for.'

Joe knew that the priest was right. His show of bravado had been foolhardy, and any movement in the confines of their hiding-place would echo around the whole house, giving them away in an instant. He strained to listen for the soldiers.

They're coming upstairs. They're coming upstairs, he realized, with a sudden feeling of dread. He heard them clattering nearer, beating at the panels and listening for the hollowness which would betray secret passages or rooms; he heard them yelling out for any traitors to the Queen who might be hiding in the dark recesses of the house; he heard his own heart beating louder than anything else.

And the pounding kept going.

Kerry stood, shaking, behind thick velvet curtains as the intruders battered the doors down.

Joe sat, quaking, in the cramped and dark hideaway while the soldiers continued their noisy search.

*

'Kerry! Joe!' came Great-Aunt Eleanor's voice as she stood on the landing outside their bedrooms, knocking on both their doors. 'Rise and shine; you're missing the best part of the day.'

'OK,' said Joe.

'Coming,' said Kerry, pulling Mr Simpkins out from the uncomfortable position he'd taken up under her shoulder and dragging herself out of bed.

What Great-Aunt Eleanor had said was true. They *were* missing the best part of the day. Even as their scrambled eggs on toast were being demolished, heavy, black clouds were rolling in from the west and shutting out the sun.

'Blast!' said Joe, looking out. 'It's beginning to rain.'

'Hmm. And it doesn't look as though it's going to be clearing for some while either,' said Great-Aunt Eleanor.

'Never mind,' said Kerry, trying to make the most of the situation. 'We'll explore the rest of the house. If that's all right with you,' she added to her great-aunt.

'Perfectly all right,' she replied.

'Is there that much for us to see?' said Joe, not sounding particularly enthusiastic.

Great-Aunt Eleanor sighed deeply: 'I can't be sure, of course, but I rather think there is.'

'What do you mean?' said Joe, becoming interested, once again, almost despite himself. The old woman had a curious knack of making the simplest of statements sound enigmatic.

'Well, I can only talk from personal experience,' she said. 'I've combed the house from top to bottom and found all that I . . . well, that I was meant to find, but . . .'

She paused, and her eyes took on the now familiar intense stare.

'Ever since you came,' she continued slowly, 'I've noticed a certain . . . quality to the atmosphere.'

Joe looked at Kerry sceptically.

'Yes, you can call me daft if you like,' she said sharply, 'but I *know* this house. And since the two of you arrived — in fact

31

before that: since I heard you were coming to stay — there's been a certain tension, a sense of expectation.'

'What about when Mum came to stay?' said Kerry.

'Oh, good grief,' said Great-Aunt Eleanor. 'Totally different kettle of fish: she wasn't the slightest bit interested in anything down here. No, it's definitely something to do with you two. I can't say what, but . . .'

Kerry shuddered.

'Of course, if you *were* to discover something,' Great-Aunt Eleanor went on, 'no one could be more happy than me — although I must confess, I think I'd be a little bit envious. More toast, either of you?' she asked, suddenly switching the subject back to the mundane.

'No thanks,' they both said.

'Fine,' said Great-Aunt Eleanor. 'Well, I suggest that for this meal Kerry washes and Joe dries. You can swap round next time.'

There was nothing Joe, in particular, hated more than helping his mother with the things which needed doing around the house. And yet he didn't seem to have much option here. He picked up a tea-towel and started drying the cutlery and crockery without a murmur. Not for the first time, Kerry looked at him curiously. She was beginning to have the feeling that she had come on holiday with a complete stranger. But this version of Joe was infinitely preferable to the sullen brother she knew from home. Ever since he'd turned thirteen he'd become increasingly moody. He'd sulk around the flat and snap at both Kerry and his mother, and more often than not he'd come back from school with the scuffs, cuts and bruises of another playground scrap.

'Ignore him, Kerry,' her mother would say. 'It's just a phase he's going through.'

Yet there was something about the house, or about Great-Aunt Eleanor that had brought the old Joe back. Kerry was pleased.

'Right, come on, then,' he said, as he finished with the last plate.

'Don't get lost,' said Great-Aunt Eleanor, winking at them both as they left.

'We'll try not to,' said Kerry.

'We'll send you a postcard if we do,' said Joe.

They started off back at the huge staircase, down near the front door. Sitting on the bottom stair, Kerry looked up over her head at the carved oak banisters. Everything looked so solid, made to last for centuries and centuries unlike the flimsy little flat the three of them had in London. You could hardly turn round there without chipping or cracking or breaking something. Here, you had the feeling that a whole contingent of soldiers could march through and not do any damage at all. And as she was letting her mind wander, Kerry's dream almost came back to her, but Joe spoke and it was gone again.

'You know, I've been thinking: the house looked pretty symmetrical from the front when we came in, didn't it, with the front door bang in the middle of the wall? So, where is *that* half of the house?' he said, pointing to his right. 'I mean, the kitchen is there, but . . .'

He got up and walked over to the wall. It was panelled to a height of about six feet. Pressing his ear to the wood, he tapped gently with his knuckles to see if he could hear any hollowness.

'You look a real nerd,' said Kerry.

'Come and give me a hand, then,' said Joe. 'She said that there were a whole load of secrets to the house. And I'm fairly sure there must be a room behind this wall if we can just get to it.'

Despite all their careful experiments with the wall, no secret passages became apparent. Joe was all for giving up, and suggested an exploration of the attic when Kerry suddenly discovered something. Standing on the skirting-board to reach up as high as she could, she found herself slipping back to floor-level, and when she looked down she found that a section of the skirting-board, the same width as one of the panels, had

33

slid down into the floor. Behind it was a small lever and when Joe lifted this up a wide door creaked open.

'Wow!' said Joe, as they walked into the hall.

'But . . .' said Kerry, as her dream finally returned to her.

'It's fantastic,' said Joe, walking round the ballroom, imagining all lords and ladies who would have attended masked balls and spun round and round to the sound of string quartets playing waltzes and polkas. 'Look at those chandeliers,' he said. 'They must have cost a million.'

But Kerry knew all about the chandeliers already, *and* the black and white patterns on the tiled floors, *and* the thick, velvet curtains at the French windows which she had taken refuge behind as the soldiers had beaten the doors down. Without even thinking, she ran her fingers down her front and it was the shock of finding herself still dressed in jeans and a T-shirt which brought her out of her dream of lace and finery.

'I dreamt of this room,' she whispered. The words echoed eerily around them. 'I was here, but it was a long time ago. In the days that Great-Aunt Eleanor told us about, when Queen Elizabeth I was on the throne.'

Joe was tempted to laugh at her, but as she spoke something of his own dream came back to him.

'Soldiers, soldiers,' he muttered.

'There *were*,' said Kerry defensively.

He ignored her and headed for the huge fireplace at the far end of the hall. It was about eight feet wide, large enough for a massive yule log which would have burned for the twelve days of Christmas while the guests of the household celebrated. At each side of the recess were two seats set in the stonework where the old folk could sit and warm themselves by the embers. Without hesitating for a moment, Joe sat down on the left-hand seat and fiddled around underneath.

'What on earth are you doing?' asked Kerry.

'Shush a minute,' he said irritably, and continued feeling

around with his fingers. 'Here we are,' he said finally, and the heavy stone alcove behind him opened up.

'This whole house is honeycombed with secret passages and doorways,' said Kerry. 'But how did you know this one was here?'

'You weren't the only one to dream last night,' said Joe, crawling through the hole. 'Come on.'

On the other side of the door was a spiral staircase which led both upwards and downwards. Because of his dream, Joe didn't pause for a second before going up the stairs.

'I don't like it,' said Kerry. 'It sounds all spooky.'

'It's just the wind howling,' said Joe. 'You can always stay here if you want.'

'No,' said Kerry. 'I'll come with you.'

'Come on, then,' said Joe, glad he wouldn't have to go up the winding stairs on his own.

Outside the storm was really beginning to rage. Rain was beating against the windows down in the ballroom, and the sound of the whistling wind was interrupted only by the echoing boom of the thunder. As the lightning illuminated the walls ahead of them for a split second, they saw they were at the top.

They found themselves in a long, narrow room just under the roof, judging by the slant of the ceiling. There was a row of four windows, glazed with diamond-shaped, leaded panes, which looked out on the garden and, beyond that, the lake. It looked much more threatening than it had done the day before. The wind was whipping the dark-grey water up into waves which broke over the jetty and set the tiny rowing-boat bobbing helplessly around its moorings. The lightning grew brighter and the thunder followed it with increasing rapidity as the eye of the storm approached.

'It's fantastic,' said Kerry.

'Look at the way those trees are bending over,' said Joe, pointing to the far side of the lake.

The storm out here in the country was a thousand times more

impressive than its London equivalent. Kerry and Joe stood spellbound as the elements continued their battering of Nature.

'Come on, then,' said Joe, dragging them both away from the windows as the storm began to subside. 'I'm sure that there's somewhere near here. Hang on a minute.'

The dream wasn't at all clear, but . . . He struggled to remember. It had something to do with one of the windows. The fourth window. The one over near the corner of the room.

'Yes,' he muttered. 'The window catch.' He lifted the handle of the window and heard a sound below him as the bar it was connected to released a panel under the window-ledge.

'This was it,' said Joe excitedly, as he got down and crawled into the dark, triangular passage. 'This was where the priest and me were hiding.'

'Wow!' said Kerry. 'Just think of all of those people hiding away then.'

Joe sat down with his back against the wall. 'It's so cramped,' he said, remembering how uncomfortable he'd felt in his dream and wondering if he would have been caught if Great-Aunt Eleanor hadn't woken him up in the nick of time.

'Hey, look,' called Kerry. 'This bit moves.' She pulled at a section on the floor but couldn't quite lift it.

'I'll try with this,' said Joe, taking his Swiss Army knife out of his pocket. With the largest blade slipped between the moving section and the rest of the floor, the square panel lifted out easily to reveal a tiny hidey-hole.

'It's like a whole load of Russian dolls,' said Kerry. 'One inside the other, inside the other, inside the other . . .'

Joe crawled over on his knees and lowered himself down into the hole. The bottom had been designed to take a human shape snugly.

'Put the top back on a minute,' he said.

'Are you sure?' said Kerry.

'Yeah, go on,' said Joe.

As the panel slid into place, everything was plunged into

darkness. Joe waited for his eyes to grow accustomed to the lack of light, but the moment never came. Although some air was coming in from somewhere, the lid was made so well that no light could penetrate.

'OK, let me out now.'

There was no movement above him. Nothing at all.

'Come on, Kerry, let me out now,' he repeated, pushing at the lid as hard as he could.

He *knew* that he was just in a little secret hole under the floor; he *knew* that his sister was only a matter of inches away from his head; he *knew* that he was perfectly safe and it was absolutely ridiculous to get frightened. Why, then, did he feel such an overwhelming panic beginning to rise up inside him? It must be because of the darkness. No one likes being in the dark and this was altogether too dark.

'Let me out, Kerry!' he shouted, and beat his fists against the wood above his head. The sound of the pounding was amplified in the restricted space. But Kerry evidently had not finished with her little game just yet.

Just wait till I get hold of you, he thought. He let his arms relax and rest on his stomach. But the pounding continued. All around him, like echoing thunder. And as he lay there, motionless, the stories Great-Aunt Eleanor had told him the previous night filled his imagination, with the cries of the soldiers calling out for their 'traitors and heretics', cursing the Pope, egging one another on as they thrust their swords into the panelling, between the floor-boards, through the plaster. Strange as it was, Joe couldn't help being more fascinated than frightened by what was going on inside his head.

This is really weird, he thought.

Gradually, the angry voices went, but as he waited for Kerry to open the lid, something else began to make itself known. Something altogether more peculiar.

His eyes had still not become accustomed to the absolute darkness of the hole, but, as he stared blindly up at where the floor-boards must be, two pinpricks of light appeared ahead of him. With every second they grew larger, and, as he watched, they began to move, tracing bright lines across the blackness in apparently random patterns. Almost indiscernibly at first, the lines started to assume the shape of a face, feature by feature, painstakingly building themselves up.

Joe was so fascinated by this display of lines — now forming a nose, now completing the hairline — that he had hardly noticed the storm developing above him. It was raging with such force that it sounded as if it would bring the entire house down. The thunder was louder than ever, battling in volume only with the sound of the wind that howled furiously through every crack and crevice. And although he couldn't actually see the lightning, just before each roll of thunder, the lines of light which were still forming themselves into the face became increasingly bright.

Joe continued to stare into the face. Shading was now being added to give the whole image depth. A moment later, he found himself staring deep into the mask-like face of an old woman. As with all nightmares, what he saw was familiar but subtly altered. Despite its resemblance to Great-Aunt Eleanor,

the face was altogether more gaunt, more harsh, with narrower lips and harder features. But there was something else far more dramatically different.

It was the eyes. Where Great-Aunt Eleanor's eyes were bright and full of life, these eyes had the expressionless stare of the dead, chilling Joe to the bone.

Suddenly, as he was looking into the lifeless gaze, the whole face became blindingly bright. Simultaneously, a deafening crash of thunder filled the hole where Joe was lying. For a moment he remained still, stunned by the scale of light and sound. Then, as he looked back into the woman's face, he noticed how the thin mouth had twisted round into a silent cackle of evil glee.

Nightmare it might be, but Joe couldn't remain silent a moment longer. He opened his mouth and screamed out in terror:

'HELP ME!'

THREE

'That wasn't even slightly funny,' said Joe, as the panel finally slid open.

There was no reply. He peered down the narrow, triangular section but Kerry was nowhere to be seen.

'Stupid little idiot,' he muttered to himself. Joe still felt far from easy. The discovery of just how powerful his own imagination could be had shaken him up. Even now, sitting in the attic, he still couldn't quite believe that he hadn't seen the face of the old woman watching him: it had all been so real. And the storm? He listened carefully, but there wasn't even a trace of distant thunder and the wind had dropped completely.

Staying down on his hands and knees he moved silently along the floor and felt for the opening to the main room. It had been locked.

This is going a little bit too far, he thought to himself, but still he remained silent. Although he couldn't put his finger on it, something very definitely felt wrong.

Perhaps I'm still asleep, he thought, with a sudden shock. He pinched himself hard on the arm. Nothing changed. Perhaps I just dreamt I pinched myself, he thought, and smiled. It was all becoming a bit *too* ridiculous. How could you not know if you were awake or not? If only he could see properly, that would be a start. He took the Swiss Army knife out of his pocket and fumbled around for the torch attachment. The beam it produced wasn't particularly bright, but anything was better than nothing in the nasty, dark, little room.

'I'm not going to shout out,' he promised himself, determined that he wouldn't let Kerry know he'd been frightened. 'I'm not.' He leant back against the wall and shone the torch through his fingers to make them glow all red, over his hands to cast distorted animal shadows on the slanted ceiling opposite, and up and down the narrow space of his temporary prison.

'Come on, Kerry,' he mumbled to himself irritably. He moved his arm round in circles, sending the beam of light spinning down the passage. As it passed through the air, it caught the millions of particles of dust, making them glitter and whirl like a snowstorm. And the faster he moved the torch, the thicker the snow seemed to become. It drifted down and began to settle evenly across the floor-boards. Joe leant down, scooped up a handful and blew it back into the thick air.

As the last few flakes settled on the ground, Joe noticed a heap of something or other at the far end. He couldn't make out exactly what it was, and crawled along to inspect. Just before he got to it, though, his hand pressed down into something sticky and wet.

'Ugh!' he said involuntarily, and inspected his fingers. There was no doubt about what the dark-red, congealed substance was, and as he cleared away the soft covering of snowy dust, the torch-light came to rest on the source of all the blood.

It was the dead body of the priest Joe had dreamt about. Almost anything else and Joe would have been frightened out of his wits. But not the priest. It just confirmed that this was all going on in his head again. The bloody body of the priest disappeared.

Knowing that your imagination was playing tricks with you was one thing, but doing something about it was quite another. An icy shudder ran down his spine as it suddenly occurred to Joe that he might be going mad. He looked round anxiously. Whereas the priest hadn't made him jump at all, the sight of the hideously familiar, death-like face peering down at him from the end of the passage chilled his blood. He knew somehow that he shouldn't, but the shock of discovering that he was being watched was too much. He simply couldn't stifle it. And the scream echoed into the darkness.

As the sound of his shock died away, the wind and the thunder started up, and once again, almost lost in the tumultuous racket, came the voices.

'Who was that?' he heard a gruff voice saying, from the other side of the wall.

'There's another damned traitor in there,' said a second man, and Joe heard footsteps running towards the panel.

Joe panicked. Perhaps it *was* a nightmare, or a trick of the light, or some stupid charade his aunt was playing. It could be any one of a hundred perfectly logical causes, but at that moment Joe was unable to think anything through rationally. All his instincts told him that the only chance he had was to hide, and the only place he could possibly hide was back in the tiny hole.

The bolt which secured the dividing panel slid open with a grating sound. Joe crawled back to the hole as fast as he could, fell down into it and pulled the lid over his head. He flicked the switch of his torch off and was, once again, enveloped by the total blackness. Above him, he could hear the sound of feet and knees on the floor-boards.

'Please don't find me, please don't find me,' he found himself praying.

But it was hopeless. Already he could hear the sound of something metallic sliding down between the lid and gently levering it up.

'No,' he said quietly, too frightened now even to scream as light suddenly streamed down into his hole. He closed his eyes and prepared for the inevitable.

'You all right?' said a familiar voice.

Joe cautiously opened his eyes. 'Kerry?' he said.

'Well, who else did you think it was?' she said.

'Ohhhh!' he shuddered, letting his tensed muscles relax with relief. 'You wouldn't believe me. You just wouldn't believe me.'

When both Kerry and Joe had finished telling their versions of what had happened, the room fell silent. Great-Aunt Eleanor, whose expression had remained totally impassive while the two children had been talking, leant back in her chair.

'Well, my dears,' she said finally, 'I told you that the house had a lot of secrets, but I certainly didn't realize just how many it would reveal to the couple of you. I hardly know whether to congratulate you or pity you.'

Both children felt the increasingly familiar sensation that they were being watched. Joe glanced up at the mirror.

'Let me have a look at that verse again,' said Great-Aunt Eleanor.

Kerry handed her the piece of thick, yellowed paper with the four lines of large, floral script written on it. It had been difficult for Kerry to decipher, but Great-Aunt Eleanor seemed to have no problems.

> 'A haven made for safety's sake
> Became a prison 'neath the lake
> For if by now the coast be clear
> The watery bars should disappear.'

She read it out slowly and carefully, as if weighing up every word in turn.

Although it came to an end there, the verse was clearly not the end of the entire poem. The rough edge to the parchment showed where it had been ripped in half, and on the jagged right-hand edge Great-Aunt Eleanor managed to make out the word 'time', from the following verse.

'It's a shame the rest of it's missing,' she said, handing it back to Kerry. 'You're quite sure there was nothing else up there?'

'Positive,' said Kerry, going over the whole episode in her head to check whether she might be mistaken.

Joe had lowered himself into the tiny hole and asked her to put the cover back on, which she had done. She remembered thinking how dust-free the whole loft area was for somewhere no one ever visited. And then a peculiar feeling had come over her. Difficult to describe: it was like that party game when you go out of the room and something is hidden. Back with the others, they guide you towards your goal by shouting out, 'Cold, cold, warmer, warmer, warm.' It was just like that.

Nobody was actually calling anything out, but she felt almost compelled to crawl along to the far end of the room. And as she made her way, down on her hands and knees, the feeling that she was somehow getting 'warmer' became stronger. Near to the corner her hand suddenly went down on a wobbly section of floor-board.

'Hot! Hot! Hot!' screamed the feeling inside her.

By pressing down firmly on one end of the board, she flicked it up, and there, in the little gap underneath, lay the scrap of yellowed paper. She noticed at once that someone must have torn it in half, and instinctively looked around for the other half, but there wasn't anything else in the hole. Yes, as far as the piece of paper was concerned, she was sure. A hundred per cent!

What had happened immediately after finding the verse was completely different, however. First, she heard her brother shouting.

'Help!' came the muffled, though definitely panicky cry. 'HELP!'

She hurried over to the secret hole but was unable to lift the lid. 'PUSH!' she yelled, but nothing happened. She rushed back through the secret panel, down the spiral stairs to the ballroom, through the hall and back into the kitchen. Without saying a word to Great-Aunt Eleanor, who was stirring some soup, she grabbed a butter-knife and belted back up again.

'Open, open, damn you,' she muttered, trying to lever the cover up. Not a sound came from beneath the floor-boards now and she was terrified that her brother had suffocated.

When the lid finally did shift and she looked down on Joe's face — all twisted up in terror with his eyes clamped tightly shut — she felt a cold shudder pass through her whole body.

'You all right?' she remembered saying. And he had looked at her as though she was a complete stranger. Slowly, painfully slowly, a look of recognition had crept over his features.

*

Kerry would never forget those feelings of horror, panic and relief all mixed up together. She looked over at her brother: he was still obviously shaken up. What on earth was going on here?

'Did you know the house was haunted?' Joe asked Great-Aunt Eleanor.

'I don't think it is actually haunted,' she said.

'Well, there's something weird here,' said Joe.

'I certainly can't disagree with you on that one,' said Great-Aunt Eleanor. 'It's a very old house and a lot has undoubtedly happened here. For whatever reasons, you two children are exceptionally sensitive to the place — you are, after all, related to Megwyn Nashe, however distantly.'

So are you, thought Joe suspiciously.

Unaware of what was on his mind, Great-Aunt Eleanor continued, 'You seem to be picking up on the . . . the echoes, shall we say, of what once took place.'

Joe and Kerry looked at one another and shrugged.

'I've often thought of houses as being like tape recorders,' she continued, 'picking up on all the sounds which take place in them. Anyone with the right equipment can . . . can . . .'

'Play them back,' suggested Joe.

'Precisely,' said Great-Aunt Eleanor. 'Having said that, though, I would say that you two are being treated to a remarkably spectacular display. Two separate dreams, voices from the past, a vision of a face, some kind of display of the elements, and the retrieval of a lost poetic document. Quite, quite wonderful! I've lived here all my life, and nothing like this has ever happened. I must confess to feeling more than an eentsy bit envious. But then, I knew I would,' she added, with a guilty smile.

'But what does it all mean?' said Joe.

'Who knows?' said Great-Aunt Eleanor, gesturing with her hands theatrically. 'Who knows? The one thing I *am* sure of is that something has been started, probably triggered off by the two of you being here, and whatever it is, it's not just going to go away.'

'I can do without the personal thunder and lightning, thanks very much,' said Joe.

'I don't think I even want to go to sleep tonight,' said Kerry.

'Oh, don't be so timorous,' said Great-Aunt Eleanor. 'This could turn into the best adventure you'll ever have.'

'It could turn into the *last* adventure we'll ever have,' said Joe, laughing. Despite his moment of terror up in the attic, he was totally hooked on the whole situation and wouldn't be happy until he knew exactly what was going on. He looked up at his Great-Aunt Eleanor and knew that she knew just what he was thinking. It was unnerving.

'Right,' she said. 'Practicalities. Anyone for lunch?'

Joe and Kerry stirred from their individual thoughts, expectations and worries and looked at each other. Both realized that they were extremely hungry.

'What time is it?' said Joe.

'About half-past one,' said Great-Aunt Eleanor.

'Is that all?' he said. 'I'm starving.'

'Good,' said Great-Aunt Eleanor. 'There's masses of carrot and celery soup waiting.'

'I don't like celery,' said Kerry, a bit sheepishly.

'You'll like this little concoction,' said Great-Aunt Eleanor.

And, as had been the case since they first set foot in Clee Manor — had it really only been the day before? — she was right again. With wooden spoon in hand, she stirred the various steaming mixtures round and round in her massive kitchen cauldron, adding a pinch of this and a touch of that until the perfect potion had been created. The soup was creamy and delicious and both Joe and Kerry had three bowlsful before finally laying their spoons down.

The unpredictable weather had changed again, this time for the better, and the sunshine streaming in through the kitchen windows created two thick bars of glittering dust.

'You never realize how dirty the air is until the sun shines, do you?' said Great-Aunt Eleanor.

Kerry blew at the dust particles, causing tornadoes and hurricanes to take place right in front of her eyes. Joe walked over to the windows and looked out.

'I can't see any clouds at all,' he said.

'Cleared up beautifully, hasn't it?' said Great-Aunt Eleanor. 'I always think the sun seems so much brighter after a spot of rain, too. As though everything's been cleaned and polished. Why don't you two go down and have a look at the boat? If there isn't too much water in the bottom, you could go out in it if you wanted.'

'Great!' said Joe.

'Shall we help with the washing-up first?' said Kerry, trying her best not to sound reluctant.

'Oh, I don't think so,' Great-Aunt Eleanor replied. 'There's hardly anything to do and you never know just how long the sun's going to stay shining around here. No, you two get along and enjoy yourselves. You'll find the oars leaning up against the back door.'

Neither Kerry nor Joe needed any more prompting. They ran upstairs to put on boots for the mud, and swim-suits under their jeans, just in case it got warm enough for a swim.

'See you later, then,' Joe called out.

'What time should we be back?' asked Kerry, poking her head round the corner of the door.

Great-Aunt Eleanor was down on her hands and knees near the skirting-board.

'Are you OK, Auntie?' said Kerry, wondering whether the old woman had fallen down and hurt herself.

'Perfectly all right,' she said. 'And call me Eleanor not Auntie, there's a dear.'

'What *are* you doing?' she asked, creeping up behind her.

Great-Aunt Eleanor sat back on her heels and sighed. She

47

wiped a streak of white down her face as she pulled the hair out of her eyes.

'Oh, it's the mice,' she said. 'Dear little things, but I really don't like them being in the kitchen. Nibbling at the bread and leaving their droppings everywhere; it can't be healthy.'

'You've got mice?' said Kerry.

'I'm surprised you didn't hear them in the night,' said Great-Aunt Eleanor. 'That wretched gnawing.'

'Why don't you put a couple of traps down?' said Kerry.

'Now, I'm sure you don't seriously think that I could do that,' said Great-Aunt Eleanor. '"Live and let live" has always been my motto.'

'Kerry,' Joe called.

'It's quick and painless, though,' said Kerry, ignoring him.

'True. Better than cats in that respect. I hate the way they play with them. You know, a year or so ago I found something called a humane trap. Wonderful little device it was. A sort of box and the mouse ran in for a little snack of something like cheese and biscuits, and the trap door locked it in. Then, the idea is that you take it out into the country, a long way from the house and release it.'

'Sounds like a good idea,' said Kerry.

'Yes,' said Great-Aunt Eleanor, shifting about a bit with embarrassment. 'Except they really shouldn't be allowed to sell it to the absent-minded. I forgot to check the thing for a couple of weeks and when I did, there was this poor little mite all twisted up and beginning to decompose.'

'Ugh,' said Kerry.

'Kerry!' shouted Joe from outside.

'Coming,' Kerry called back.

'I just couldn't stop thinking about it,' said Great-Aunt Eleanor, apparently unaware of Joe's mounting impatience. 'That poor little mouse running round and round in the dark and gradually getting weaker. No, I've decided that the only way to deal with the mice is to keep them out of the kitchen altogether.'

'So you're blocking up all the holes,' said Kerry.

'I'm trying,' said Great-Aunt Eleanor. 'One trick I learnt is to mix a little bit of washing-up liquid with the filler. They're not supposed to like the taste.'

'Isn't it all going to take rather a long time, though?'

'Probably,' she said. 'But that's one thing I've got plenty of. The problem is the mice themselves. I've been reading up about them. Did you know that they have a special sort of swivelling skull so they can squeeze through really tiny gaps? They can get through an opening of an eighth of an inch with no problem at all. And you know how sleek they are. Well, they found some in a butcher's freezer and they'd grown really thick coats to cope with the cold. It's amazing how nature adapts, it really is.'

'Kerry, I'm going,' said Joe crossly, and she heard him tramping off down the path.

'I'd better go,' said Kerry.

'Of course you had, my dear,' said Great-Aunt Eleanor.

'What time did you say you wanted us to be back?'

'I didn't. There's no rush. Come back whenever you want to and we'll rustle up something for dinner.'

Kerry smiled. It was one of the most pleasant things about not being at home. Always having to be in at a certain time for meals was really boring.

'Off you go then, my dear,' said Great-Aunt Eleanor. 'Have fun, and take care.'

'You're so impatient,' said Kerry, as she caught her brother up.

'And you're so slow. What on earth were you talking about?'

Kerry told him all about the mice, and the filler, and the humane trap that had sentenced the mouse to a slow and agonizing death, and the hairy freezer-mice which had taken over cool rooms, and, as she was telling the story, it all became increasingly ludicrous.

'You can just imagine her,' said Joe, 'walking through the

village with her little box. Morning, Mrs Smith, just taking the mouse for a walk.'

'And then letting it out of the box and hoping it wouldn't follow her home,' said Kerry, laughing. 'Stay. I said stay, you naughty mouse!'

'And just when she thought it was safe to go back into the kitchen, she'd open the fridge, and there'd be a hairy little mouse, like a mini-mammoth, skating round the ice tray,' said Joe.

'Getting fat on bowls of lettuce soup and veggie-burgers,' said Kerry.

The path down to the jetty was muddy and slippery, but the sun was hot now, and wisps of steam were coiling out of the drying earth. From close up, neither the jetty nor the rowing-boat looked in such good repair as they had from the house. A couple of the planks of wood were missing, and they had to be careful not to slip into the water as they made their way to the end where the boat had been secured.

'It doesn't look too bad,' said Joe. A little bit of water had collected, but not enough to get their feet wet. 'Right, I'll get in first,' he said.

'Naturally,' said Kerry.

'All right, clever Dick, you get in, then.'

'No, it's all right,' she said, as the boat bounced around underneath her.

Joe stepped down, holding on to the post the boat was tied to. The boat lurched and rocked, but he managed to steady it by keeping his legs apart. He sat down on the bench.

'Right, now pass me the oars and I'll get them into the row-locks.'

'All the technical terms, eh?' said Kerry.

Joe ignored her. 'Do you want to get in now?' he said. 'Come on, it's easy. You can hold on to my shoulder.'

After a considerable amount of swaying, splashing and squeal-ing, Kerry was finally sitting down opposite her brother at the stern, or, as she called it, the blunt end.

'Ooh, I feel seasick,' she said.

'Don't be so wet,' said Joe, slipping the rope off the post and pushing them away from the jetty with one of the oars.

'It's you that's wet,' said Kerry, cupping a handful of water and throwing it at him.

'Cut that out,' snapped Joe. 'Which direction shall I head for?'

'Does it really matter?' asked Kerry, as Joe struggled to coordinate the two oars. He glared at her. 'OK,' she said. 'Over there, where the stream comes out.'

Gradually the rowing became easier, and, with Kerry giving the occasional instruction as to whether to pull more to the left, or more to the right, they made their way across the lake. The sun was still beating down on the water, which glistened, dazzlingly bright. There was a very slight breeze and the weeping willows lining the stream waved their branches welcomingly.

'It's so beautiful,' said Kerry, letting her hand trail along in the water.

'It's hot, I know that much,' said Joe. 'Especially here,' he said, rubbing his hand over the top of his cropped scalp. 'I'll probably get a sunburnt head. And then it'll peel.'

'That's all right,' said Kerry, 'it'll just look like dandruff.'

'T'riffic,' said Joe. He laid the oars across the boat and pulled off his jumper and T-shirt.

'Come on, slave,' shouted Kerry. 'No slacking. Pull, PULL, PULL!'

The whole lake seemed to have come to life under the warm sun. Herons waded and stabbed for fish near the banks, grebes and kingfishers, coots and moorhens, skylarks and swallows paddled, dipped, dived and swooped for food. Newts and frogs scuttled and hopped around between the water-lilies, duckweed and reeds, chasing after the insects which had filled the air with a constant drone of activity. Neither Kerry nor Joe knew what the birds, or the plants, or the trees, or the insects were called.

They saw 'hovering brown bird' and 'diving blue bird', watched 'walking-on-water insects' and were stung by 'stinging insects'. Joe made a note that he would have to look some of the things up in Great-Aunt Eleanor's reference books when they got back, and yet, sitting there, half-asleep on the lake, it occurred to him that being able to categorize everything he could see and hear was a bit pointless. It was enough just to *be* there.

Both of them drifted off into a state of wonderful drowsiness; everything other than the warm sun, the rocking boat and the hypnotic hum of the insects seemed a million miles away. London, and their mother's fears that they would start sniffing glue or trying heroin; Clee Manor, and the weird dreams and hallucinations they'd been gripped by there; the torrential rain and spectacular display of thunder and lightning they'd watched; where were they all now? Away and gone. This was the life.

'Hey, what was that?' said Kerry, looking round her.

'What?' said Joe, refusing to open his eyes.

'I thought I heard something splashing,' she said. 'It came from over there. Yeah, there it was again!'

She scanned the bank for any clues as to what might have caused the noise. A sudden flurry of fur shooting down a mud slide, followed by a splash into the water, gave her the answer.

'Joe!' she said, as quietly as her excitement would allow. 'Look. Quickly!'

Joe pulled himself up and turned to where Kerry was pointing. A moment later and he was rewarded with the same sight.

'They're otters!' said Kerry. 'Otters. I've always wanted to see them.'

'Are you sure?' said Joe.

'Of course I am. What else do you think they are?' she asked.

'Freezer-mice?' suggested Joe.

'Wally,' she said. 'Can we get any closer?'

'If we use the oars we'll frighten them away,' said Joe. 'Let's try just paddling over with our hands.'

As they got closer to the bank, they counted six of them. They looked like children playing; one after the other they would run up the grassy bank in a series of leaps and then slide back down the muddy chute into the lake. Twisting and turning in the water, they would play rough-and-tumble with each other for a few moments before diving back down under the water.

'Aren't they sweet?' said Kerry. 'Look at their little noses and ears. Oh, and the whiskers!'

'They're not very big,' said Joe.

'Perhaps they're young ones,' said Kerry.

The otters continued their exhibition, apparently unaware of the two children watching them from the boat. They all seemed to be enjoying themselves splashing around in the water and sliding down their chute, but occasionally another side to the fun and games became clear. This time of the day, with the sun slowly turning to red and sliding down behind the hills ringing the lake, was evidently feeding time. After a sudden darting movement or a particularly deep dive, the otters would break the surface of the water with a frog or a crayfish in their mouths.

'I could watch them for ever,' said Kerry.

'It's getting a bit late,' said Joe. 'And cold,' he added, pulling his T-shirt back on. 'I think we ought to start rowing back.'

'Oh, just a couple more minutes,' said Kerry. 'Look at that one there,' she said, pointing at the largest of the otters. It had evidently struck lucky on a dive and was carrying a big wriggling fish in its teeth. As they watched, the otter clamped down hard and shook the fish until it was motionless and then swam with it to the bank. Up on its tiny back paws, it flicked the fish round so that the scales wouldn't catch in its throat as it swallowed. The head disappeared first, followed by the body, and finally the tail was bitten off and spat out.

'Right,' said Joe, picking up the oars. 'We're going now.'

'All right,' said Kerry sulkily. 'If you say so.'

As he placed the oars back in their rowlocks and started to row, the otters noticed the boat for the first time. They didn't panic at all. On the contrary; apparently interested by the new creature in the lake, they simply stopped what they were doing, whether they were in the water or on the land, and looked over.

'Bye-bye, otters,' said Kerry, as Joe manoeuvred the boat round and started to row back to the opposite bank.

They both fell silent as they gradually made their way across the lake. Kerry was remembering everything she could about the otters: their faces as they'd eaten the fish, the movements they had made as they wrestled with each other, the way they had climbed out of the water and leapt up the bank to the top of the chute. It was a million times better than watching one of those nature programmes on telly. If only they lived nearer the country, she thought. Joe was thinking about the boxing lessons he had at the community centre and how much stronger he'd be in the autumn when they started up again if he went out rowing every day. He could feel his shoulders, neck and stomach tense and relax with every stroke as the boat glided across the water. The sun had set by now, but if he kept up the same steady rhythm, they should be back before it got dark.

Then suddenly, and without any warning, the boat lurched and rocked. Kerry and Joe looked at one another accusingly, each suspecting that the other had done something.

'What happened?' said Kerry.

'I haven't got a clue,' said Joe, starting to row again.

The second jolt to the boat was even stronger and both children had to grab hold of the side.

'Dammit!' shouted Joe, as one of the oars plopped into the water and drifted out of his reach. 'Kerry, quick! Grab the oar.'

She leant over the side of the boat as far as she could, but it floated just past her fingertips.

'Give me the other one,' she yelled. Joe passed it to her. 'Come on, come on!' she shouted, as the floating oar continued to drift out of reach.

Joe leant over and paddled with his hands to get them to move towards it, but the oar continued to outstrip the boat.

'I said we should have left before,' he yelled.

'What difference would that have made?' said Kerry. 'You'd still have dropped the bloody paddle.'

'Oar!' shouted Joe.

'Or what?' yelled Kerry angrily.

'It's called an oar, not a "bloody paddle", and it wasn't my fault I let go of it. We must have hit something.'

Joe was feeling very worried. Looking around him, he estimated that they were slap-bang in the middle of the lake. It couldn't have happened in a worse place.

'Be careful,' he said as Kerry wobbled to her feet and leant out with the oar, trying to hook it round the other one.

'Grab hold of me round the waist,' said Kerry.

Joe got to his knees and had just started inching himself along to the stern, trying to keep it from rocking when the boat hit something for a third time. It was the hardest jolt of all, and Joe watched powerlessly as his sister stood, flailing her arms around and around like a broken windmill, trying to regain her balance. It all seemed to be happening in slow motion. A long-drawn-out scream echoed round and around the lake as Kerry finally gave up the struggle to remain upright and toppled over, twisting through the air seemingly for ever before plunging head first into the lake. There was hardly any splash at all as the body cut through the surface and disappeared from sight. For an instant Joe sat, motionless, watching the ripples coming out from the spot where his sister had fallen in. And then it struck him.

'KERRY!' he yelled.

He tried to get his jeans off, but the legs wouldn't go over his boots, and he was shaking so much that he couldn't untie the double-knotted laces.

'Come on, you stupid, awkward little . . .' he muttered angrily, trying to shift the knot. But it was all wet and his fingers couldn't get a proper grip. 'I'll never bite my fingernails again,' he promised himself.

'KERRY! WHERE ARE YOU?' he screamed down into the water. 'COME UP.' He felt all hot and scratchy inside his head. Why had she still not surfaced? What if she had drowned?

He peered down into the still, dark water for any sign of a body, but the surface of the water was totally flat and calm, giving nothing away.

He stood there in the tiny rowing-boat as it rocked backwards and forwards. 'Please don't drown,' he whispered quietly. He remembered hearing of people who had drowned because of swimming downwards in their panic to get out of the water.

'KERRY! LISTEN TO ME!' he screeched as loudly as he could. He couldn't stop shaking and the painful lump in his throat was getting worse.

'KERRY!' he yelled again.

There was no alternative. He couldn't just stand there doing nothing. And, hoping desperately for the best, he launched himself off from the side of the rowing-boat and dived down into the cold, darkening water of the lake, in search of his missing sister.

FOUR

The water was freezing cold. It soaked through Joe's T-shirt instantly, seeped through his jeans to his legs and filled his boots. He dived down, peered through the murky water for Kerry. But she was nowhere to be seen. Becoming short of breath, Joe tried to swim back up for air, but as his clothes had become saturated with water they had become increasingly heavy. With sudden horror, he realized that resurfacing was going to be a problem. The thick denim and the restricted movement the boots allowed his feet combined to drag him down still deeper into the lake. He struggled desperately to try to force his body back up to the surface, but the water seemed to have taken on the consistency of treacle and the more he pulled, the weaker his arms felt. Suddenly, instead of trying to rescue his sister, he found that he was trying to save his own life.

'Up, up, up!' he encouraged himself, but all the while he felt as if his feet were pulling him down towards certain drowning. The further down he sank, the more his heart began to pound; and the more his heart pounded, the greater the need for oxygen became. But if he breathed now, his lungs would simply fill with water and that would be that. He tried all the harder to drag himself back to the surface for a gulp of fresh, life-saving air. But it was hopeless. He was caught in a whirling current tugging him further down, down to the bottom of the dark lake. Unable to hold his breath a moment longer, he was finally forced to breathe in.

He had expected the tickly sensation he got when he was doing back-stroke to fill his head. But it didn't come. And then he'd expected everything to go black, as if someone had turned off the light. But that didn't happen either.

To his complete surprise and considerable relief, he found he could . . . But no, it sounded too ridiculous. He inhaled again. Yes, it *was* true. Somehow, he could breathe under water.

The current which had gripped him by the ankles was by now spinning much faster. He looked about him as he hurtled round and round, and realized that he was in a long, narrow tunnel, like an underwater whirlwind. Trapped in the same downward spiral were a whole collection of animals. There was a large green frog with a wide comical mouth, struggling futilely against the downward pull. A mandarin duck was trying in vain to launch itself off into the middle of the air stream to find its way back up to the surface, but was failing to get both wings out of the water at the same time. Below him, Joe saw that one of the otters was also being dragged down to the bottom of the lake. Rather than panicking, however, the otter was using the opportunity to grab at the confused fish which poked their heads out into the vertical column of air.

The rate of descent all seemed to be dependent on how heavy the particular object was, Joe noticed.

Different to what Galileo said, he thought to himself, remembering the story of the old Italian scientist dropping different weights from the top of the Leaning Tower of Pisa to prove that gravity worked. Or something like that.

It wasn't possible to see the bottom of the lake as the column of air was twisting and writhing, never allowing a clear view all the way down. But as Joe looked, he saw that just below his feet was a hedgehog. It knew that something was wrong but couldn't decide what. Curling itself up, it remained in a tiny ball for a few seconds. Then, presumably hoping for a change in its predicament, it would stretch open and pedal its legs wildly in the air before giving up and retreating again. As Joe was watching, he soon caught up with the confused little animal, and overtook it. Meanwhile, a massive log which must have been washed into the lake, was coming down on him with frightening speed. As it spun past him, Joe had to duck to prevent his head being knocked off.

How deep *is* the lake? Joe wondered. He seemed to have been spinning down and round now for ages. The only comforting thought in the whole episode was that if Kerry had been dragged down by the same mysterious current, she might still be alive.

Suddenly, just as Joe was beginning to feel that he couldn't take much more of being spun round and round, he found he had been ejected from the base of the watery tornado. Out he popped, like a cork from a bottle of champagne and, after a brief flight through the air, he came to earth with a soft, if somewhat prickly, thud. As everything stopped turning, he realized that he had landed on top of a haystack.

'A haystack?' he said to himself, in amazement, as the fact dawned on him. 'What on earth is a haystack doing at the bottom of a lake?'

Above him, like a huge, blue cathedral dome, was the water. The colour was a deeper, more violet blue than the sky and he could see exactly where the air stopped and the water began. But it didn't make any sense. He slipped off the haystack and ran over to where the water arched right down to the ground. Scarcely daring, in case the water suddenly came cascading in on top of him, he poked his finger into the wall of water. At first, the skin caused by the water tension merely dented inwards a little, but as he continued to push, he punctured it. He thrust his finger, then his hand and then his whole arm in, right up to the shoulder. When he pulled it out it was soaking wet.

'This is crazy!' said Joe, looking around him. 'Absolutely crazy!'

Crazy as it might be, there was no doubt about where he was. No doubt at all. Joe was standing in a giant air bubble at the bottom of Lake Clee.

'Now what?' he said to himself.

Just as night had been drawing in while Kerry and Joe were crossing the lake, so here, *under* the lake, it was also getting dark, certainly too dark to explore, even with his penknife torch. Joe didn't know what to do for the best: everything was getting too much for him. Kerry was still missing; he was trapped under countless thousand gallons of water; he was aching and tired from being tossed around by the current; and now, to cap it all, it was getting dark. All his instincts told him that he ought to continue searching. But his body simply wouldn't let him.

'I just can't,' he murmured quietly. 'But tomorrow . . .' He returned to the haystack, pulled off his wet clothes and curled up under the warm hay.

Unlike the previous night, which had been filled with violent nightmares and peopled with soldiers who were out to get him, Joe, rolled up snugly in the haystack below the lake, slept like a baby. If he did have any dreams, then, by the time the warm glow of morning woke him up, he had already forgotten them. If anything, it was the curious bubble of air itself which he hoped he had conjured up in his sleep, but rubbing his eyes and pinching his arm soon confirmed that he was, indeed, awake.

His clothes had all dried overnight and he dressed quickly so that he could explore this curious underwater world without any more delay. The whole area was suffused with a shade of blue which had a strangely calming effect. Joe was no longer worried that Kerry had drowned: he was sure that she was all right. Nor was he afraid for himself. Everything was going to be fine.

Looking around at the circular disc of water above his head, he set off towards the centre of the air bubble. It was a beautiful day. The turquoise-tinged sun beat down through the air and cast soft, grey shadows across the countryside. As he left the haystack, it occurred to Joe that it was one of the old man-made ones, pointed and sealed with a thatched top.

'Like in old picture books,' he thought, remembering a story he'd had as a boy about a town mouse and a country mouse.

In contrast, the ones in the fields near Great-Aunt Eleanor's house had obviously been made by machines and looked like nothing so much as giant, circular Shredded Wheats. And as he continued his walk, the feeling that he was wandering through a picture from the past continued. There were no tractors, no ploughs and no combine harvesters. The wheat fields were small and dotted with the reds and blues of unwanted plants which would normally be sprayed with weed-killer. And the animals grazed in fields which were enclosed and separated by clipped hedges, rather than the strips of electrified wire Joe had noticed being used on the land around Clee Manor.

He kept walking, and above him, the dome of water was getting higher and higher as he approached the middle. He crossed a field of sheep, all scrawny from their recent shearing, and looked down to the bottom of the valley. Although the obvious care and attention the fields had received ought to have prepared him, he couldn't help being shocked by the sight of a village down below him.

'But this is crazy!' he said to himself, for the umpteenth time.

There was a church, a hall with a red and white flag fluttering from the front wall, a village green surrounded by a ramshackle collection of little houses with orange and grey tiled roofs and tall chimneys, and a small main street lined with various shops. Peering more closely, Joe could even make out the presence of people. Judging by the number of cottages there, he estimated that the village must be home to some five hundred or so people. Would Kerry be one of them?

He ran down the hill, round the edge of a field of barley, across a meadow full of cows and through a wood which bordered on the main street. From close up, he saw that it was an untarmacked dirt-track with none of the familiar road signs, central white lines, yellow no-parking lines, or drains. Just a plain and simple muddy track. The state of the road didn't hold his attention for long, though: far more interesting than that was the sight of the villagers themselves.

'It's like a film set,' Joe muttered to himself.

He remained out of sight, crouched down behind a low wall and from this vantage point he watched the men, women and children going about their daily business.

But it can't just be for a film, thought Joe. The buildings are all real. And anyway, there are no cameras.

Almost directly opposite him was the village smithy. He could see the glow of the hot furnace deep inside the shop and hear the metallic sound of the blacksmith beating the horseshoes to the right shape on his anvil. He came to the door, a big, burly man with dark hair and, having plunged the new shoe, hissing, into a butt of water, he leant against the horse and hammered the shoe on to its hoof. A plump, red-cheeked woman wearing a shawl and a lacy bonnet walked past, greeting the smith as she did so. A group of four children were crouching in the road, playing some kind of game with a handful of stones and two sticks. It all looked real enough, but Joe couldn't rid himself of the sneaking suspicion that they were all actors, and that at any moment, the director would leap out from behind a tree and yell, 'CUT!'.

To his left, the sound of two women arguing caught Joe's attention.

'But it does matter, it does,' one was insisting.

'Oh, you're always worrying your head about something or other, Anne,' said the other. 'You've managed up to now and I daresay you can manage a little longer.'

'You'd be concerned yourself if you were in my shoes, Betty Clegg. If he doesn't get christened soon, there's no knowing what might happen to the little mite. You know what they say about changelings and the like.'

'Superstitious nonsense, if you ask me.'

Joe listened, but the conversation made little sense. If it was for a film, he definitely wouldn't be going to see it. It sounded really boring. And what was a changeling? Perhaps he had misheard: Joe found their accents difficult to understand. In fact, at first, he'd thought they were speaking some foreign language.

'Better get ourselves out of the way,' said Betty, pulling her companion to the side of the road as a herd of cows, their udders swollen with milk, approached them. They were being driven by a gangly man with long, greasy hair who was carrying a stick which he switched the cows' rumps with, when they threatened to dawdle.

'Morning, Mrs Cartwright, Mrs Clegg,' said the man, grinning inanely, and revealing a mouth full of missing teeth.

'Morning, Dan,' they replied.

As Dan passed out of earshot, Joe heard Anne whispering to her friend:

'See what I mean. Now, you wouldn't wish that on me, would you?'

'But Dan's an idiot, not a changeling,' said Betty. 'Everyone knows that.'

'Well, I'm not so sure,' she replied.

'Anne Cartwright!' said Betty with mock horror.

'Anyway, I can't stand around talking all day,' said Anne. 'I've got the boys' washing to get done.'

'Yes, be a shame to miss this good drying weather,' Betty agreed. 'You never know what that Megwyn's got in store for us, do you?'

'And that's the truth,' said Anne.

'Megwyn,' Joe repeated to himself. The unusual name rang a bell. Hadn't Great-Aunt Eleanor said that one of her ancestors was called Megwyn? Megwyn Nashe. The so-called witch who had supposedly concealed the village from Queen Elizabeth's soldiers when they had come to destroy it? 'In . . . what was the year? 1589,' he remembered, repeating the date slowly.

'Fifteen hundred and eighty-nine!' He looked around at the high street again, and his whole body began to shake with apprehension. He looked at the horse being shod: there were no cars. He looked at the pump at the end of the street: there was no tap water. He looked at the lantern hanging up outside the bakery: there was no electricity.

'But what's happened to the last four hundred years? They can't have just vanished,' he said, trying to argue himself out of the situation logically.

'You must be Joe,' came a voice from behind him.

Joe was so wrapped up in his own thoughts that the sudden sound of another person, and one who apparently knew him, threw him into even more of a panic. He screamed out loud, so loud, in fact, that the blacksmith looked up.

'It's only me, Father,' said the boy standing next to Joe.

'If you're fighting again, I'll tan your hide, my lad,' said the blacksmith.

'I'm not. I just hurt myself on some stinging nettles.'

The smith resumed his work and the boy crouched down next to Joe.

'My name's Thomas Cartwright,' he said.

'I don't care what your name is,' said Joe sharply, angry that he'd been made to jump. 'How did you know who I was?'

'From your sister's description,' said Thomas simply.

'You've seen Kerry?' said Joe, jumping up with excitement. 'Where is she?'

'Back at our house,' said Thomas. 'Yes, she described you well,' he continued, looking Joe up and down.

'What did she say, then?' said Joe, so relieved to hear that Kerry was OK, that he couldn't remain angry for a moment longer.

'Let me see,' said Thomas. 'Blue trousers that she called "jeans", is it?'

'Yeah, jeans, it is,' said Joe grinning.

'Boots. And this must be the "T-shirt". She described the flag quite well, but she didn't know whose it was.'

'It's the Confederates' flag,' said Joe. 'The Deep South of America,' he added, noticing the blank expression on Thomas's face.

'America?' he said, continuing to look puzzled.

'The Civil War,' said Joe. 'Oh, it doesn't matter. What else?'

'Well, the obvious,' said Thomas, 'your funny haircut. No one round here looks like you do — but I reckon I'd have recognized you, anyway.'

'How's that?' said Joe.

''Cos I know everyone else, that's how,' said Thomas.

'Logical,' said Joe.

'Do you want to see her, then?' asked Thomas.

'Who?' said Joe.

'Kerry, of course,' came the reply.

'Oh, yeah, I do,' said Joe. Everything else around him was so strange that, having ascertained that his sister was OK, he had promptly forgotten all about her.

'She's back at the house at the moment with Sarah.'

'Who's that?' asked Joe.

'She's *my* sister,' he said. 'You know, I was really glad when Kerry turned up out of the blue yesterday. It meant I didn't have to go to school today.'

'Is it that bad?' asked Joe.

'Worse,' said Thomas. 'You can come along and see for yourself tomorrow, if you like.'

'May as well,' said Joe. At least history lessons ought to be shorter, he said to himself.

Thomas laughed. 'We'll see,' he said.

As they walked along the narrow street Thomas kept up a constant stream of conversation and gradually, as he spoke, Joe got used to his strange accent. At the same time, Thomas found he had to concentrate less and less on the way Joe was speaking, although from time to time, he would stop him in mid-sentence to check what particular words meant. The Underground, a record, a video (nasty or otherwise), a computer, GCSEs, a bus, trainers, the telly, disco, hip-hop ... almost everything that they talked about ran into problems of understanding at some point or other, and Joe had to describe the problem word as well as he could.

'It's like talking to a Martian,' said Joe.

'What's a marsh'un?' asked Thomas.

'Never mind,' said Joe, 'it doesn't matter.' It was hard enough trying to describe things that did exist, let alone getting on to science-fiction creatures.

Although there weren't that many people on the muddy road, the few who were around stared at Joe as though *he* was a Martian.

'Had your penny's worth?' he yelled at one woman, who stared all the more intently on hearing the stranger speak.

'They don't mean any harm,' said Thomas, noticing his rising agitation. 'They're like me. They haven't seen a new face for so long, they're just fascinated.'

'But I don't understand,' said Joe. 'Why haven't they?'

'I'll explain everything once we get home,' said Thomas. 'Look, over there is the church. All the windows and statues were done by men from the village. Some of the really talented ones went to seek their fame and fortune in Venice and Florence.'

'Yeah, very nice,' said Joe, who had never been particularly interested in churches.

'And up there is the squire's mansion,' he said, pointing to a grand-looking house on a hill behind the village green. 'He's the main landowner from hereabouts, but he keeps himself to himself.'

To the right of the mansion were four stalls and Joe could see the cows being milked one after the other by young girls with white cotton bonnets on their heads. Sitting on the gate at the bottom of the drive was Dan, the toothless cowherd who Joe had seen driving the cattle along the road earlier. He was sucking on a piece of straw.

'Good morning, Dan,' said Thomas.

'Morning,' said Dan, more as a statement of fact than a greeting. 'Yes, that much is true. The sun has not yet reached its highest point, so morning it is. Whether or not it is a "good" morning is not for me to say. I daresay for some it is good; for myself, it is a morning much like any other. Neither good nor bad.'

'Joe,' said Thomas, 'meet Dan Boggle.'

'So-so morning, Joe,' said Dan, giggling and swinging back and forth precariously on the gate.

'Dan used to be a sailor,' explained Thomas, 'but he was shipwrecked after a storm for six weeks, and drinking the salt water turned his mind, didn't it, Dan?'

'I'm the village idiot, if that's what you're saying,' said Dan. He looked at Joe and winked. 'You'll be wanting to go off and be reunited with your sister at the moment, but you and I have got a lot of tales to tell each other.'

'How did you know who I was?' said Joe, astounded, once again, that somebody totally unknown knew him. It was unnerving.

'I'm not as green as I'm cabbage-looking,' said Dan, and resumed his straw-sucking.

'Come on, then,' said Thomas. 'We're nearly there. Bye, Dan.'

'Yeah, see you, Dan,' said Joe.

'As sure as eggs is eggs,' said Dan, without looking up.

At that moment, a small boy came careering down the street, knocking along a wooden hoop with a stick.

'Back in a minute,' said the boy, racing past them.

'That's William, my younger brother,' said Thomas. 'He's got the day off school as well. Your sister was so worried, you know, that we were all sent out looking for you.'

'My little sister, Kerry,' said Joe to himself. It occurred to him that most of the time he didn't give her much thought, and yet when she'd fallen off the boat, he'd suddenly felt really close to her and responsible for her. What Thomas had just told him confirmed that she had felt exactly the same way.

'Here we are, then,' said Thomas, breaking Joe's thoughts.

Joe looked up at the building they'd stopped in front of. It was a half-timbered house with a thatched roof and small windows with leaded, diamond-shaped panes. They walked round to the side door. A powerful-looking dog, like a cross between a mastiff and a boxer, growled at them and strained on his lead.

'He's all right,' said Thomas, as Joe flinched. 'Aren't you, Rex?' he added, rubbing the big dog's head.

'What kind of dog is it?' asked Joe.

'A bandog,' said Thomas. 'He guards the house. Not that there's anyone who'd steal anything. But, well, we like him anyway.' Thomas lifted the latch and the two of them walked through, into the kitchen.

'Joe!' yelled Kerry immediately, and rushed across to give him a big hug.

He was glad to see her as well, of course, but her enthusiasm made him feel all hot and awkward.

'Hi,' he said. 'I thought you'd drowned.'

'Same here,' said Kerry. 'I'm still not convinced I haven't,' she added. 'This place is so *strange.*'

'Have we come back into the past, or something?' asked Joe.

'Well, not exactly,' said Kerry, 'although this is an Elizabethan village. But only here — above the lake, everything else is going on just as normal in the good old twentieth century.'

'So how do we get back there?' said Joe.

'That,' said Kerry, 'seems to be the problem.'

'Oh, what!' said Joe, screwing his face up impatiently.

'Everything will turn out fine in the end, you'll see,' said the girl standing next to Kerry.

'Oh, yes,' said Kerry. 'This is Sarah.'

'Thomas's sister,' said Joe.

She nodded.

'And how long have *you* been down here?' Joe said angrily. The prospect of being trapped below a lake for the rest of his life did not appeal: he felt his mood turning decidedly sour.

'Well,' said Sarah a little sheepishly. 'Four hundred years or so. But there was a reason for that . . .'

'From what I can make out,' said Kerry, 'the actual reason we're here is to get the village out from under the lake.'

'Great!' said Joe, sarcastically. 'What are we supposed to do — drink it away?'

'Boy of autumn, girl of spring,' came a cracked, old voice from the corner of the kitchen.

Joe looked over and saw an old woman with her long hair pulled up into a bun, rocking back and forth in a chair.

'That's Grandma Mary,' explained Thomas.

'What did she say?' asked Joe.

'"Boy of autumn, girl of spring". She's said it loads of times since I arrived,' said Kerry. 'But I haven't got a clue what it means.'

'She's old,' whispered Thomas. 'Not everything she says makes a great deal of sense.'

'What a surprise!' muttered Joe. 'This whole place is full of weirdos: village idiots, senile delinquents . . .'

'I heard that,' Grandma Mary rasped. 'I'm not that old. And I'm certainly not stupid.'

'I didn't mean that you were, Grandma Mary,' said Thomas.

'Come over here, children,' she said to Kerry and Joe, ignoring her grandson. 'Come over into the corner and let me look at you.'

Grandma Mary seemed to be made up of various shades of yellow. Her skin was the tone and texture of old maps; her crooked teeth were the colour of mustard; her greasy hair was lemony-yellow, while her nails and even the whites of her eyes were stained a nicotine shade of ochre. Neither Kerry nor Joe could remember ever having seen any of their grandparents, and apart from the old people they met queueing up in the post office for their pensions, they never came into contact with anyone older than their parents. Being old seemed so peculiar, so far away.

Joe felt a cold shiver of apprehension as he shook her cold, dry, papery hand. And Kerry couldn't help the thought that kept going round and round her head: I'll never get to be this old.

'So, my dears,' began the old woman, pulling her grey shawl closer round her body, 'you two have come from up there, have you?' She pointed to the ceiling and beyond with her bony finger.

'From above the lake?' said Joe. 'Yes, we have.'

Grandma Mary nodded slowly. 'It's been so long,' she said. 'So very long. I'd almost begun to give up hope. But then, that's the one thing you must never lose. Hope,' she repeated quietly.

Joe stole a quick look at Kerry, who was doing the same. *Was* the old woman senile?

'How much do you already know?' she asked, suddenly back in full possession of her faculties.

'About this place?' asked Joe. 'Not much at all, really.'

'We were told a story about the village of Cleedale by our Great-Aunt Eleanor,' said Kerry. 'She lives in Clee Manor, that big house next to the lake, and she said that when Queen Elizabeth's soldiers came to destroy the village, it was the only house they could find. The rest of the village had disappeared.'

'So the story got through, did it?' said Grandma Mary. 'We often wondered whether it would or not. It only needed one generation to neglect to tell their children and the story would have been lost for ever.' She rocked back in her chair with her eyes closed for a couple of moments. 'And so would we!

'Who's on the throne now?' she asked abruptly.

'Another Elizabeth,' said Joe. 'Elizabeth the Second.'

'Good grief!' said Grandma Mary. 'Did the woman finally marry Philip of Spain and have a daughter?'

'Oh no!' said Joe, desperately trying to remember what had happened to whom, and when. 'Let's see. Elizabeth I died in 1603 and James I came to the throne.'

'What, the son of that Scottish usurper, Mary!' exclaimed Grandma Mary, evidently scandalized.

'I think so,' said Joe, attempting to be diplomatic.

'And then?' Grandma Mary persisted.

'Oh, a Charles. But he was beheaded. And then there was a

Civil War between the Roundheads and the Cavaliers. And then another Charles. And then later there were lots of Georges. Six of them in all and another queen, called Victoria, who was on the throne for about seventy years.'

'Loads has been going on outside, but what about here?' said Kerry, trying to get the conversation back to what *she* wanted to hear about.

'Ah, here,' said the old woman quietly, and sighed. 'Here, nothing has changed at all. Nothing. It is the same today as on that day in 1589, when, as the soldiers were marching on the village, the calendars came to a standstill.'

'But what *actually* happened?' asked Kerry. It was her turn now to be persistent.

'It was a Thursday,' Grandma Mary began. 'A messenger had brought word that the Queen had ordered our village to be destroyed for harbouring Catholics. He said that the troops were little under a day away.'

Coming from a century with motorways, instant telecommunication and speedy vehicles, the whole idea of travel within Britain taking days rather than hours sounded crazy to Joe and Kerry.

'At first we didn't believe the young man, but when he himself abandoned the village, we were forced to take his claims more seriously. We held a meeting in the town hall and decided what measures should be taken.'

'Father was all for making a stand, fighting rather than hiding,' Thomas interrupted.

'So he was,' said Grandma Mary. 'The impetuous fool – he wouldn't have lasted ten minutes. And even if he had won that particular battle, she would only have sent more and more soldiers, until every last one of us had been murdered. It was the arrogance of the menfolk of Cleedale that caused all the trouble in the first place,' she added.

'At least it wouldn't have been cowardly,' said Thomas sullenly.

'"Discretion" as they say "is the better part of valour",' continued Grandma Mary, 'and it was discretion which won the day. For better or worse, we decided to enlist the help of Megwyn Nashe.'

Kerry looked over to Joe.

'That was who Great-Aunt Eleanor was talking about, wasn't it?' she said. 'Her great-great-something or other?'

'I think so,' said Joe. 'And that's the second time I've heard her name today.'

'Who is she?' asked Kerry.

'Megwyn Nashe,' croaked Grandma Mary dramatically, 'is the most brilliant, the most talented, the most self-sacrificing witch that ever lived.'

'She's related to us, you know,' said Kerry proudly. 'We're not actually called Nashe, but our mum was before she got married.'

'I know you are, my dear, you are the twenty-first in line,' said Grandma Mary calmly.

Joe did a quick calculation: 'Yeah, that's about right,' he said.

'And she was a real witch?' said Kerry. 'I didn't think there was ever any such thing.'

'What a peculiar remark to make,' commented Grandma Mary, looking puzzled. 'I am ninety-two now, and as far back as I can remember witches have been alternately revered and persecuted, but no one has ever doubted their existence. Of course they exist! And the greatest of them all, as I say, is Megwyn Nashe. While all the stupid men were drawing up their ridiculous plans of action to combat the Queen's forces, it was Megwyn who kept her head and made plans to truly protect the village.'

'So you're saying that it was Megwyn who, somehow, managed to conceal the village under the lake?' said Kerry.

'Indeed it was,' said Grandma Mary. 'It was her greatest feat ever. For over fifteen hours she boiled up the necessary ingredients, adding a drop of this and a pinch of that with the expertise of a master alchemist, and when the whole concoction was prepared, she was able to take control of the elements to save the village. What a day. Lord above, what a day it was!'

'It really was,' said Sarah, and Thomas nodded too.

'The skies turned the colour of wet slate,' said Thomas. 'We could hear rumbling beyond the horizon and see, beyond the hills, the distant flashing of the brightest lightning the world has ever known.'

'And then the rain started,' said Sarah. 'It rained and rained and rained. And when you looked up, rather than seeing raindrops, it was like whole buckets of water being poured down on to the village.'

'But not a single drop landed on the village,' said Grandma Mary in a hushed, mysterious whisper.

'It's true,' said Sarah excitedly. 'We could see the water landing above our heads, but neither we, nor the roofs, nor the fields became wet. Instead, we stared high above us as the sky slowly disappeared behind a great watery bowl which kept us safe and dry underneath.'

'And by the time the soldiers arrived, all they could see was the newly formed lake: there was no trace of the village,' said Sarah.

'And we're still trapped here today,' added Thomas angrily.

'"*A haven made for safety's sake, became a prison 'neath the lake,*"' murmured Grandma Mary quietly to herself.

'Hey!' said Joe. 'I recognize that.'

'Everyone recognizes it,' said Thomas, scathingly.

'Everyone here might,' said Joe, 'but we're not from Cleedale, are we? We found it in the attic at Clee Manor.'

'You were obviously *meant* to find it,' said Grandma Mary.

'Let me have a look, then,' said Thomas.

Kerry took the old piece of parchment out of her pocket and showed the three members of the Cartwright family the verse.

'But this is only half of it,' said Thomas.

'That's what we thought,' said Joe. 'But we could only find this bit, so we don't know how it goes on.'

'Go on, Grandma,' said Thomas, 'you tell him.'

Grandma Mary took a deep breath and recited the whole poem.

> 'A haven made for safety's sake
> Became a prison 'neath the lake
> For if by now the coast be clear
> The watery bars should disappear
>
> The time will not become the time
> Till come the twenty-first in line
> The boy of autumn, girl of spring
> Will freedom from this prison bring.'

As Kerry and Joe listened, everything became both clearer and yet much more curious. And as she finished, they could only look at one another, wondering what they should do next. The old woman looked from Joe to Kerry.

'Welcome,' she said. 'Welcome boy of autumn, welcome girl of spring.'

'I don't get it,' said Joe.

'Look at you both,' said Grandma Mary. 'Joe, your hair is cropped like the fields of stubbled wheat in autumn, and here,' she continued, running a dry and bony finger down the tramlines the barber had etched in, 'are the ploughed furrows for the new year's sowing. And you, Kerry, with the colours of bluebells and red campions in your hair: the very hues of spring. You two, my dears, are the boy and girl of the poem that Megwyn wrote all those years ago.'

'But how could she know?' said Joe. 'How could she possibly have known?'

He felt thoroughly disoriented hearing that even a haircut could somehow have been predicted by some old woman over four hundred years earlier. It made no sense. But then like so much else that had happened over the previous forty-eight hours, the fact that something was illogical made no difference whatsoever to the situation. Everything was following a logic of its own.

'So it's all up to us, is it?' said Joe.

Grandma Mary nodded.

'And what if we don't want to do anything?' said Joe belligerently.

'Then you'll be spending a longer time with us than you bargained for,' said Thomas. 'And how are you going to like it without your underground video, disco trainers and computles?' he added.

Kerry burst out laughing. 'What have you been telling him?' she asked.

'Just gave him the run-down on the inventions of the twentieth century,' said Joe. 'The poor boy's just a bit confused, that's all.'

Thomas blushed angrily as he realized they were making fun of him. 'Well, whatever they're called, you're not going to see them again unless you help us, and that's for certain,' he said.

Kerry looked at Joe. 'We don't seem to have much option, do we?' she said.

Joe didn't answer her. He'd wandered over to the window and was looking out on to the street where a crowd of people had gathered. As he stood watching, their angry shouting grew louder and louder.

Rex was snarling and barking at the assembled people, trying his best to chase the intruders away.

'What on earth is going on out there?' said Kerry, feeling more than a little uneasy. 'I hope they're not shouting about us being here.'

'I've no idea, but I think we're soon going to find out,' said Joe, as their spokesman strode towards the door with his clenched fist raised.

The heavy pounding sound echoed round the room and everyone inside froze. Four children and one old woman would be no match for the mob outside if they really were intent on violence.

'Who's going to open it, then?' whispered Sarah nervously.

No one moved a muscle.

FIVE

In the end, it was Grandma Mary who made the first move. She pulled herself out of her rocking-chair, straightened up and slowly hobbled over towards the door.

'All right, all right, I'm coming as fast as my old bones will allow,' she croaked irritably.

Outside, the chaotic chorus of shouts and cries had become unified into a single, repeated chant:

> 'Boy of autumn, girl of spring
> Freedom from this prison bring!
> Boy of autumn, girl of spring
> Freedom from this prison bring!'

The shouting of the two lines over and over gradually built up to a deafening, roaring crescendo. The prophecy of the poem was being turned into a demand, and there was no doubting whom they were addressing.

And as they shouted, so Rex kept up his accompaniment of barking, yelping and whining while he tugged and jerked at the lead which was preventing him from sinking his teeth deep into the flesh of the unwanted visitors.

Having reached the door, Grandma Mary took hold of the heavy bolt with both hands and wrenched it across. The man on the porch heard the sound and motioned to the others to be still. Silence fell. The door creaked open to reveal a sea of faces outside.

'What do you think you're doing here?' asked Grandma Mary. Even though her voice was weak and frail, the now silent group of villagers heard her every word. They shuffled about awkwardly, looking at their feet.

'Ebenezer Cudlip, Silas Jenkins, Joseph Adams,' she said, picking out some of those in the front row and making them blush a deep crimson. 'Just what do you hope to achieve by standing out in the street reciting poetry?'

'We've no argument with you, Mary Cartwright, we ...' began the ringleader.

'And as for you, Dr Beamis Kelly,' snapped Grandma Mary. 'You, sir, are a disgrace to your profession. Your job is to cure people of ailments, not to go around frightening old ladies half to death.'

A snigger arose from the centre of the crowd.

'I was merely elected to be spokesman,' he said sheepishly.

'And what, pray, did they elect that you should say?' asked Grandma Mary, apparently warming to her task.

The doctor remained silent.

'We want to see the children!' came an anonymous voice from within the crowd.

'Yeah, we want to see the boy of autumn,' shouted another.

'And the girl of spring,' added another.

'And we want them to get us out of the damned prison under the lake once and for all,' shouted yet another person.

The group was rapidly regaining its confidence as, one by one, the men and women once again started up with their demand to see Joe and Kerry, the children who, it had been foretold, would lead them back into the real world. Realizing that it would not be in the villagers' best interest to do them any harm, Joe walked over to the front door and stood behind Grandma Mary. Kerry followed him. Confronted finally by the boy of autumn and girl of spring, the villagers were thrown into total silence for a second time.

'Ever felt like a chimpanzee?' Kerry whispered to Joe, as the people gawped at them, mouths open wide.

Joe laughed and proceeded to leap around making wild chattering sounds and scratching under his armpits like the monkeys in the zoo. Horrified, the crowd took a step backwards.

'What's going on here?' came a slow, deep, booming voice. It was the blacksmith Joe had been watching earlier.

'Father!' shouted Sarah, and rushed up to him. He wrapped

his arms protectively around his frightened daughter and turned towards the crowd.

'What are you all doing here?' he asked.

'We came to see the children,' said Dr Kelly.

'Did you indeed?' said Henry Cartwright calmly.

'We wanted to see the boy of autumn and girl of spring,' added Ebenezer Cudlip.

'Is that so?' said Henry Cartwright in the same calm manner. 'Well, it seems to me that you've seen them now, so,' he took a deep breath, 'BE GONE. GET OUT OF IT, THE LOT OF YOU!'

To a man, woman and child, the crowd leapt six inches into the air. Then they turned tail and ran.

'GO ON! BE OFF WITH YOU!' he yelled, and helped a couple of the ditherers to leave with a well-placed boot up the backside.

Thomas and Joe cheered.

'Right, come on, you lot,' said Henry Cartwright. 'Inside.'

Back in the house, everyone's heartbeats began to slow down to normal speed. Grandma Mary hobbled back to her rocking-chair, mumbling something about not knowing what the world was coming to, while Thomas and Sarah constantly interrupted one another in their attempts to tell their father exactly what had been happening. In the meantime, Henry Cartwright sat himself down in the largest chair in the room and listened patiently to his children's garbled account of the events that had occurred.

'So,' he said, when Thomas finally got to the part in the story where he himself had entered and got rid of the crowd, 'this is young Joe, is it?'

'Yeah, that's me,' said Joe, and came forward to shake hands. He had liked the blacksmith immediately. He was big, strong and friendly, like an affable bear – and Joe realized sadly how much he had missed his own dad since he'd left home.

'And you must be Kerry,' he said, smiling at her. 'And the

pair of you are here to release the village, is that right?' said Henry Cartwright.

'Well, I suppose so,' said Joe. 'Though we didn't know that when we fell into the lake.'

'I'm sure you didn't,' he said. 'Still, you've certainly not come a moment too soon, I can tell you.'

'But it seems so lovely here,' said Kerry. 'All quiet and beautiful. And no pollution, no unemployment, no wars . . .' she added, thinking of all the things her mother was always moaning about when the news came on.

'And no one's sick, no one's hungry . . .' added Joe.

'And nothing ever happens,' said Thomas, sighing. 'Just day after day after day of exactly the same.'

'Where we come from, people would think this place was Heaven,' said Joe.

'But you can't *live* in Heaven,' said Thomas.

'Only angels can live in Heaven,' said Henry Cartwright, nodding as his son spoke. 'And angels is one thing we are not.'

'And that's a fact that no one could dispute,' came Grandma Mary's truculent agreement from the corner.

Both Kerry and Joe were puzzled. True, they hadn't been in the village for very long but it seemed to have everything going for it. They'd both done so many projects at school – projects on London, proving that city life caused nothing but problems, that small groups work better and more fairly than multinational companies, that processed food with all its Es was bad for you – proving, in short, that the twentieth century was bad for your health. After all, hadn't their working, single-parent mother been forced to send them both away from London for the summer holidays because she was afraid of them turning to drugs or crime – or both – in her absence? And here were the people of Cleedale, apparently in the best of all possible worlds, and yet still not satisfied. They were all so bored that they were clamouring to get out.

Henry Cartwright seemed to know what was going through their minds.

'A prison is a prison, however perfect it may seem,' he said. 'When we asked Megwyn to save the village, I don't think any of us properly understood the consequences.'

'As every second goes by in the outside world, you get a second older,' said Thomas. 'I've been exactly this age for four hundred years.'

'But everyone wants to live for ever,' said Joe.

'Only because they can't,' said Thomas. 'I've tried it, and I've had enough now. I *want* to get older.'

Joe didn't know what to say. He'd dreamt of being immortal – all those things you could do! Why couldn't they all see that?

'Perhaps it's a case of the grass always being greener on the other side,' said Henry Cartwright quietly. He looked up, grinned and clapped his hands together loudly. 'But come on, now, this is all getting far too serious. Everything'll work itself out, one way or another.'

At that moment, the latch of the kitchen door moved and Anne Cartwright came into the house carrying two baskets full of provisions.

'Ah, Anne,' said Henry, getting up and taking the bags from her. 'We *are* glad to see you. We're all famished, right, children?'

'I'm sure you are. It's getting late and I've been chatting away with that silly old gossip, Betty Clegg. Ooh, she does go on.'

Joe thought back to the conversation he'd overheard about the changelings – whatever they were – and realized that Betty wasn't the only one to gossip.

'Right then,' said Anne, and proceeded to hurry back and forth from the cupboards to the table with food and drink.

'Anne, this is Kerry and Joe,' said Henry introducing the two children. 'They're from up there,' he added pointing upwards, through the ceiling.

'And about time, I'm sure,' said Anne, apparently totally

unsurprised by their appearance. 'Now, come on, all of you. There's lots of cold beef and good cider, so come and sit yourselves down.'

Joe and Kerry watched how, before sitting at the table, the other members of the family went over to the sideboard and washed their hands, using the bowl and pitcher there. Not wishing to offend the Cartwrights, they followed suit.

In the centre of the table was a large pewter plate with a huge chunk of roast beef, a basket with slices of bread, and a massive jug full of the clear cider.

'What are you two staring at, then?' asked Thomas. 'Tuck in.'

'Oh,' said Kerry, 'I was waiting for a plate. And a knife and fork.'

She looked around her and saw that Mr and Mrs Cartwright were eating off the table. They had poured a little pile of salt from the carved salt-cellar on to the wood and were dipping the slices of bread and beef into it, before washing the whole load down with a swig of cider.

'A plate, eh?' said Henry Cartwright, looking up. 'You won't find any china in this house. A waste of money, if you ask me: with all the money that you lose in broken plates and glass, you could furnish a whole cupboard with pewter. And when a man's bought once, he is furnished for his children, and his children's children. Isn't that right, Anne?' he added, including his wife in the conversation.

'It is,' said Anne. 'But if they're used to eating their food from something . . .' she said, with slight embarrassment, and went over to the dresser. 'Put your food on these trenchers,' she said, 'if that's what you're used to.'

'Thanks,' said Kerry, and laid her bread and meat on the round cutting-board.

'It's all a bit different,' said Joe, trying to make it clear that his sister wasn't just being difficult. 'If we cut anything on the dining-room table at home, Mum would go mad. It's varnished, not scrubbed like this one.'

'And we have a knife, fork and spoon at every meal,' said Kerry.

'What's a fork for?' said Sarah.

'A nasty Italian fashion,' said Henry Cartwright gruffly. 'You mean that they have become fashionable, eh?'

'You use it for getting the food from the plate to your mouth,' said Kerry, 'so you don't have to use your fingers.'

'What's wrong with the knife?' asked Thomas, feeling, like his father, that somehow they were all being criticized.

'We just don't do it with the knife,' said Kerry.

'You could cut yourself,' said Joe.

'You'd have to be pretty stupid,' said Thomas sullenly.

'More cider?' asked Anne, in an attempt to get the subject off the pros and cons of forks.

'I've got a good knife,' said Joe, also trying to avoid the matter of table etiquette – something which had always been lost on him anyway. He reached into his pocket and pulled out the Swiss Army knife Mick had given him.

'What's the metal?' said Thomas looking at the bright shiny finish to the first blade Joe pulled out.

'Stainless steel,' he said.

'Stainless?' repeated Henry Cartwright.

'It means it doesn't rust,' said Joe.

'Doesn't rust,' whispered Henry Cartwright reverently. 'You have knives which don't rust?' He was evidently impressed.

Joe continued to show the blades: the nail file, the cork-screw, the miniature saw, the tweezers and magnifying glass, the pen-torch and the bottle-opener.

'Oh, and this one's good,' he said to Henry. 'It's for getting out those little bits of gravel that get in the crack of a horse's hoof.'

'Let's have a look,' he said.

Joe handed the knife over to Henry Cartwright, who laid aside his bread and beef to inspect it.

'Useful,' he conceded, almost despite himself. 'And what is this red material?' he asked, fingering the outer cover.

'Plastic,' said Joe.

'What's that?' he asked.

Joe realized he hadn't really got a clue *what* plastic was. 'Well,' he said. 'It's cheap and hard and man-made, and it doesn't rust or rot. And you can get it in any colour.'

'It sounds perfect,' said Henry Cartwright, in genuine amazement. 'It's very light, as well,' he said.

Joe watched his face as the advantages of this new material occurred to him. He had never given plastic much thought before. It was just there. And yet if he could have invented it four hundred years earlier he'd clearly have been able to make a million selling it to the Henry Cartwrights of the time.

When they had finished their beef, Anne brought in a large earthenware pot full of the previous year's soft fruits, steeped in brandy.

'Hey,' said Thomas to Joe and Kerry, 'you must be special, we don't often get this for dinner.'

'Stop telling such awful lies,' said Anne Cartwright to her son. 'There's a big L forming on your forehead.'

'This is delicious,' said Kerry, spooning up the syrupy juice left in the bottom of her bowl.

'Really good,' agreed Joe, with a slurp.

'So,' said Henry Cartwright, as he laid down his spoon at the end of his meal. 'Joe and Kerry. You know now that you've been brought down here to fulfil that old prophecy. And I don't think you can be in much doubt as to what the villagers of Cleedale would like you to do.'

Thomas and Sarah remained silent. Anne Cartwright busied herself around the kitchen.

'We can't force you to help us,' continued Henry. 'But I doubt whether you will want to stay here for ever, and while you are trying to get yourself out, you might bear the rest of us in mind.'

Joe gulped involuntarily. 'But we haven't got a clue what to do,' he said.

'Well, I can't tell you what comes next, of course,' said

Henry, 'but I'd have thought you could have done worse than pay a visit to Megwyn Nashe. After all, she was the one who put us – and you – in this situation.'

Both Kerry and Joe shuddered. It was the same chilled unease which had passed through their bodies when they were sitting in Great-Aunt Eleanor's sitting-room. It seemed to confirm that they were still where they were *meant* to be, doing what they were *meant* to be doing. But more than that: they both realized that every, single move they made was being carefully monitored. Even at that very moment.

Outside, the light had dimmed and torrential rain was threatening to pour down.

'She's at it again,' said Thomas bitterly.

'We all need rain,' said his mother.

'Yes, but does it have to be this afternoon?' he said.

'I don't understand,' said Kerry. 'Who's at what, again?'

Anne Cartwright laughed. 'It's difficult to have normal weather when you're under a lake,' she explained, 'so, after old Megwyn had learnt how to control the elements, she took it upon herself to give us our daily weather. And she still does it.'

'And half the time, she sees fit to dish up the worst weather imaginable,' said Thomas. 'She's a vindictive old witch.'

At that moment, an exceptionally dazzling flash of lightning illuminated the whole room. The thunder which followed less than a second later rattled everything on the shelves.

'I'd keep my voice down if I were you,' said Anne to her son.

'Oh, what do I care if she *can* hear me?' said Thomas.

'There's no sense in deliberately trying to rile her,' Anne persisted.

'You mean she can hear us here?' said Kerry.

'We've never really been sure how,' said Sarah, 'but she must have her methods.'

'There have been too many coincidences,' said Thomas. 'Things that she knew about that she couldn't have known about, if you see what I mean.'

Kerry and Joe knew exactly what he meant and they looked around the room warily. In Great-Aunt Eleanor's rooms they'd had the feeling that someone had been observing them, perhaps through a two-way mirror. Both of them stole a look at the oak-framed mirror above the mantelpiece. But it gave away no secrets. If there was anyone looking through it, they would have to be on the other side of the wall, and neither of them could imagine the indomitable Megwyn hiding herself away in the chimney.

The feeling that they were being watched was not so easy to rid themselves of, however, even if they knew that it wasn't logically possible.

'Let's go and say hello, then,' said Joe, with as much confidence as he could muster. 'Thomas, Sarah, do you want to come with us?'

'I think,' interrupted Anne Cartwright, 'that this first time, you ought to go alone.'

'Oh, Mother,' complained Thomas.

'After all,' she continued, ignoring her son, '*you* are the fulfilment of her prophecy, not my children.'

'I think she's right,' said Kerry, albeit reluctantly.

'Me, too,' said Joe.

'That's settled, then,' said Henry Cartwright, in his deep and forthright voice. 'You two go off to meet Megwyn Nashe and find out exactly what she expects of you.'

'Well, I want to go next time,' said Thomas, angry at being excluded from the action.

'You can, you can,' replied his father.

Joe looked at the blacksmith. There was something about the briskness of his manner which he didn't quite trust. He seemed too keen to get him and Kerry out of his house and down to see the old woman. Were they both being led into some kind of trap?

'It *is* going to be safe, isn't it?' said Joe.

'Of course it is, of course,' Henry and Anne replied in unison.

But Joe had noticed the little look they had shot at one another as they had spoken. It made him feel even more nervous. Why had Anne Cartwright been so determined not to let Sarah or Thomas go with them? Was she keeping something from them, as well? Joe's imagination began to run wild again. He foresaw all kinds of horrors lying in wait for them, growing more monstrous, more malevolent, more menacing by the second. It was Kerry who brought him back to earth, making him jump as she did so.

'Hey, Dumbo,' she said, 'are we going or not?'

'Oh . . . Yeah. Sorry, I was just thinking . . .' said Joe. 'Come on, then.'

Now that it had been agreed that they would go and see Megwyn Nashe on their own, the Cartwrights seemed determined to speed up their departure as much as possible.

'No time like the present,' said Anne Cartwright.

'Make hay while the sun shines,' said her husband, 'even if it is overcast!' he added and laughed loudly, though rather hollowly, at his own joke.

But before the pair of them had managed to usher Kerry and Joe right outside the door, Grandma Mary called to them from the corner.

'Boy of autumn, girl of spring,' she said hoarsely. 'Come over here a moment.'

'They really have a lot to get done,' said Anne Cartwright a little impatiently. 'Is this absolutely necessary?'

'We have waited four hundred years for this moment,' said Grandma Mary. 'I scarcely think a minute here or there now is going to make that much difference.'

Kerry and Joe went over to the old woman and crouched down in front of her rocking-chair. Grandma Mary leant forwards and whispered roughly so that the others in the room could not hear her.

'You mustn't mind Henry and Anne if they seem anxious to see the back of you,' she hissed. 'They mean well. But everyone is so tired of being imprisoned, and Megwyn interprets their irritation as ingratitude. There is mistrust all round. But don't be afraid. Do not forget that you are meant to be here; harm can only come to you if you attempt what you were not intended to attempt.'

'But how are we supposed to know if we're intended to do something?' exploded Joe angrily.

'You *will* know,' said Grandma Mary.

'Humph!' snorted Joe.

'There is only one piece of advice I can give you,' she whispered, taking no notice of Joe's scepticism. 'I've known Megwyn Nashe a long, long, long time. She can be an unpredictable old stick, like the weather. Just remember that, like the weather, there are hot spells and cold spells and they're both as unpleasant as each other. Do you understand?'

'Not really,' said Joe and Kerry together.

It was Grandma Mary's turn to snort. 'Well,' she said, 'even if you don't understand, then at least remember what I said and beware of any hot or cold spells.'

'All right, then,' said Kerry.

'And thanks,' said Joe.

They both stood up and made for the front door. Some kind of a disagreement seemed to be going on between father and son about whether or not Thomas should go to school for the rest of the day now that Kerry and Joe had both been found.

'Oh, Father!' Thomas was whining. 'Do I have to?'

'I think you should,' said Henry.

'But one afternoon can't hurt,' he persisted.

'The thin end of the wedge,' said Henry, 'the thin end of the wedge. And it wouldn't be fair on William, either, if I let you stay away. He's already gone back to school.'

And, while father and son continued to argue about the advantages and disadvantages of missing one afternoon, Joe and Kerry slipped out of the front door.

'Poor old Thomas,' said Joe. 'Can you imagine being at school for so long. No wonder he wants to get out.'

'I'd have thought that anything he hadn't learned after four hundred years was pretty much unlearnable,' said Kerry, laughing.

'That's true,' said Joe.

As they were walking along, the enormity of the task ahead gradually occurred to both of them. They fell into silence and thought about their situation. Two ordinary children from a London comprehensive had somehow been hijacked by the past in order to release a four-hundred-year-old village from a spell which had originally been designed to save them, but which had become a curse. Kerry looked at her brother. He was staring down at the muddy path.

'What are you thinking?' she asked.

'Oh, I don't know,' he said. 'I just can't work out what we should do — assuming we can do anything. I mean, can you imagine this lot in the twentieth century?'

'It would be a bit of a shock to the system,' agreed Kerry, 'but it's what they want. If we do find a way to get ourselves out, we can't just forget about the people here.'

'I suppose not,' said Joe. 'But I can't help thinking that they'd be better off staying hidden. By the way,' he added, 'I hope you know where we're going, because I haven't got a clue.'

'Everything's under control,' said Kerry. 'Sarah told me where Megwyn lives yesterday. Look out for an oak tree with a hollow trunk.'

The trouble was as they had no idea what they were going to encounter when they entered Megwyn Nashe's house, it was almost impossible to make any plans at all. She could be glad that they had arrived and make immediate preparations for the evacuation of the village. On the other hand, she could object vehemently to the twentieth century being let loose on the unsuspecting villagers and oppose any change. Even Grandma Mary's parting words hadn't really given away any clues. There was no way of knowing what they might expect to find.

'Psst,' came a sound from behind the hedge.

'Was that you?' said Kerry.

''Course it wasn't me,' said Joe, looking around.

'Psssst,' came the sound again.

'There,' said Kerry, pointing at a face peering through a gap.

'You were in the crowd outside the house, weren't you?' said Joe, recognizing the face of the man Grandma Mary had called Ebenezer Cudlip.

'That I was,' said Ebenezer, 'and I've got the bruises on my bum from that oaf of a smith to prove it.'

'Well, he's not here now,' said Joe, 'so you can come out from behind that hedge.'

He checked around him, darting his head around as if sniffing at the air to check that Henry Cartwright was nowhere in sight, and then scuttled through the hedge and introduced himself to the two children.

'Ebenezer Cudlip,' he said, and extended a scaly hand to be shaken.

'Kerry,' said Kerry, wincing as his long, claw-like fingernails dug into the palms of her hands.

'And Joe,' said Joe, similarly recoiling from the touch of the little man. His stoop brought him down unnaturally low, and he was forced to twist his bony, twitchy, little face round to look up at the two children. He held his hands in front of him like a praying mantis and, as he spoke, his nose crinkled and sniffed at any new odour which wafted past, while his beady, black eyes darted round keeping a constant check on every nearby movement, however tiny.

'It is such an honour, such a great and wonderful honour to meet the boy of autumn and the girl of spring,' he said.

His voice was curiously high and squeaky, like the sound of polystyrene rubbing on glass. It was almost unpleasant to listen to, but Kerry and Joe waited patiently for the purpose of his interruption to become apparent.

'We've all waited so long for you to arrive, and now that the day finally seems to have arrived, we are all the more impatient to escape the confines of this prison beneath the lake, except . . .'

And he suddenly stopped speaking, so his hands, which had been twisting and writhing round one another, also came to a standstill.

'Except?' said Joe, after a while.

'Except, well,' said Ebenezer, 'is it a very clean place in the twentieth century?'

'Quite clean, I suppose,' said Joe.

'The sea's dirty,' added Kerry.

'Oh, I'm not interested in the sea,' squeaked Ebenezer quickly. 'But the streets, and the . . . waste. Do people dispose of all that . . . cleanly where you come from?'

'What're you on about?' said Joe.

'Well, it's just that . . . Listen to my rhyme. I say it as I'm passing through the village to try and drum up trade, you know . . .

> Rats or mice, ha' ye any rats, mice, polecats or weasels?
> Or ha' ye any old sows sick of the measles?
> I can kill them
> And I can kill moles
> And I can kill vermin that creepeth up and creepeth down
> And peepeth into holes.'

'Ugh!' said Kerry, stepping backwards.

'You're a rat-catcher,' said Joe, grimacing and stepping back with his sister.

'It's a job,' said Ebenezer defensively. 'And someone has to do it. At least they do these days, and that's why I wanted to ask you about the future.'

Joe started to laugh. 'What, you mean whether there are any rats on earth?' he said.

The little man, who resembled nothing so much as a rat himself, played with his hands and nodded nervously, apparently expecting the worse.

'Well,' said Joe. 'There are over five billion people on earth now, and rats still outnumber us. At least ten to one.'

The look that came over Ebenezer Cudlip's face was one of pure joy. His sharp, yellow teeth came into view as his lips curled back in a delighted grin.

'I knew it,' he squeaked. 'I knew there would still be a job for me.'

Kerry looked at him with increasing distaste.

'We really ought to be going,' she said. 'It's getting late.'

'Oh, indeed,' said Ebenezer. 'I would hate to delay you for an instant. I know only too well how important your task is. Yes, go, go. Get us released from this place.' And, as he evidently thought of the countless millions of rats that 'creepeth' and 'peepeth' in the twentieth century, his face burst into another grin.

'Bye, then,' said Joe and Kerry.

'Fare thee well,' said Ebenezer, 'and God speed.' And with that, he scuttled off the road and disappeared from sight behind the hedge.

'What a revolting little man,' said Kerry.

'You're not kidding,' said Joe.

'If we do get the spell taken off the village, perhaps an exception could be made in his case.'

They kept walking along the road. So far they had encountered unanimous support from everyone in the village for trying to persuade Megwyn Nashe to release Cleedale. They wondered, once again, what she herself would say when they appeared. Some way in the distance, Kerry saw a strange-looking tree which seemed to be standing with its legs apart.

'That could be it up ahead,' she said, pointing.

'I think you're right,' said Joe, as they got nearer to it.

The tree had evidently been struck by lightning at some

time in the past and the resulting fire had burned a hole right through the trunk, without actually killing the tree itself.

'Hey,' said Joe, 'it's great. You can get right inside it.'

'It is an oak, is it?' said Kerry.

'I dunno,' said Joe. 'What do oak leaves look like?'

'No idea,' said Kerry. 'Look, there's a path behind the tree — I'm sure this must be the right way.'

'It'd better be,' said Joe.

They followed the track, and continued slowly up the steep hill. According to Sarah, Megwyn Nashe's abode should come into view once they reached the crest. As they walked upwards, it was as though the watery dome of the lake was coming down to meet them.

'That's the trouble with building villages in valleys,' puffed Joe. 'You always have to go upwards to get out of them.'

'Are we nearly there?' said Kerry, who was keeping her eyes on the ground just in front of her, rather than looking ahead at the distance they still had to cover.

'A hundred yards,' said Joe.

The land levelled out ahead of them as they reached the crest of the hill. At the top end of the meadow stood a weird and wonderful house. Both Joe and Kerry stopped walking and stared in awe at the bizarre building in front of them. It looked as though thirty different architects had all been given a little bit to do and then, with no attempt to reconcile the varying styles, had thrown it all together like a fairy-tale, nightmare house.

'Who designed *that*?' said Kerry.

'A six-year-old?' suggested Joe.

Some of the walls had been constructed with local stone, some of them with small red bricks arranged in intricate patterns, while some were white plaster in between oblique wooden beams. The only thing that all of them had in common was that not a single one was a hundred per cent vertical. Set into them were an odd assortment of windows, apparently placed totally at random. Some were filled with traditional, diamond-shaped panes of leaded glass, some were huge, stained-glass affairs, while along one stretch of wall a line of round windows resembling a row of portholes gave that particular part of the house a nautical look. The roofs suffered from the same disparity. To the left of the house, one part had been thatched, while adjoining it to the right was a tiled section. The tiles were various shapes, sizes and colours and gave the appearance of a patchwork quilt. To the extreme right was a flat area of roof; not only was there grass growing up there but also a couple of goats were happily grazing. In front of this particular roof and partially obscuring it was a tall tower. Arrow holes spiralled their way up the wall to the crenellated top. If the house in any way resembled its owner and occupant, then Megwyn Nashe would be a very strange woman indeed.

'Well, here we are,' said Joe.

'I suppose we ought to go and introduce ourselves,' said Kerry.

'I suppose so,' said Joe reluctantly. 'Here goes nothing.'

They began to trudge across the meadow, but before they had gone more than a couple of steps, the air around them began to turn an evil shade of yellowy-grey. A thick, curdling mass of dark vapours swirled round the dome above Joe and Kerry's heads. It seemed to be emanating from the assortment of chimneys decorating the house in front of them.

'I don't like this much,' said Kerry, looking around nervously.

Suddenly, a dazzling thunderbolt came hurtling out of the centre of the clouds and struck the ground a yard in front of Joe's feet.

'My God,' he yelled and jumped backwards.

The smell of scorched grass filled the air and the smoke coiled up to join the ever-thickening clouds above them. A second, third and fourth bolt of lightning hit the ground in rapid succession. They seemed to quiver there like javelins for an instant before disappearing.

'What do we do now?' yelled Kerry.

'We'd better take cover,' said Joe.

'Where?' she screamed. The situation was so terrifying that she could feel herself becoming hysterical. Lightning wasn't even supposed to strike twice, and there, by her feet, were the four smoking holes in the ground that made nonsense of that theory.

'Calm down a minute,' said Joe.

'Calm down?' shouted Kerry. 'We're almost burnt to a frazzle and you tell me to calm down! It's that woman doing this, isn't it?'

'What woman?' said Joe.

'Stop being thick: Megwyn Nashe. She's the one who's in charge of the weather around here, and now she's using it to keep us away.'

'Well, it isn't going to work,' said Joe defiantly.

'I hope you're right,' said Kerry.

Joe didn't hear her words, though, because at that moment the skies opened and torrential rain came pouring down. The smouldering earth hissed and was instantly saturated. It was the heaviest rain either Joe or Kerry had ever experienced, soaking through to their skin almost immediately and transforming the slope into a squelchy, slippery slide.

'This is getting ridiculous,' muttered Joe, picking himself up out of the mud for the second time.

'Whoops!' yelled Kerry, as her feet slid from beneath her and she too came down with a crash.

A stream of muddy water was, by now, pouring down the field, swirling round the two grounded children and out on to the road. And still the rain fell. It was so hard that it bounced back on itself like stones tossed into a lake; so torrential that it filled the air like a blinding blanket of fog; so relentless that it pinned Kerry and Joe motionless to the ground. Shielding his eyes with his hand, Joe peered through the thick, rain-filled air to see if there was anyone up at the windows of the weird house, watching them and seeing how they were coping with the display of violent elements. But the heavy rain had made everything around them disappear. He couldn't see the building, let alone its windows and, turning round, even the nearby oak tree had been swallowed up by the rain.

As he continued to look, however, Joe thought that he could make out something moving around in the gloom. He dismissed it at first as a trick of the light – surely no living thing could be out in the downpour – but there it was again. And another one beside it. And over to the left, another couple. He turned to Kerry and was going to point out what he'd seen, but she had already noticed the shadowy forms.

'What are they?' he saw Kerry mouthing to him.

He shrugged and resumed his surveillance. They, whatever 'they' were, had moved nearer, moving slinkily, stealthily, prowling round as if completely oblivious to the driving rain. One, nearer than the rest, paused in mid-stride and rolled around on to its back. A couple of seconds later, as it leapt up and trotted off, Joe gasped.

In that brief moment, it had more than doubled in size.

'I think I preferred the thunderbolts,' Joe whispered into his sister's ear. She nodded and clutched hold of his arm.

With their cruel yellow eyes shining out of the thick rain like flames, it was as though Kerry and Joe had been surrounded by a ring of fire. But the creatures came nearer still, and as they did so, their lean, muscular bodies became more clearly defined. Half of them were like massive Dobermans, sleek and powerful with lolling tongues hanging almost carelessly over razor-sharp teeth. The feline half of the pack were smaller, but with their glinting fangs and claws, looked no less dangerous for that.

'We're surrounded,' whispered Kerry.

Joe nodded. The animals reacted to his tiny movement furiously. The dogs growled and slavered menacingly. The cats hissed and spat; one of them pounced at the crouching children. They both ducked. After a parting snarl, the cat padded away to rejoin the circle of prowling dogs and cats.

There was nothing that either Kerry or Joe could do. Even the slightest stirring on their part resulted in a vicious display of teeth: they wouldn't stand a chance if they tried to get away. Their hearts raced with terror at the prospect of being ripped to shreds. And still the rain kept beating down, stinging their hands and faces, adding to the muddy sludge their knees were sinking into. Their animal captors continued to be undeterred by the rain. Every so often one or more of the dogs would roll around in the soft earth and even the cats, traditionally no lovers of water, would occasionally lift their angular faces and let the raindrops beat into them.

'They're still growing,' said Kerry.

'I know,' Joe replied.

It was true. The dogs had grown to the size of small horses, while the cats stalked back and forwards like caged leopards.

'I'm frightened,' whimpered Kerry, hiding her head in her hands and trying to block out both the sound of the driving rain and the snarling and hissing coming from the pack of savage beasts surrounding them. 'I wish it would all stop.'

But there seemed little chance of that. The rain continued to pour down like a million nails being hammered into the earth. And as it did so, the snarling, ever-growing cats and dogs began to prowl increasingly restlessly. It seemed as if it would only be a matter of time before they grew bored with their waiting game, pounced on the children and tore them to pieces in their wild frenzy.

SIX

'My little pets been worrying you, have they?' came a strident voice from in front of them.

Kerry and Joe looked up to see that the circle of animals had been broken by a gaunt old woman. Joe wasn't the least bit surprised to see that this was the face of the death-like mask which had stared down at him in the attic. It was inevitable. The woman stood there, looking down at them impassively, her gnarled hands resting on the heads of the gigantic beasts at her side. The massive dog wagged its tail, while the cat noisily purred its contentment.

'Pets?' said Kerry shakily.

'Well, they double as watchdogs, of course — and watchcats,' she added, with a smile. 'You can't be too careful, you know.'

'Is it all right if we stand up now?' asked Joe irritably. He, for one, was not at all impressed with having had to sit in the cold mud for the past quarter of an hour, surrounded by slavering beasts, not knowing whether they were about to rip his throat out or not.

'Of course it is,' she said sweetly, 'and I think it's about time I switched the alarm system off, as well. Follow me.'

Kerry and Joe helped one another up and slithered and tripped their way up the hill after the old woman. As they broke through the circle of cats and dogs, the animals gave one final threatening snarl as if to let them know that it was only the apparent seal of approval they had received from the old woman that had prevented them from being torn limb from limb.

As Megwyn pushed it open, the heavy oak door creaked dramatically, like something out of a Dracula movie. Joe looked at Kerry and raised his eyebrows: it was all a little bit too predictable.

However, what they were confronted with inside was anything but predictable. Both Kerry and Joe gasped.

'You get used to it,' said Megwyn matter-of-factly. 'Shut the door behind you, please, I don't want any of it to escape.'

In contrast with every single style of architecture on the outside of the house, the hallway was like something straight out of a science-fiction novel. Hexagonal in shape, each of the six walls was a giant mirror. Above them, the ceiling was formed into an angular dome by reflecting triangles extending beyond the tops of the walls and meeting directly above their heads. Looking up was like gazing into a kaleidoscope as thousands upon thousands of images shifted and changed, reflecting infinitely in upon themselves. But the design of the hall was nothing in comparison with the spectacular display that was going on within its six walls.

'It's incredible,' said Joe.

'Fantastic,' said Kerry, ducking out of the way of a shower of hail-stones the size of golf balls. 'But what's going on?'

An electric storm appeared to be in progress above them. Forks of lightning and fire balls were spinning round the hall, bouncing off the angular walls in all directions. And as the dazzling blue and yellow flashes vanished, the hall echoed with the deep, sonorous bass of pounding thunder. Snow flurries materialized out of thin air and massive flakes, each one unique in its intricate design, swirled and spun in wild sequences of movements down to the floor, where they disappeared without a trace. As the snow fell, it was mirrored back on itself, creating the optical illusion of falling in criss-cross patterns. At the same time, oblivious of the impossibility of snow and rain falling simultaneously, a fine drizzle was drifting down in a different part of the hall. A ball of intense light in the centre of the room caught the tiny droplets and caused a multi-coloured rainbow to arc through the air and disappear into the mirrors, where it rolled away in stripy waves.

'This is the weather centre,' explained Megwyn. 'I can offer you any weather you care to see.' She went over to a display panel and twiddled around with some knobs.

'I give you a hurricane,' she said, and instantly a howling wind started up. It got stronger and stronger, pulling at Kerry's hair and tugging at Joe's T-shirt. Both children found it almost impossible to remain upright and were forced to lean into the wind at an increasingly acute angle, as it whistled past them, round and round in the strange mirrored hall.

'And a tornado,' screeched the old woman, turning a large wheel in front of her. The hurricane immediately altered its course and character. It started to turn and Kerry and Joe watched, awestruck, as it formed itself into the familiar funnel shape of a whirlwind. The narrow bottom bounced on the floor, sucking up anything it could find there and spinning its booty up towards the ceiling. Kerry stepped back nervously and grabbed hold of her brother to stop herself from being drawn towards the hoovering action of the artificial wind.

'Fog!' they both heard Megwyn announce, as they disappeared into a suffocating blanket of the thickest fog either of them had ever experienced.

'Where are you?' called out Joe. But the fog seemed to deaden his voice as if his whole body had been wrapped in cotton wool.

'I'm over here,' came a distant reply.

'Or frost!' Megwyn called.

The fog disappeared in an instant and Kerry and Joe found themselves standing back to back in the middle of the hall. When they breathed the chill into their noses, their eyes watered and as they looked around they saw that the floor, the display panels, the various articles of furniture – even Megwyn's matted hair and hotch-potch assortment of clothes – were all covered in a thick, furry covering of pure white frost.

'And my favourite of all,' continued Megwyn, 'a display of the Northern Lights. Kerry, Joe, I give you the aurora borealis.'

As she spoke, the edges of the hall were filled with the most beautiful shimmering colours – reds and purples, oranges and greens, all rippling like vast, translucent curtains in a breeze.

And there were sudden flashes and sparks of dazzling light, piercing the pastel shades and leaving after-images of deep violet and fluorescent green. The entire hall was pulsating with colour, and when Kerry and Joe looked at each other and at Megwyn, they saw that they too had taken on the shades of the mysterious performance of lights.

'There,' said Megwyn. 'That'll do for the time being. It tends to be a bit hypnotic if you watch it for too long.' She turned down a dial on the console and pressed a couple of buttons. The colours gradually faded away and the hexagonal hall re-appeared.

'That was the most beautiful thing I've ever seen,' said Kerry, still gazing into mid-air.

'How did you do that?' asked Joe.

'Oh, it's easy when you know how,' said Megwyn modestly, 'although it did take years of practice to get it right. Now, where was I?' she mumbled to herself absent-mindedly. 'Ah yes, the alarm system.' She flicked up a switch on the side of the panel.

'What alarm was that?' asked Joe.

'Against intruders,' said Megwyn. 'As I said before, you really can't be too careful.'

'But nobody from the village would want to steal anything, would they?' said Joe.

'Secrets. Secrets,' said Megwyn and tapped the side of her nose. 'Secrets that would do little good and could do a lot of harm if they got into the wrong hands. After all, the good men of Cleedale might try and leave, mightn't they?'

Joe looked at Kerry. He was beginning to have the horrible feeling that things might not run as smoothly as they had hoped.

'And your alarm system keeps everyone away, does it?' said Joe, trying to keep the conversation away from releasing the village from under the lake.

'Well, would *you* like to chance your lives with my stormy little concoction a second time?' she asked.

Joe shook his head.

'Not particularly,' admitted Kerry, thinking back to the power of the fiery thunderbolts.

'What I don't understand,' said Joe, 'is why you need to do all those tricks with the weather when you've got so many dogs – and cats – to guard the house.'

'But they *are* the weather,' said Megwyn.

'What?' said Joe.

'My dear child,' said Megwyn, 'have you never heard of the expression "raining cats and dogs"?'

Kerry and Joe looked at each other for a second and then burst out laughing.

'You *are* joking?' said Joe. Of course he had heard of the expression; they both had, but they had never had the slightest suspicion that it might have any literal meaning.

'Much more practical all round, really,' said Megwyn. 'I could never afford to feed that many animals. But enough of all this: let's leave my little laboratory here and go and have a nice chat in more comfortable surroundings.'

She led them across the hall, past the work benches covered in their array of bottles, flasks, teat pipettes, pestles and mortars, towards the door on the far side. Before leaving, though, Kerry was determined to have a last look out at the field and, as Joe followed Megwyn, chatting about the weather which – for the first time in his life – had become a subject of some interest, Kerry poked her head outside.

The rain had stopped, and as she watched, the last remaining cats and dogs disappeared down into the ground. Even if she had been tempted to doubt what the curious old witch had told them, the evidence of her own eyes spoke for itself. Megwyn had been telling the truth. *How* she could control the elements remained a mystery, but that she *could* do it was undeniable. It occurred to Kerry that Megwyn Nashe would make an extremely formidable opponent if pushed into that role.

Kerry pushed the door shut quietly and ran across the hall.

She caught up with Megwyn and Joe just as they were reaching the door.

'Believe me now?' said Megwyn sharply, without turning round.

Too stung to speak, Kerry could only blush with embarrassment.

The whole house was like a labyrinth. At first, Joe had tried to remember the route they were taking so that he'd be able to find his way around if they came back to the house. But after the eighth or ninth turn, he realized that there wasn't a hope, and he gave up. They walked along narrow corridors, through doorways, across tiny courtyards with fountains playing, up stairs and under ornate arches.

'It's deceptively large inside,' said Joe, stating the obvious.

'Yes,' was all Megwyn deigned to reply.

And on they continued. And on and on and on and on. If the whole exercise had, indeed, been designed so that they wouldn't know their whereabouts at the end of it, then it had worked perfectly. When Megwyn finally announced that they had arrived where they were going, neither Kerry nor Joe had the faintest idea where they were in relation to the front of the house they'd looked at from the bottom of the field.

For the second time since they had entered Megwyn's strange residence the appearance of one of the rooms took the breath of both children away.

'But it's . . .' Joe started to say.

'So modern,' said Kerry, completing his sentence.

'One tries one's best,' said Megwyn.

The entire room was done out like a twentieth-century sitting-room. There was a large settee and a couple of chairs strewn with cushions, a coffee-table with magazines on it, and pine shelves filled with paperbacks. Most peculiar to Kerry and Joe, however, was the sight of all the electrical goods. Lamps, spots, and fluorescent tubes illuminated the room brightly. There was a stack stereo-system with a deck, double cassette and CD player. Shelves full of records, cassettes and CDs reached up to the ceiling. Over by the window was a pine desk with a home computer on it. And there, in the corner of the room, with the beanbags and low chairs all pointed in its direction, was the most familiar object of all: the television. Kerry and Joe looked at one another and smiled. It was like meeting an old friend. They might be stuck down under a lake in the middle of the English countryside, but the presence of the telly suddenly made everything considerably more bearable.

'It's like the one we've got at home,' said Kerry, nodding over to the telly.

'I wonder what's on,' said Joe.

Megwyn gave them a withering look. 'Real children of the twentieth century, aren't you?' she said. 'Happy at last because you've rediscovered your little electric picture box.'

'Well, you've got one too,' said Kerry.

Megwyn just snorted unpleasantly.

Joe went over to check it out. It seemed to be on, but there was no picture on the screen, just the familiar snowy effect you get when the test-card isn't being run. He fiddled around with the channel knobs, the colour, contrast and volume buttons but to no avail. The snowstorm effect continued.

'Something's not right,' he said finally. 'Something is definitely up.' He looked round the back of the TV. Everything *looked* all right but Joe was far from convinced. 'How come you've got all these mod-cons here while the people outside in the village are living so primitively?' he asked.

Megwyn chose to ignore the question and asked them instead whether they would like something to eat.

Joe was far more interested in the workings of the television, though. He followed the flex from the back of the set

along to the socket in the skirting-board. The plug was curiously cold to the touch. He pulled it out and looked back up
at the screen. The snowstorm was still going on inside the
box.

'You're quite sure you wouldn't like a nice drink and some
cake?' said Megwyn, trying to distract their attention. 'I made it
myself.'

'Have a look at the computer, Kerry,' said Joe, taking no
notice of the old woman. 'See if it works.'

And while she was taking care of that, Joe inspected the
other objects in the room. The lamps were tiny balls of fire, like
miniature suns glowing from inside the lampshades; the fluorescent tubes were nothing of the sort: somehow, Megwyn had
learnt how to tame the power of lightning and fix it permanently as strip lighting. The chrome coffee-table with its glass
top was constructed wholly from ice: opaque and transparent
for the different finishes. The air-conditioning unit led nowhere.
Behind the fake grill was a small alcove and there, presumably
trapped by Megwyn, was a small breeze, constantly blowing
cool air into the room. Strangest of all were the cushions. One
of them was very slightly torn and the contents had spilt out
on to the settee. Neither foam rubber nor feathers had given
the cushions their bounciness. The pillows had been filled with
soft flakes of unmeltable snow.

'The whole place is a fake,' said Joe.

'The materials at my disposal were a bit limited,' said
Megwyn slightly peevishly.

Joe looked at her more closely than he had before. He could
see that she was a very, very old woman indeed. Her face was so
dry and lined that it looked more like elephant hide than human
skin. Her hair was wispy and grey and hung loosely around her
jaws, softening the hard lines of her cheekbones and chin. Skin,
hair, teeth, posture, all of these take on familiar characteristics in
the old, but there was another feature which separated Megwyn
Nashe from others of her age. Her eyes. Joe had never seen a

person with such lifeless eyes before. And yet this was not the first time he had found himself staring deep into the dead depths of so impassive a stare, those horribly familiar yellowed eyes watching him, without anything seeming to register in them. Joe returned their gaze, shivering uncomfortably as he remembered the chilling terror he had felt when, lying in the priest's hole, the eyes had fixed their morbid gaze on him for the first time.

Megwyn sat down on the edge of the settee. 'I see all these strange new devices from the future,' she said wearily. 'But I haven't the means to re-create them here. I'm a witch, not an electrical engineer or a computer whizz-kid.' Megwyn looked exceptionally tired.

'Hey, something odd's happening over here,' Kerry called out. She was standing in front of the computer, pressing buttons and the keyboard at random. The screen was made of glass, the keys of wood, and the floppy discs of black ice, but despite the obvious trickery Megwyn had used to reproduce a facsimile of the future by manipulating the forces of nature, there was definitely something taking place on the screen.

'You've got it the wrong way round,' said Joe. 'This is what the television should be doing.'

There, on the screen of the visual display unit, a soap opera seemed to be in progress. They saw a middle-aged woman nervously pacing up and down a large, over-furnished room. She walked over to the window, pulled the curtains out of the way and looked out for a moment. Whatever she had hoped to see was nowhere in sight and she turned round mumbling indistinctly to herself. The pacing resumed.

'Where are they?' she said. 'Where *are* they?'

With a shock, both Kerry and Joe recognized the voice simultaneously and, as that became familiar, so also did the chaotic appearance of the main character. They realized that, although the perspective of the room was different, they were looking into Great-Aunt Eleanor's sitting-room.

'She looks so worried,' said Kerry.

'She's talking about us, you know,' said Joe.

'I'm not stupid,' said Kerry. 'Oh, look at her. She must think that we've drowned.'

'Or run back to London,' said Joe.

'I wonder if she's contacted the police,' said Kerry.

'I hope not,' said Joe.

Great-Aunt Eleanor paused in mid-stride and walked towards the mirror hanging over the mantelpiece, towards Kerry and Joe – or so it seemed. She looked as though she sensed something, but wasn't quite sure what.

'We're over here!' yelled Kerry.

'Look into the mirror,' shouted Joe encouragingly. 'We're here.'

They saw Great-Aunt Eleanor's face coming closer and closer. It felt as though she was staring deep into their eyes, but she merely fiddled around with her hair, pulling a wayward strand away from her forehead.

'You're making me grey before my time,' she said into the mirror. Clearly, she hadn't the slightest idea that they could see her, but it was eerie being addressed like that through a television screen.

'Hey,' said Kerry, 'that's not fair. You were grey anyway.'

'Eleanor,' shouted Joe. 'Great-Auntie Eleanor, can you hear me, you deaf old boot? We're all right! Don't worry about us! WE'RE OK!'

'She can't hear you,' said Megwyn, from the settee.

'I know that,' said Joe, 'but it can't do any harm.'

'I'm not so sure she can't anyway,' said Kerry. 'We felt we were being watched when we were in the house. And we knew what *you* were feeling when you heard us,' she said to Megwyn.

'Oh, you did come out with a load of nonsense,' said Megwyn.

'Yeah, maybe,' said Kerry, 'but anyway, I'm sure that Great-Aunt Eleanor can somehow feel that we're watching her and sense that we're all right.'

And when they looked back, although they might have been imagining it, a look of relief *did* seem to have spread all over her face.

'Probably just having an adventure on the other side of the lake,' Great-Aunt Eleanor reassured her reflection. She turned round, and as she did so, her elbow caught a vase of roses and sent them crashing to the floor.

'Oh, blast,' she said, and unaware of Kerry and Joe laughing at her, she left the room in search of a cloth, dustpan and brush.

'Is this the only room you can see?'

'Not at all,' said Megwyn, pulling herself up from the settee. 'I can tune in to anywhere in the world. Although, of course, the reception isn't quite as good the farther you go.'

'So you see the whole world through mirrors?' said Kerry, suddenly feeling very self-conscious about the amount of time she spent pouting and posing, trying on new clothes, new make-up, interviewing herself, miming along to records, dancing, dressing, stripping in front of her full-length mirror.

'I do,' said Megwyn.

'And you've watched the pair of us?' said Joe, also feeling a bit of an idiot, knowing that someone had been looking while he'd been prancing about either shadow-boxing with his reflection or playing an invisible guitar.

'I have,' said Megwyn. 'But then that's hardly surprising, is it? You are my own flesh and blood, so to speak, and after all, I did have a somewhat vested interest in your whereabouts.'

She walked over towards the computer screen where the children were standing and pressed a few of the keys. The picture changed. They found themselves looking into an unknown dining-room scene with mother, father and three children tucking into roast pork. Another change and a long, luxurious hall in a hotel appeared with women in furs having their bags carried by uniformed bellhops. Yet another, and a small, dirty bathroom came into view: a haggard woman was miserably inspecting the bruises on her cheek.

'There was always one way that the people of the world could have stopped me, and people like me, prying on them,' she said.

'What, you mean that there's lots of other witches looking in on us as well?' said Joe, horrified, realizing that this increased the odds of him being watched at some time doing something he would rather not have been seen doing!

'The fact that people in your century have stopped believing in witches doesn't mean they no longer exist,' said Megwyn curtly.

'Go on,' said Kerry, returning Megwyn to her point. 'How could we have stopped you?'

'It's obvious. By getting rid of all your mirrors,' she said. 'But then men and women are such vain creatures that that was never really on the cards. No, I'm afraid that your vanity has condemned you to a life of constant observation.'

Kerry and Joe looked away guiltily.

'Of course,' continued Megwyn brightly, 'this isn't a real computer. It's more of a camouflaged crystal ball. In fact, there was never any need for witches and fortune-tellers to have those spherical ones, you know. It was all hocus-pocus, pure and simple. Anyway, I like to pretend that I'm a part of the new technological age.'

'But you could be,' said Kerry. 'All you need to do is to release Cleedale from under the lake, and you and all the others could be living in the technological twentieth century.'

Kerry felt quite chuffed with the way she had slipped the purpose of their being there into the conversation, but Megwyn chose to ignore her. Selective deafness seemed to be a symptom of her old age and she picked and chose what she wanted to hear.

'It does look like a typical room from your decade, doesn't it?' she said, sounding a little unsure of herself.

'Definitely,' said Joe. 'And I think it's all the more clever that you can do all this sort of thing without electricity. I mean, we all use things like computer games and videos, but no one I know understands how they *really* work.'

'Babes in the high-tech wood,' said Megwyn.

'But we wouldn't swop it for anything,' said Kerry, once again bringing the conversation back to the matter in hand.

'You're so keen to destroy everything we've got here in Cleedale, aren't you?' said Megwyn slowly. 'Just watch this.'

She tapped out a series of letters and numbers on the keyboard, pressed 'enter' and waited. After a short while, a series of pictures started to come up on the screen. They remained there for a single second before being replaced by a subsequent image.

A street full of bricks and broken bottles with youths throwing stones at police carrying riot shields . . . four marines in combat gear beating an immobile body . . . the bloody aftermath of an explosion in a nursery school . . . the shivering desperation of a teenage girl injecting heroin into her arm in a public toilet for the last time . . . machine guns stuttering as the sun rises over a bombed city . . . water cannons . . . bullets . . . lethal gas canisters . . . nuclear tests mushrooming into the sky . . . soldiers on every street corner . . .

'But . . .' Kerry started to say. She turned round to talk to Megwyn, but the old woman had wandered off to the far side of the room.

Joe turned away from the screen. There was a lump in his throat but he was determined not to start crying. It wasn't fair just selecting this series of horrible events: there were millions of nice things going on as well, and he told Megwyn as much.

'Joe, Kerry,' she said calmly. 'Come and sit down on the settee with me.'

Although reluctant, they did as they were told. Megwyn patted them both on their knees.

'I'm not blaming you,' she said. 'You do understand that, don't you? But how can I condemn the people who entrusted me with their safety to a world which hasn't changed at all?'

111

'But it has,' Kerry protested. 'It must have.'

'Very little,' said Megwyn, 'and certainly not for the better. Everything you saw was just a fraction of what is happening today. A tiny fraction. Perhaps in your part of the world children are no longer sent up the chimneys to sweep them, but equally horrible things are happening elsewhere all the time.'

'But . . .'

'Joe, do you remember how terrified you were when you were hiding in the little priest's hole and you could hear the soldiers outside? Do you remember that feeling? Do you? That absolutely intoxicating, blind panic, knowing that at any second a soldier with orders to hurt you, to kill you, could carry out those orders? That's the feeling which afflicts millions and millions of people every day in your twentieth century. *That* is why I have been keeping an eye on the outside world to see whether anything has changed. And *that* is why I cannot, with any clear conscience, let the people of Cleedale back out into the real world. They're innocents. They'd be swallowed up in an instant.'

'But they *want* to get out,' said Kerry quietly and simply.

'Yes,' said Megwyn.

'Shouldn't it be up to them to make their choice?' said Joe.

'Even if it turns out to be the wrong choice?' said Megwyn.

'You're being as unreasonable to them as Queen Elizabeth was,' said Kerry.

'You know they're frightened of you,' said Joe.

'I know,' said Megwyn, and her eyes filled up with water. 'It isn't the way I wanted it. I really, truthfully and honestly believed that the world would be a better, safer, fairer place to live in by now. I thought that four hundred years would easily be long enough for the soldiers to have got their marching orders once and for all.'

'It really isn't *that* bad,' said Kerry.

'Isn't it?' said Megwyn.

'*We're* both OK,' said Joe.

'Are you?' said Megwyn.

The old woman seemed to be weakening, her resistance softening, and Kerry and Joe decided to take advantage of the situation. The silly thing was that Megwyn had come up with all the arguments and reservations that they themselves had had about releasing the village. They knew only too well the difficulties the people of Cleedale would have to face. And yet, if the alternative was that they too would have to remain in the village for ever, then they were determined to get the old woman to remove the spell.

'You just can't imprison people for ever and ever,' said Kerry.

'I can't?' said Megwyn.

'They'll thank you for releasing them,' said Joe.

'They will?' said Megwyn, continuing to repeat their words weakly.

Both Kerry and Joe looked at Megwyn: their eighteen-times-great-grandmother. There definitely was a family resemblance. Joe noticed that the pointed nose and chin were like his mother's and sister's. Most of all, though, Megwyn looked like an older version of Great-Aunt Eleanor. It was such a bizarre feeling looking at someone who had been born nearly five hundred years earlier.

She, in turn, looked from side to side at her two descendants: at Kerry, and Joe.

The moment was charged with tension. Would she accede to their request and free the village, or would she obstinately try to keep the people of Cleedale, and now Kerry and Joe too, under lock and key for ever? Would she say yes? Would she say no? The knife-edge seconds silently passing were to prove the closest the three of them would ever be.

'No! I *won't* allow it!' she said, suddenly powerful and strident again. Any show of apparent wavering weakness vanished with those five little words.

'But . . .' said Kerry.

'No "ifs", no "buts",' she said. 'I will not allow all my work to be destroyed.'

'And what about us?' shouted Joe furiously.

'You're very welcome to stay here,' said Megwyn. 'And one day you may even thank me.'

A moment earlier it had almost seemed as though the old woman would come round to their way of thinking. But then suddenly she had made up her mind and any hope they'd had of being able to leave Cleedale had been cruelly taken away from them. Kerry and Joe leapt up from the settee and Joe shouted down at the old woman:

'You evil old hag!'

'You can't keep us here!' yelled Kerry, frustration threatening to turn to tears at any moment. She thought of her mum and dad, all her friends, and of her life at home — where she belonged. And looking down at this ridiculous, self-righteous old woman who was determined to take it all away from her, a sudden fury surged through her body. She leapt forward and began scratching and punching at her hateful, ugly, old face.

'Kerry,' said Joe, and tried to restrain her. 'Not this way.'

'HOW DARE YOU!' screeched Megwyn, pulling herself up with a force and violence that totally belied her frail appearance. 'YOU IMPUDENT LITTLE WRETCH!' she screamed and raised her bony fingers dramatically.

'NO!' yelled Joe. 'She didn't mean it. She didn't. Honest. She was just upset.'

But it was too late. Joe watched, in horror, as dazzling flashes of lightning darted out from her fingernails and found their target in his sister's helpless body.

Kerry felt a numbing thud in her chest which sent excruciating tingles of pain to her fingers, toes, eyes. The next thing she knew she was hurtling through the air and crashing against the far wall.

'I'll show you both,' continued Megwyn, furious now to the point of frenzied madness. 'I'll teach you to cross me. I'll show you what'll happen if you meddle in things stronger than you are.' And she raised the palms of her hands towards the ceiling. Instantly, a viciously cold wind began spinning around the room. Hail and sleet drove into the children's faces. Joe pushed his sister over and took cover himself on the floor next to her, shielding her body from the icy attack. Suddenly, the temperature reversed, and searing tongues of flame whipped round, licking at their feet like dragons' breath.

'Enough,' yelled Joe, cowering behind a table. 'You've proved your point.'

But still the alternating extremes of cold and heat continued to be driven round the room by Megwyn's hurricane.

'You'll kill us!' said Joe. 'Is that what you want?'

Megwyn must have realized, with horror, what she was doing. She lowered her arms again and the elements calmed down. The wind dropped and the extremes of temperature united as a warm compromise. Finally able to check how his sister was, Joe rolled her over on to her front and crouched down next to her.

Her lips were blue and she had stopped breathing. Joe took hold of her wrist and felt for the pulse. He couldn't find it. If they hadn't done first-aid training at the swimming baths he wouldn't have known what to do next, but he'd got a gold medal for life-saving, and the whole kiss of life procedure was as familiar to him as riding a bike. He held the head back, pinched the nostrils gently closed and breathed air into her lungs. Pressing her chest down, he prayed she was all right.

On the second attempt, she spluttered and began coughing violently.

Joe helped her to a sitting position and leant her against the wall. He looked up at Megwyn.

'So the pair of us don't even get to be immortal?' said Joe.

'I can't repeat that original spell,' said Megwyn quietly.

'So there really isn't anything at all for us to gain by staying here, then?' he persisted.

Megwyn simply shook her head.

'You brought us to this place. We didn't ask to come,' said Joe calmly, 'and you're going to pay for it! We're going to leave here, and so is everyone else. If they can live with you for four hundred years, they can cope with my world. You're as wicked as anything going on out there.'

He helped Kerry to her feet.

'Come on,' he said, 'we're going.'

The thunderbolt had taken its toll and Kerry could hardly stand, let alone walk. She tottered around uncertainly, until Joe put her arm round his shoulder and helped her.

Megwyn watched as the boy of autumn and girl of spring she had predicted all those centuries earlier walked defiantly, if shakily, towards the door.

'You won't ever leave Cleedale, you know,' she said, as Joe opened the door.

It was becoming a battle of wills. Joe knew that he couldn't appear to weaken, even for a second. He turned round and stared at Megwyn, hatred and contempt blazing in his eyes.

'Do you want to bet?' he spat out, and slammed the door behind him.

SEVEN

Joe leant back against the door and breathed deeply. It was a relief to be out of the claustrophobic atmosphere of Megwyn's house and yet they still had the infinitely bigger problem to solve: how to get away from Cleedale itself.

'Oh Joe, that did frighten me,' said Kerry.

'I'll bet,' said Joe. 'Come on, let's get away from here so we can do a bit of thinking.'

They walked back down the grassy slope towards the road. At first, both of them were uneasy about crossing the field in case they triggered off the alarm system again. They walked on tiptoe as if picking their way carefully across a minefield. This time, however, there were no thunderbolts, no torrential cloudbursts, no cats or dogs. Megwyn was not putting up any obstacles to prevent their leaving.

'Hey!' said Kerry. She had looked back at the house to see if Megwyn was watching them, making sure that they actually were leaving, and what she'd seen had taken her breath away. 'Am I going crazy, or has it all changed round?'

'What?' said Joe.

'The whole house,' said Kerry. 'Wasn't the thatched roof on the left? And I thought that grassy bit with the goals was over on the right.'

'You're right,' said Joe. 'And the tower's moved as well.'

'It's *all* been jumbled up,' said Kerry. 'But that's impossible, isn't it?'

'It seems to me that everything's possible down here,' said Joe. 'That's what's so worrying.'

Both of them felt totally despondent. It was all very well shouting threats at the old witch, but when they looked at the situation more rationally they really didn't seem to have a lot going for them. She had created this little hideaway section of Elizabethan life and preserved it for the past four centuries: it seemed almost madness for them to expect to be able to undo her work now.

Ironically, the one thing which offered any hope at all was the rather disappointing discovery they had made that *they* were not immortal. What was it Megwyn had said? She couldn't repeat the original spell. Now, there was no reason why she wouldn't have wanted them to live for ever, which meant that she was simply incapable. Did this suggest a weakness? If so, maybe it was something they would be able to exploit later on.

'Psst,' came a familiar sound.

The sound roused both Kerry and Joe from their thinking and dreaming and planning. They turned round to see the rat-like Ebenezer Cudlip emerging from behind a wall.

'So when do we all leave?' he asked, in his squeaky little voice.

'What?' said Joe irritably.

'I am, of course, assuming you got on well with dear Miss Nashe.'

'Well, you assumed wrong,' said Joe.

'You mean there was an unforeseen hitch?' said Ebenezer, twitching his nose nervily.

'You could say that,' said Kerry.

'Oh dear, oh dear,' he continued. 'We were all counting on you. I do hope things aren't all messed —'

'Look, you,' Joe interrupted aggressively. 'Why don't you just get lost!'

'Well, I —'

'I think what my brother's trying to say is that you've had over four hundred years to escape, if that's what you really wanted. We've been here one day. Just one day. It's a bit soon to start getting at us.' She turned to Joe, 'That *is* what you meant, isn't it?'

'Yeah, get lost!' Joe repeated. '*Now!*'

'All right, no need to shout,' said the rat-catcher and scurried off.

Kerry and Joe were left feeling considerably more confident. The time scales involved had put everything back into perspective and as they continued walking along the road to the Cartwrights' house, they managed to convince themselves that things weren't as bad as they'd seemed. It was just a matter of time before they got back to the real world.

'How are you feeling now?' asked Joe.

'Much better,' said Kerry. 'But it was horrible. I felt as if I'd been hit really hard on the back of the head – and then there was nothing.'

'You were better off out of it,' said Joe. 'She went totally spare. Hurricanes, fire and ice: the whole bag of tricks.'

'I can't remember any of that,' said Kerry.

'So you don't remember me giving you the kiss of life,' said Joe.

'You didn't?' said Kerry.

'You'd be dead now if I hadn't,' said Joe.

'Ugh!' said Kerry, wrinkling up her nose.

'What's that for,' said Joe, 'the thought of being dead or the thought of me blowing down your throat?'

'Well, both,' said Kerry.

'Thanks a lot,' said Joe, pretending to be offended.

'No, I mean I'm very grateful,' said Kerry. 'But "ugh" all the same.'

Joe laughed.

'At least *you* were unconscious,' he said.

They were nearing the village again by this stage and both of them realized how hungry they were. The streets were empty, and ahead of them they could see smoke coming out of the chimneys as the women of the households prepared supper for their families.

'Who's that?' said Kerry, pointing to a lone figure sitting, hunched up, on a gate post.

'How should I know?' said Joe.

As they got closer, though, he realized that there was something familiar about the man.

'I think it's Dan Boggle,' said Joe.

'Who's he?' asked Kerry.

Dan, if it was he, seemed to be looking at something in the air above his head. Both Kerry and Joe tried to see what had attracted his attention, but couldn't make anything out. Turning his head this way and that, the man was following the movements of whatever it was so intently that he didn't notice the children approaching. Suddenly, the invisible object must have darted back over his head, because without any warning the figure jerked backwards. So violent was the movement that he totally lost his balance and rolled back off the gate, disappearing from view.

'The village idiot,' answered Joe.

'That figures,' said Kerry.

They both ran over to see whether the man had been hurt. It was indeed Dan Boggle, sprawling on the ground on the other side of the gate. The piece of straw he liked to chew was still there in the side of his mouth.

'Whoops,' he said when he noticed the children looking down at him. 'Head over heels, I bin 'n gone.'

'What were you looking at?' asked Kerry, as Dan stood up again.

He scratched his head in a puzzled way.

'Looking at?' he repeated.

'Something in the air?' prompted Kerry.

'Can't say as I remember,' said Dan. He climbed back on to the gate. 'So,' he said, continuing to chew the straw. 'No go at the Nashe residence, eh?'

Kerry and Joe looked at one another.

'How did you even know we'd been there?' said Kerry.

'Not the biggest village in the world, is it?' he said.

'Well, how did you know what happened there, then?' Kerry persisted.

'A little bird told me,' said Dan.

'A little rat, more like,' said Joe under his breath, thinking of Ebenezer's nasty little face.

'She's a tricky old girl,' said Dan, presumably returning to the subject of Megwyn Nashe. 'I can't say as I envy you your task.'

It was the first time that anyone in Cleedale had acknowledged the fact that what they had to do might not be easy. Everyone seemed to assume that just because they had arrived in the village in fulfilment of the prophecy, they would free it all at once. It was rather a wild assumption anyway: the poem didn't say that they would bring freedom, but simply that freedom definitely would not come before they arrived. And there was all the difference in the world between the two.

'I hope you are successful, though,' said Dan. 'And do you know why?'

'No,' said Joe.

''Cos I've travelled. I've crossed the seas many a time with the Royal Navy of Good Queen Bess. Battled with the Armada of the Spaniards, I have, and sailed with the best of them: the Drakes, the Frobishers, the Hawkinses, the Effinghams. You name them, I've sailed alongside them.'

'And where have you been?'

'Where haven't I been, more like,' said Dan and grinned his black, toothless grin. 'To America and Araby, Ethiope and Egypt — I've been round the Mediterranean so many times it would make you dizzy, it would.'

'Sounds like you've seen it all,' said Joe.

'No,' said Dan, with a firm and serious expression on his face. 'I haven't seen everything. There's just one animal I've still got to clap eyes on and then I can die a happy man.'

'And what's that?' said Joe.

'You know, I've seen some beasts in my time,' said Dan, apparently deaf to Joe's question. 'I've seen massive dark animals, ears the size of doors, noses the length of a man and all coiled round like a snake, with ivory tusks like the branches of a silver birch. And the noise they makes, bellowing louder than anything you ever heard in your life.'

As he spoke, Dan's voice rose from a hushed and intimate whisper to a loud declamation. 'And I've seen animals taller than houses, with necks like chimneys and black, black tongues ripping off the juiciest leaves from right at the top of the trees.'

'Yeah,' said Kerry. 'Elephants and giraffes.'

Dan sensed that they were less than impressed. 'And I've seen dragons,' he announced conspiratorially.

'Dragons, eh?' said Joe. 'And what did these dragons look like?'

'Oooh. Horrible,' said Dan. 'Dragons there are in Ethiope, ten fathoms long. Ten fathoms long! And do you know what they live on?'

'No, but I'm sure you're going to tell us,' said Joe.

'Eggs,' said Dan. 'And do you know how they eat them?'

'Fried,' Kerry whispered to Joe.

Both of them sniggered, but Dan seemed completely unaware of their scepticism.

'Well, the grown-up dragons swallows them whole and then rolls round and round on the ground till they're all crushed up into little pieces inside them. But the little ones don't do that. They can't, 'cos their mouths are too small.'

'So what do they do?' said Joe, gradually being drawn into the superstitious old tales, and wondering how they had been received by the others in the village.

'They're clever little fellows,' continued Dan. 'One of them will take the egg in the coil of its tail and squeeze it. Then he holds it fast till his sharp little scales open the shell up like a knife, and he sucks out the juicy bit inside. Isn't that remarkable?'

'Certainly is,' said Joe.

'Have you actually seen this happening?' asked Kerry.

'With my own eyes,' said Dan. 'As God is my witness.'

'And weren't you frightened, getting so close?' said Kerry, continuing to humour him.

'Not really,' said Dan. 'They won't harm you if you don't

harm them. Anyway, I always carried an apple around with me, just in case one turned a bit nasty.'

'An apple?' said Joe.

'Apples is poison to dragons,' said Dan. 'Didn't you know that, even?'

'I'd forgotten,' said Joe.

''Course, if they *must* eat an apple, they always eat a little bit of wild lettuce first. But I wouldn't have given them the chance, see? First sign of any snapping around or breathing of fire, and I'd have pushed the apple straight into its gob and presto, it'd have been a goner.'

'I'll remember that if I ever come across one,' said Joe.

'You do that,' said Dan earnestly. 'And don't forget that a good turn will always tame a dragon. Don't try and trick them, mind, 'cos they never blinks.' Dan's eyes glazed over as he reminisced about his life on the ship and in distant lands.

'You haven't told us what the one thing is that you haven't seen,' said Joe.

'Nor I have,' said Dan. 'I've always, always, always wanted to see a unicorn. If I could see one of those ... Oh, what I wouldn't give just for a tiny glimpse. 'Course, there's none here in the village, so I've got to get out just to have one last trip around the globe to see if I can't find one.'

Neither Kerry nor Joe had the heart to tell him that unicorns belonged to the pages of myths and legends rather than to real life. Kerry remembered that she herself had dreamt of riding a unicorn when she was young and it was strange talking to a grown man who thought they existed – like meeting an adult who still believed in Father Christmas or the tooth fairy. But then that was what Megwyn had created: a village full of people who hadn't grown up with the rest of the world.

'We've got to be going now,' said Joe.

'See you soon,' said Kerry.

But Dan didn't register their farewell at all. He had resumed his straw-chewing and was staring into mid-air, perhaps imagining his future encounter with the unicorn.

As they walked along the last two hundred yards or so to the house, Kerry had the constant feeling that the people of Cleedale were peeking at them from behind their curtains. She wanted to shout out, 'We didn't succeed!' and have done with it. But she held her tongue. Perhaps it was simply her own disappointment making her feel under observation.

Even Rex seemed to look at them both quizzically as they arrived at the Cartwright house.

'Sorry, lad,' said Kerry, putting out her hand for the dog to lick.

'Next time,' said Joe, and patting Rex on the head he steeled himself for the question that would assault him as he opened the door.

From the very first second, both Kerry and Joe knew that all the members of the Cartwright family had already heard, if not the details of what had happened, then certainly the result. Unlike Ebenezer Cudlip, however, they were a little more tactful. Nevertheless, the immediate silence that greeted their arrival seemed to last almost indefinitely. It was finally broken by Grandma Mary.

'Welcome back, the pair of you. Bet you thought you'd bitten off more than you could chew, eh?' she said, and cackled gently to herself.

'You're not kidding,' said Joe.

'Come and tell me what happened,' she said.

Joe and Kerry nodded a greeting to the others in the room and went over to the old lady. No one seemed to mind the fact that it was Grandma Mary who had taken control of the situation. They were content to wait their turn to talk to the children and carried on with what they were doing. Henry Cartwright was sitting in the chair smoking his pipe and reading a book, Thomas and William were playing cards, while Mrs Cartwright, Sarah and Betty Clegg, the woman Joe had seen on the street earlier, were in the corner busy with a baby.

'I didn't know they had another kid,' said Joe to his sister.

'That's baby John,' whispered Kerry. 'He hasn't been christened yet and there's some problem with changing, or something.'

'Changelings,' Joe corrected her, remembering the conversation he'd heard.

But before he could ask what it all meant, Grandma Mary had indicated with her hand that they should sit down next to her rocking-chair.

'So how did you get on?' she asked.

'Not very well,' said Joe.

'Right, then,' said Grandma Mary, 'I want to hear all about it. Everything from the word go.'

And so Kerry and Joe told her: about the alarm system that had set the cats and dogs raining down on them; about the hexagonal hall where she did all her experiments with the elements; about the room she had done out like a twentieth-century lounge; about the mock-computer and the pictures from the real world. And lastly, they told her about Megwyn's fit of rage and how she had almost killed Kerry.

'I did warn you about the spells she could cast,' said Grandma Mary.

'Did you?' asked Kerry.

'The hot spells and the cold spells; surely you didn't forget,' said Grandma Mary. 'Sounds as though you had more than your fair share of the both of them.'

'Hot spells and cold spells,' Kerry repeated, 'I thought you were talking about the weather, not magic.'

'They're much the same in Megwyn's case,' said Grandma Mary. 'She is the Weather Witch, after all.'

'You mean there are different kinds?' said Kerry.

'Oh yes. After their apprenticeship they all have to specialize. Animals, cures, fertility, that sort of thing. Megwyn chose the weather. Mind you, she was so indecisive that we used to nickname her the "Whether Which". She could always see the opposite point of view. It was almost impossible to pin her down to any sort of concrete opinion. And then when she did finally make up her mind she'd be all the more determined to stick to it because of the time it had taken her to decide.'

Joe explained the way they had almost seemed to convince her while they were sitting on the settee. She'd been simply echoing their points when suddenly, completely out of the blue, she'd started shouting and vehemently refused *ever* to release the village.

'You see what I mean?' said Grandma Mary. 'That's typical.'

'Ever?' came a voice behind them.

'Pardon?' said Joe.

'Did you say that she refused to release the village ever?' said Mrs Cartwright, and burst into tears. 'Oh, my poor baby,' she wailed, and hugged the infant to her chest.

'That's what she said,' Joe told her, getting up. 'But I, for one, am not taking that as her final word on the subject.'

'Well said, young man,' said Grandma Mary.

Joe went over to see the little baby, John. He looked a contented little bundle: even his mother's sudden outburst hadn't wiped the happy smile off his face.

'My name's Betty Clegg,' said the other woman, extending her hand.

'Joe,' said Joe, 'and this is my sister, Kerry.'

Betty Clegg was a short, plump woman with bright red cheeks and curly grey hair. There was something immediately likeable about her. Joe watched her sympathetically calming Mrs Cartwright down while tickling the baby under his chin, and it occurred to him that she would be a good person to have around in a crisis.

'Oh, I'm sorry,' said Mrs Cartwright, 'but I do get so . . . so worried about the baby, his not being christened and all.'

'I don't understand,' said Joe.

As far as he knew, neither he nor his sister had been christened either, but he kept this titbit of information to himself until he found out what significance this had had four hundred years ago.

'It's a problem with changelings and all,' said Betty confidentially.

That word again. Joe and Kerry exchanged glances.

'I don't think we have them nowadays,' said Kerry. 'That is, outside in the real world.'

'You don't?' said Mrs Cartwright. 'Oh, what a marvellous place that must be then, mustn't it, my little darling?' she said to the baby and laid him back down in his cot.

As she covered up his little body with a woollen blanket, Joe noticed something glinting from the bottom of the cot. He looked closer and there, at the edge of the mattress, was a sharp and shiny knife.

'What on earth's that doing in there?' he asked.

Mrs Cartwright made no effort to explain, so it fell to Betty Clegg to reveal all. But instead of speaking, she recited some kind of verse to them.

> 'Let the superstitious wife
> Near the child's heart lay a knife,
> Point be up and haft be down,
> (While she gossips in the town)
> This, 'mongst other mystic charms
> Keeps the sleeping child from harms.'

'Surely he's more likely to come to harm sleeping next to a blade,' said Joe.

'You don't understand,' said Betty. 'Baby John hasn't been baptized yet and he's in mortal danger of being stolen by fairies and replaced by some monstrous little changeling.'

'Or they could just bewitch him,' added Mrs Cartwright.

'And if he died, God forbid, then he couldn't go to Heaven,' said Betty.

'I can't bear the prospect of any of those alternatives,' said

Mrs Cartwright. 'That's why we've got to get out of here, we've got to get time moving again so that I can get the poor little soul to a church.'

'But why can't you, anyway?' said Joe.

'Because every day is a repetition of the day before,' said Mrs Cartwright, threatening to start crying again. 'And it goes on and on. I can't take much more of it. I really can't.'

'But if every day is the same,' reasoned Joe, 'and he wasn't stolen or swopped or killed yesterday, then he won't be today or tomorrow.'

'Just because Megwyn has stopped us from getting older, it doesn't mean that she's had any influence over the little people, does it?' said Mrs Cartwright. 'Oh, I don't know. If it wasn't for Betty Clegg here, I don't think I could go on.'

'I helped deliver the baby,' explained Betty.

'You're a midwife?' said Kerry.

'Indeed I am,' said Betty. 'I was there when all this lot were born. Thomas, Sarah, William and John, and even their mother, Anne. Wasn't I, my dear? The whole caboodle — well, except for Grandma Mary,' she added and laughed. 'Of course, since we've been trapped under the lake there haven't been any new babies at all. There's one woman in the village and she's been seven months pregnant now for four hundred years!'

'I quite wanted to be a midwife,' said Kerry, 'but most babies are born in hospitals.'

'You don't say,' said Betty, looking thoughtful. 'It hadn't occurred to me that my skills might not be necessary in the future.'

'Perhaps you could become a nurse,' said Kerry. 'Although it's very badly paid,' she added.

'Oh, I'm sure I'd find something to do,' said Betty brightly again.

'I'm sure you will,' said Mrs Cartwright. 'She was a wonderful midwife,' she added to Kerry. 'She never blabbed or gossiped about anything she saw or heard in the houses where she helped with the deliveries. Her fingernails were always clean and nicely clipped, and she would always use the best butter to rub into her hands at the birth. Not like some I could mention who use nothing better than pig fat.'

It dawned on Kerry how little training, if indeed any at all, Betty had received. And at a time when there were no antiseptics, no antibiotics and no anaesthetics to ease the pain, childbirth must have been a terrifying experience at the best of times.

'And of course she is of unimpeachable character,' continued Mrs Cartwright, 'which is essential, you know. If the midwife has any history of being a criminal or a drunkard, the infant could easily take after her.'

'I'll tell you something else,' said Betty. 'When you're feeding the baby you have to be *so* careful that no blood gets into the milk. The slightest drop, and the child could grow up to be a murderer.'

Both Kerry and Joe had to stifle a grin. Neither of them had heard so many old wives' tales in their lives. Knives in the bed, butter on the hands, blood in the milk. But then as they were listening to the original 'old wives' themselves, it was hardly surprising.

'Well might you smirk,' said Betty, 'but I could tell you some stories as would make your hair curl.'

'Be difficult in young Joe's case,' Henry Cartwright called out, looking up from his pipe. 'When are you two old gossips going to stop chattering and start getting my dinner ready?'

Kerry and Joe looked at each other again. That was the sort of comment that had led to a considerable number of their parents' rows. Mick would come in, make some demand and Susan would just about hit the roof. One birthday, she had given him a huge inflatable pink pig and labelled it 'to the biggest chauvinist in the world'. This little gesture had led to the most impressive slanging match either Kerry or Joe could remember them having. After he'd popped the pig with the end of his cigarette, their father had left the flat and not come back for over a week.

Anne Cartwright, on the other hand, didn't bat an eyelid.

'I'll just get the baby to sleep, dear,' she said.

As she, Betty and Sarah were singing baby John a lullaby, Kerry turned and whispered into Joe's ear: 'I don't think mum would have liked the sixteenth century much.'

'I think I might have, though,' he whispered back.

'Pig!' said Kerry, and elbowed him in the ribs.

The lullaby the three of them were singing was familiar:

> 'Rock-a-bye, baby, on the tree top,
> When the wind blows the cradle will rock;
> When the bough breaks the cradle will fall,
> Down will come baby, cradle, and all.'

'Just think how many times that nursery rhyme must have been sung over the last four hundred years,' said Kerry.

'It's still the most stupid one I've ever heard,' said Joe. 'What kind of idiot would put the baby up a tree, anyway?'

Baby John was fast asleep even before the song came to an end. Mrs Cartwright went over to the stove and stirred a large pot of stew which had been bubbling and filling the room with increasingly mouth-watering smells.

'Soon be ready,' she said. 'I'll just do some dumplings. Betty, if you're staying for supper, could you do me a favour and get some suet out of the pantry.'

Henry Cartwright had laid his book aside.

'So,' he said to Kerry, 'you still sing "Rock-a-Bye, Baby" to your little ones, do you? What others do you know?'

'Oh,' said Kerry, 'there are lots. "Baa, Baa, Black Sheep".'

'Yep,' said Henry. 'I know that one.'

'"Little Boy Blue" and "Bye, Baby Bunting".'

'Those as well,' said Henry.

'"Humpty Dumpty",' added Joe.

'That's new on me,' he said. 'Still, it's nice to know that, by and large, so little has changed.'

'I wouldn't go that far,' said Kerry. 'This whole village is pretty weird for us. No gas, no electricity, no television, no cars . . .'

'Whoa! whoa!' said Henry. 'Now start at the beginning: what do you mean, "no gas"?'

Thomas and William, who had been listening in on the various conversations while they were playing cards, decided that this one was worth paying proper attention to. They laid the pack down and pulled their chairs over to where the others were sitting.

'Well,' said Kerry. 'We get gas from under the North Sea, and it's piped all over the country for –'

'Under the sea!' interrupted Henry Cartwright and guffawed with laughter. 'That's ridiculous!'

'No more ridiculous than your village being under a lake,' retorted Kerry.

'She's got you there, Father,' said Thomas.

Henry reddened a little, but said nothing.

'And it's used for cooking and heating, you know, central heating – heating all round the house,' she explained. 'And electricity is the other form of power. And it's also used for lighting all the streets and buildings, so it's as bright as day all the time if you want. And running the Underground trains. And . . . Oh, Joe, help me, my mind's gone blank.'

Joe had been watching the expressions on the faces of the three Cartwrights. He'd already faced the same kind of brick-wall response when he was talking to Thomas. There was no meeting point. Just as he found it hard to believe half the things that were going on around him, so the Cartwrights would have to experience the modern world at first hand before any of the words Kerry was using could take on any real meaning.

'And then there are the cars,' continued Kerry.

Joe winced. He'd hoped she wouldn't bring them up again, but it was already too late.

'What are cars?' asked Thomas.

'They're vehicles. The way people travel about, you know,' said Kerry.

'You mean people don't travel on horseback?' said Henry Cartwright slowly.

'Oh no!' said Kerry enthusiastically. 'Most adults have got a car: they're much faster than horses. Seventy miles an hour you're allowed to go on the motorways – although most people drive even faster than that.'

Joe watched as the incomprehension spread over the Cartwrights' faces. Seventy miles an hour and over. They simply couldn't take in that sort of speed.

'So people don't have horses, then?' Henry persisted.

'No, I told you,' said Kerry. 'They're too impractical. Oh, there are a few rich people who ride them at the weekend for a hobby, but that's all.' Kerry looked around the four sombre faces. She couldn't understand what they were all looking so glum about.

'It's all right,' said Thomas. 'There'll be lots of new jobs that you can do.'

As he tried to comfort his father, it suddenly clicked with Kerry what she had been saying. She kicked herself mentally for being so stupid, but it was too late to take back her words now. Anyway, she thought, they ought to know what was awaiting them.

'Hey, I've just remembered something. You'll like this,' she said, and ran up to the room she'd slept in the night before. She was back a moment later carrying a small box. 'I was wearing this when I fell into the lake,' she explained. 'As long as no water's got inside the casing it should be all right.'

'What is it?' asked the two Cartwright boys together.

Kerry put the little headphones on and pressed the button on the side of the Walkman. Thomas, William and Henry looked at one another, obviously totally unimpressed with the tinny, percussion noises that were escaping from the ear-pieces.

'Yeah, it still works,' said Kerry, taking them off.

She put them over Thomas's ears. Joe wished he could have photographed the expression of sudden bewilderment which flashed across his face. He sat bolt upright and then started looking desperately around the room. Finally, he wrenched the headphones off and stared at them intently.

'What is it, son?' said Henry. 'You look as if you've seen a ghost.'

'Music,' muttered Thomas. 'Right inside my head.'

'I want a go,' said William.

Kerry turned the volume down a little and put the headphones on William. Being more prepared for the sound than his brother, he didn't jump so violently and after a couple of seconds was tapping his feet along to the beat.

'IT'S WONDERFUL!' he yelled.

'There's no need to shout,' said Henry.

'I SAID IT'S WONDERFUL!' yelled William even louder.

Joe and Kerry got an attack of the giggles watching the grinning William swaying back and forwards to the music that only he could hear, and shouting out his comments, unaware of how loud he was being.

'Take them off the boy, for Heaven's sake, before he deafens the lot of us,' said Henry Cartwright.

Kerry did so and passed the headphones over to him. He slipped them on and, totally motionless, he listened to the sounds filling his head. After a couple of songs he removed them.

'And it's all inside this little box,' he said. 'What instruments were playing? I didn't recognize them.'

'Synthesizers mainly,' said Kerry, 'and it's no good asking me what they are, because I really don't know,' she added, with a laugh.

'What a strange world you must live in,' said Henry slowly.

'You have so much more than we do, and yet you don't seem to understand how even a fraction of it works.'

'True,' said Joe.

'I'll tell you what,' said Anne Cartwright, looking up from her stew pot, 'I know how I work.'

'How?' asked Henry.

'Hard!' said Anne. 'Your dinner's ready. Come to the table, everyone.'

The meal was a quieter affair than earlier. For a start it was late and everyone was tired after the long day. But there was a second and more important reason: with the exception of Kerry and Joe, who knew exactly what *they* wanted, each and every one of the people sitting at the table had to rethink their decision to get out of Cleedale.

Anne Cartwright desperately wanted time to start moving again so that she could have baby John christened. But then judging by how little either Kerry or Joe knew of the Christian customs that were common knowledge to everyone in the village, what kind of godless world were they heading for?

And when Betty had heard that the population of Great Britain was over ten times the size of Elizabethan England she had happily envisaged herself delivering babies every day, but now she had been informed that her services would probably not be needed in the future, she would have to think again.

Thomas and Sarah were still fairly sure they would like the future, although when Thomas heard he would have to study for a further six, instead of two, years if he wanted to go to college, he balked at the idea; and Sarah, almost despite herself, was shocked by Kerry's outgoing and, in her mind, unfeminine character. She was nervous about living in that sort of world. William, for his part, didn't care one way or the other.

Of them all, it was Henry Cartwright who was most concerned. He had always accepted his role as provider for his family and worked hard in his smithy, earning the money to ensure they lacked for nothing. In the future, if there were cars then there were no horses. And if there were no horses, no horseshoes would be needed. In short, he would be totally superfluous. The thought terrified him, and not even Kerry's encouraging words could dislodge his growing unease.

But then, weighed against all these negative aspects was the fact which still remained that being imprisoned under a lake, condemned to repeat the present for ever and grow no older, was intolerable. Surely it wouldn't be impossible for any of them to adapt to the future.

Kerry and Joe watched the faces of the villagers mulling over the possibilities as they tucked into their delicious lamb stew and dumplings. When they all finally laid their spoons down next to their bowls, no one seemed inclined to talk. The atmosphere was oppressive. As usual, it was Grandma Mary who punctured the gloom.

'Tomorrow is another day,' she said.

'Except it isn't, is it?' said Henry. 'It's just more of the same.'

'Oh, I don't know,' said Grandma Mary. 'Since Kerry and Joe arrived I, for one, have noticed differences.'

'Perhaps you're right,' said Henry. 'Anyway, I think we should all sleep on it: "In winter at nine and in summer at ten . . ."' he started to say.

The rest of the family joined in for the second line: 'To bed after supper both maidens and men.'

'Not where we come from,' said Kerry, laughing. 'That's when all the best programmes come on the telly.'

'You two and your television,' said Henry.

All five children were sleeping in the same room. Anne had made mattresses up on the floor for Thomas and William, so that the two guests could have beds. It probably wasn't that fair, but neither Kerry nor Joe objected.

The other occupant of the room was the children's pet, a tame red squirrel called Tag that they kept from running away by attaching it to a hook with a long, long leather thong. A little bell was tied around its neck. It jumped up on to William's shoulder and sat there, chattering.

'I've never seen a red squirrel before,' said Kerry. 'All we get now are grey ones, and you can't tame them, I don't think.'

'What does all this mean?' said Joe looking at an embroidered poem in a picture frame on the wall.

> With curtain some make scabbard clean,
>   With coverlet their shoe;
> All dirt and mire, some wallow abed,
>   As spaniels used to do.
>
> The sloven and the careless man,
>   The roynish, nothing nice,
> To lodge in chamber comely decked
>   Are seldom suffered twice.

'Basically, it means that if you're a dirty so-'n-so, you won't be asked to stay again,' said Thomas.

'What's a "roynish"?' asked Joe.

'It's like a video nasty with legs,' said Thomas, and grinned.

'Are you taking the mickey?' said Joe.

'Might be,' said Thomas. 'You're not the only one with lots of new words, are you?'

'Come on, you two,' Sarah called out from her bed. 'Put the lamp out.'

'Yeah, we should,' said Joe. 'I have the feeling that tomorrow's going to be the make-or-break day.'

Thomas blew out the flame and the room was plunged into darkness. Joe lay on his back looking upwards. At first, a chill of horror shuddered through his body as he remembered his terrifying experience in the priest's hole. But this time, after a couple of minutes, his eyes grew accustomed to the dark and he looked at the beams of the sloping ceiling.

The more he thought about their predicament, the more clear it became to him that even if the villagers were beginning to have second thoughts about abandoning Cleedale, he and Kerry would have to try as hard as they could to leave. Unfortunately, even though it was the last thing he wanted to do, a second trip to Megwyn Nashe's seemed to be unavoidable. The key to leaving the village *must* lie there.

But this time she would not find them such a pushover!

'Kerry,' he whispered, 'are you awake?'

'Mmm,' she murmured. 'What do you want?'

'Today, all we managed to do at Megwyn's was weather the storm,' he said. 'Tomorrow, it'll all be different. We're going to storm the weather! Do you get it?' he asked. '*Storm* the *weather*!'

But the only sound that came back from Kerry's bed was that of deep, sleepy breathing.

'Well, I thought it was good,' said Joe to himself, and rolled over on to his side.

EIGHT

'Come on, you two! Up you get!' came an insistent voice.

Neither Kerry nor Joe stirred. It just *couldn't* be time to get up.

'Come on!' the voice repeated more urgently.

Joe opened his eyes reluctantly and peered round the room. The mattresses and bed where the Cartwright children had been sleeping were already empty and the whole of the attic room was bathed in the curious turquoise daylight of the underwater village. Thomas was standing over by the door.

'What time is it?' asked Joe.

'It's gone four,' said Thomas.

'What, four in the morning?' said Joe irritably. 'You must be crazy.'

'The sun's already up,' said Thomas. 'And so's everybody in the house, except for you two.'

'But why?' groaned Joe.

'Your breakfast's on the table,' said Thomas gruffly, and stomped off downstairs.

Kerry rolled over and yawned. 'Welcome to sunny Cleedale,' she said. 'This happened yesterday morning as well.'

'I suppose they need to make use of all the sunlight they can get, but you'd have thought they could have made a bit of an exception in our case,' said Joe. He pulled himself out of bed and rubbed his eyes. 'I slept well, anyway,' he said. 'Where do we wash?'

'There's a jug and bowl on the dressing-table,' said Kerry.

It didn't take more than a couple of minutes before they were sitting down at the table having breakfast. It still felt a bit too much like the middle of the night to be eating, but the smell of the frying bacon woke up both their appetites. Two fried eggs, two rashers of bacon, two slices of fried bread, parsley and mushrooms, toast and honey, and two beakers of milk each later, they were feeling just about ready to start the day.

'Looking a bit more human now,' said Henry Cartwright to the pair of them, as they laid their empty beakers down. 'You looked awful when you came down.'

'This is all very early for us,' said Joe.

'We don't usually get up till about eight,' explained Kerry.

'You miss the best part of the day,' said Henry.

'That's what Great-Aunt Eleanor says,' said Joe.

'Well, I don't know who she is, but she's certainly correct on that one,' said Henry approvingly.

'More toast, anyone?' said Anne Cartwright, 'or shall I start to clear the things away.'

'None for me, thanks,' said Kerry.

'I'm full,' said Joe.

'So,' said Henry, 'have you made any plans for today?'

'Yeah,' said Joe, aware of the fact that the mirror above the mantelpiece was probably relaying the information straight back to the Weather Witch herself. 'We've got to go back and see Megwyn again.'

'Not that we want to,' said Kerry, screwing her face up.

'But we haven't got any choice,' said Joe. 'She *must* have the answer.'

'I think you're right,' said Henry.

'And *we're* going along this time too,' said Thomas, 'aren't we, Sarah?'

She nodded, rather reluctantly.

Henry looked at the pair of them as though he was about to forbid it again.

'You promised,' Thomas reminded his father.

'Well, I'm still not happy about it,' said Anne.

'They'll be all right,' said Henry.

'Thanks, Father,' said Thomas.

'If anything happens to those children,' said Anne ominously.

'What, I'd be to blame then, would I?' said Henry, turning on her.

Joe and Kerry looked at each other. This was all beginning to sound horribly familiar. How many times had they triggered off arguments between their parents? On several occasions they'd both had the feeling that they were there simply to provide the excuse for a good row. Thankfully, a timely knock on the door nipped any angry words in the bud.

'That'll be the doctor,' said Grandma Mary, from her rocking-chair.

Still far from happy, Anne Cartwright went over to let him in.

'Morning, Dr Kelly,' she said.

'Morning, Anne, Henry,' he said, nodding over towards him. 'Children.'

'Morning,' they all replied.

Joe recognized him as being the spokesman from the previous day's deputation to the front door. He had a strong Irish brogue, and both Kerry and Joe found him much easier to understand than any of the Cartwright family. It was almost like meeting someone from the present: his accent, however, was to prove the only familiar aspect of the good doctor.

'Morning, Mary,' said Beamis Kelly, going over to examine her.

'You're late,' she snapped, and looked away.

'A bit held up,' he explained vaguely. 'And how are you this bright and sunny morning?' he asked.

'No better at all,' she said.

'She still has the most awful attacks of the shivers, Doctor,' interrupted Anne Cartwright.

'Ah, the ague, the ague,' said the doctor, 'a curse on all us old'uns.'

'And I don't know how many leeches you're going to have feasting on me before my gout gets any better,' said Grandma Mary, leaning down and massaging her swollen feet.

'Leeches?' Kerry mouthed at her brother in amazement, and started giggling.

She and Joe left the table and went over to where Dr Kelly was carrying out his consultation with the tetchy old woman in her rocking-chair.

'If it isn't the boy of autumn and the girl of spring,' said the good doctor, beaming and extending a hand of welcome. He was wearing a makeshift suit of a dark material, with a tight-waisted jacket and baggy breeches. Tied around his lower arm was a small cotton bag which swung back and forth as he shook hands with the children.

'Yes, I've got a bone to pick with you,' said Grandma Mary. 'What kind of a doctor goes gallivanting around the town with a bunch of ne'er-do-wells and fishwives causing an affray, in front of one of his patients' houses, huh? Tell me that.'

Beamis Kelly fawned and cringed accordingly.

'I'm so very sorry,' he said. 'I must confess I was carried along with the spirit of the moment, the enthusiasm of the crowd, the crest of the wave of elation I felt on hearing that our four centuries of being locked away might soon be coming to an end.'

'Hmm,' grunted Grandma Mary, unappeased.

'Please accept my most humble of apologies,' said Dr Kelly, squirming painfully under her critical gaze.

'Accepted,' said Grandma Mary irritably. 'They might not be coming to an end so quickly, anyway,' she added, just to rub salt into the wound.

'But why?' said the doctor, spinning round to face the children. He looked genuinely shocked.

Joe and Kerry shrugged.

'Megwyn Nashe is a very powerful witch indeed,' said Grandma Mary. 'It's going to take an awful lot to outsmart her. Anyway, enough of that. What about me? When are you going to cure my ills?'

'One moment, one moment,' said Doctor Kelly, picking up

his black case and laying it on the table next to her chair. 'First, I think, the ague.'

'What is ague?' asked Kerry.

'Oh, a horrible illness, to be sure,' said the Doctor. 'The sufferer is afflicted alternately by hot, sweaty flushes followed by the shivers, so extreme that the teeth rattle in their sockets.'

'Sounds like flu,' said Joe.

'We take a paracetamol for that,' said Kerry.

'Parrots what?' said the doctor.

'It doesn't matter,' said Kerry.

'What do *you* do?' asked Joe.

'I,' said the doctor pompously, 'follow the advice of the great French physicians of the day.' And so saying, he unlocked his case. Inside, it was lined with royal-blue velvet and divided into innumerable tiny compartments. He pulled out a small silver box from one of them and laid it ceremoniously down on the table. Next, he took out a crystal bottle filled with a deep-orange syrup. He unstoppered the bottle in preparation and placed it next to the silver box. What was to happen next occurred in only a matter of seconds, so swiftly, in fact, that Kerry and Joe could scarcely believe what they had just witnessed.

'Here we go, then,' said Dr Kelly, flicking open the silver box and carefully removing its occupant: a large black spider. This he placed on a spoon taken from his case. To prevent it from running away, he pressed down on two of its legs with his index finger. Then, with remarkable dexterity, he poured the syrup from the bottle into the spoon, completely covering the spider with the sticky substance, and popped the whole lot in Grandma Mary's waiting, open mouth.

Kerry and Joe were so surprised, shocked and sickened by what they saw that they were never to forget it for as long as they lived.

'That's disgusting,' said Kerry.

'It's the best treatment I know,' said Dr Kelly.

'Well, thank God you're not my doctor,' said Kerry.

'Another *very* good reason for leaving Cleedale,' said Joe.

The doctor's visit was only half-over, however. There was still the problem of the gout. He replaced the bottle and box and pulled out a larger casket.

'What's in that, cockroaches?' said Joe.

'What, for gout? Don't be ridiculous, young man,' said the doctor. 'We can see how much *you* know. Gout is a very tricky complaint. Often we recommend bleeding to remove the poisons — the leeches, you understand. But I think this morning, something a little less severe.'

Kerry turned away. She felt distinctly ill just thinking about what the box might contain. She looked over to Grandma Mary, but the sight of the old woman sitting there licking her lips made her feel even more sick.

'Oh, you're not going to make her eat those,' she heard Joe saying, and looked round despite herself.

The casket was full of a line of dead mice, all lying rigid in death like a box of cigars.

'Eat them!' said Doctor Kelly, shocked. 'Most certainly not.'

He took out one of the mice and laid it carefully on a silver tray. Then, with the precision of a surgeon, he sliced the mouse in two with a single stroke of his scalpel.

'Right, feet up,' said the doctor to Grandma Mary.

She did as she was told, and when her feet were resting on the footstool, he carefully laid the two halves of the mouse on her swollen ankles.

'And that's meant to be good for arthritis, is it?' said Joe.

'Half a what?' said the doctor.

'For gout.'

'Indubitably,' he replied.

Perhaps it was shock, perhaps it was the thought that she might get some illness and have to be treated by Beamis Kelly. For whatever reason, Kerry suddenly got a fit of the giggles. The sight of the yellowed old woman sitting there with her feet sticking out in front of her, half a dead mouse on each foot and a live spider inside her, began to amuse her. And then she heard her brother humming an old song their mum had sung to them both when they were younger and the laughing got all the louder.

> 'I know an old lady who swallowed a spider,
> That wriggled and jiggled and tickled inside her.
> She swallowed the spider to catch the fly,
> I don't know why she swallowed the fly;
> Perhaps she'll die.'

And Joe started to laugh too.

'I don't know what you two find so amusing,' said Dr Kelly. 'Mice have all manner of healing properties,' he continued, with as much dignity as he could muster. 'For instance, fact number one: if you have warts, just lay a half a mouse on them for half an hour and then bury it. As the mouse decomposes, so the warts will disappear.'

Fact number one started both Kerry and Joe laughing even harder.

'Fact number two: if you've got a really bad case of the toothache, you could do a lot worse than eating a mouse which has been appropriately flayed and beaten.'

Kerry clutched at her stomach. She looked around the room at the expressions of the various members of the Cartwright family. Their seriousness only made her laugh all the more.

'Fact number three, and a tip for you, young lady,' said Beamis Kelly. 'If you want your eyelashes to grow thicker just take some young mice which have been beaten into small pieces, mixed with old wine, and boiled, and apply them twice a day.'

'Oh . . . ol . . . old wine, you say?' said Joe, trying to get the words out while holding his stomach and laughing. Tears were streaming down his cheeks.

'I think I'll stick to mascara,' said Kerry.

'And, of course, the burnt heads of mice make the base of an excellent powder for the scouring and cleansing of teeth,' continued the good doctor.

'Poor little mice,' said Kerry, regaining control a little.

'Oh, mice aren't the only animals which are used to benefit mankind,' said the doctor, and he tapped at various bottles and boxes in his case. 'Potions and syrups for all manner of complaints,' he explained. 'Dead moles are good as a cure for baldness, armadillo tail for deafness, and for leprosy there is some debate at present under way as to whether elephants' blood or the ashes of weasels are more efficacious.'

If they had thought that their laughing fit was nearly over, the new list of sure-fire cures got them going again.

'You know where you get all these things from, don't you?' spluttered Kerry.

'Where?' asked Joe.

'The Bodies Shop!' said Kerry, and burst out laughing again.

'My stomach, my stomach,' groaned Joe.

'Cramp, is it?' inquired Dr Kelly. 'Elk's hoof is what you need for that.'

'Stop it, stop it, stop it,' pleaded Kerry. 'No more. I can't stand it.'

'Well,' said the doctor primly. 'I can't force those to learn who will not,' and he snapped his case shut. 'Leave those on for another thirty minutes,' he said, gesturing towards the slices of mouse.

Kerry started to snigger again.

'And now,' said Dr Kelly, 'I shall take my leave of you all.'

Grandma Mary slipped a ten-shilling coin, called an angel, into his hand in payment for the treatment. He pocketed it deftly.

'Good morning to you, Doctor,' said the rest of the family meekly.

'Farewell,' he said, and flounced out of the house.

Gradually, Kerry and Joe quietened down. They sat down on

the large bench by the window and watched the doctor walking down the alley-way.

'*He's* going to find it fairly difficult to get a job in the twentieth century,' said Joe.

'I assume his methods seemed a little outdated to you,' said Grandma Mary.

'A bit,' said Kerry.

'So you've got a cure for gout – or arthritis, now, have you?'

'Well, no,' said Joe, thinking of the old lady in the flat below them, all bent up and slow.

'And no one gets ague any more?'

'Flu?' said Kerry. 'Well they do, actually.'

'Hmm,' said Grandma Mary, in a sort of smug 'well-I-might-just-as-well-stick-with-dead-mice-then-mightn't-I?' sort of way.

'Well, I must be getting to the forge,' said Henry Cartwright. 'You children look after one another. We all want to get out from under the lake, but it's much more important to us that you remain safe and sound. So, take care.'

'We will,' they all said.

'William,' said Henry, 'you can come with me. I don't want *you* going with the others. You're too young.'

'Oh, Father,' he protested.

'No whining, now,' he said firmly. 'Pick up your horn book and let's be off.'

Reluctantly, he did as he was told.

'Let's have a look,' said Joe, as he was walking past. He and Kerry inspected the horn book. It consisted of a piece of paper mounted on a wooden board and protected by a thin piece of transparent horn. On the horn was inscribed the alphabet and the Lord's Prayer. William had been practising copying the letters on to the paper. The whole page was covered in sentences written in both English and Latin.

'Come on,' said Henry, 'they can have a look at that later,' and with his hand on his son's shoulder he guided him towards the door.

'Bye,' said William.

'Have a good day at school,' said Thomas, deliberately trying to goad him.

William merely glared at his older brother before being shepherded out of the house.

'Shall I make you up some kind of a packed lunch?' said Anne Cartwright.

'We'll be all right, I think,' said Thomas.

'Yeah, we'd better not lose any more time,' said Joe.

'Well, good luck, all of you,' said Anne nervously, from the doorway as Kerry and Joe, Thomas and Sarah set off down the road.

'Thanks,' said Kerry and Sarah, turning to wave.

'I think we're going to need it,' Joe muttered to Thomas under his breath.

It was a bright morning and despite the daunting task ahead of them all four children felt glad that their quest was actually under way. The waiting for everything to get started was the worst part of any task and now that they were heading off towards Megwyn's, for what could prove to be the final make-or-break confrontation, they felt far more confident. Thomas and Sarah were busy comparing the signs they had noticed that constituted good or bad omens for the job ahead.

'I heard an owl hooting after daybreak,' said Sarah. 'That's bad.'

'But there are swallows nesting under the eaves,' said Thomas. 'And that's good.'

'Mother said there was a stray cow in the vegetable garden this morning,' said Sarah. 'And that can mean bad luck or even,' her voice dropped to a hushed whisper, 'death.'

'There were two magpies in the apple tree,' said Thomas. 'That cancels out the cow.'

'I thought I heard a raven,' said Sarah, 'which is bad.'

'No, it was one of the magpies, definitely,' said Thomas, 'and that's good.'

'Well,' said Joe interrupting, 'I think that proves it quite conclusively.'

'What?' asked Kerry.

'Well, it's either going to go badly or well,' said Joe.

Thomas laughed. 'You don't think much of our omens,' he said.

'They're a bit haphazard, aren't they?' said Joe. 'At least they don't involve chopped-up mice, though,' he added, with a grin.

'Oh, that reminds me,' said Kerry. 'What was in that little bag tied around Dr Kelly's arm – not more mice?'

'No,' said Thomas and, seeing the funny side of their superstitious use of animals for the first time in his life, burst out laughing himself. 'You'll never guess.'

'Ear of rabbit?' suggested Joe.

'Bum of toad?' said Kerry.

'No, you really won't ever guess,' said Thomas. 'If the left foot and claws of a hyena are bound up in a linen bag and fastened to a man's right arm,' stated Thomas, as if reading from a medical dictionary, 'then the wearer shall never forget whatsoever he hath heard or knoweth.'

'I think I *might* have guessed that,' teased Kerry, 'eventually.'

'Now I've heard everything,' said Joe.

They continued their walk in silence. Unlike the previous day when Kerry and Joe had had no idea what to expect from their ancestor and were still hoping for the best, today they knew exactly what was awaiting them, and the prospect was not a good one. In the distance they saw the curious hollowed-out tree and all four of them involuntarily slowed the pace down a little.

Nothing can be put off for ever, though, and they soon found themselves standing at the bottom of the field looking up at the weird house. It had shifted around once again, just to make them feel that little bit more uneasy.

'I'm not going through that cats and dogs thing again,' said Kerry.

'No, you're right,' said Joe, 'let's see if we can get her attention.'

He cupped his hands to his mouth and yelled as loudly as he could:

'MEG – WYN!'

The sound echoed round and round the field and over the hills behind, bouncing back off the dome of water above them. But there was no response from the house.

'Try again,' said Kerry.

'MEG – WYN!'

His voice echoed even louder this time, round and round the field. But still there was no answer. They were just about to cut their losses and chance the field anyway when Sarah caught sight of a small figure at the top of the circular tower.

'Up there,' she pointed.

They all turned and looked. There was no doubt that it was Megwyn Nashe. Motionless, apart from her hair and clothes flapping in the breeze, she was staring down at them.

'Hello,' Joe called out, for want of anything better to say.

No response.

'Can you hear me?'

They thought they could discern a slight inclining of the head which could represent a nod.

'We've come back,' said Joe, rather lamely.

'What do you want?' Megwyn said. She didn't seem to be raising her voice at all, but they could hear her very clearly.

'Two things,' said Joe, who had taken it upon himself to be the spokesman. 'Firstly, Kerry and I would like to apologize for our rudeness yesterday. And secondly, we want to talk about the prophecy and what it means to us and the villagers.'

There was a long silence that became increasingly embarrassing by the second. What was she going to do? Let them in? See them off with a further attack from the elements? Or simply turn round and disappear back into her house without a word? They were too far away to see her face and guess what she was thinking.

'Joe, Kerry,' she said finally. 'You two may come in. The

other two will have to wait for you outside. I will not allow villagers in my house.'

Joe looked at Sarah and Thomas and shrugged.

'We haven't got much option, have we?' he said. 'She holds all the cards.'

'It's all right,' said Thomas, obviously disappointed but putting as brave a face on it as possible. 'We'll get things ready here, just in case you have to make a sudden getaway.'

'That's a good idea,' said Joe. 'I've no idea what we're going to do in there, but hopefully something will turn up.'

Joe turned back to Megwyn. 'OK,' he called out. 'Just Kerry and me.'

On hearing their decision, Megwyn disappeared from sight. At Kerry's insistence, they left it a couple of minutes before crossing the field, just in case she had gone to switch the alarm off. Then, with a brief farewell to Sarah and Thomas, and the promise that they'd be as quick as possible, they set off.

Megwyn was there to greet them at the door.

'You'd better come in,' she said grudgingly.

They followed her through the door and found themselves back in the curious parody of the twentieth-century sitting-room. The computer was on and the Cartwrights' kitchen was on the screen.

'You knew we were coming, then?' said Joe, nodding over to the terminal.

'I didn't need to look at that to know you'd be back,' she said sourly.

'No,' said Joe.

Megwyn perched herself on the edge of the settee and stared at them through her dead eyes. Her silvery-black hair was all matted and dry, her features looked even more angular than before; in short, she looked altogether meaner than the previous day. Kerry was beginning to feel extremely nervous.

'Well, first of all,' began Joe, 'we're both very sorry for the way we upset you yesterday. We realize that it must be a shock for you, us suddenly appearing, but then . . .'

'I let you in here because I thought I owed you an explanation,' said Megwyn, dismissing his apology with an airy gesture. 'I am also sorry for what happened yesterday. I had forgotten what a responsibility it is being surrounded by mere mortals. The villagers learned very early on *not* to cross me,' she added. 'I can make their lives extremely unpleasant, for all time.'

'It's all right,' said Kerry. 'It's over now.'

'But it isn't,' said Megwyn sharply. 'In fact it's only just beginning. I cannot let you leave here.'

Kerry felt tears of panic and frustration beginning to rise again.

'But you can't just hold us here against our will,' she protested rather pathetically.

'Why on earth not?' said Megwyn.

'Because . . . Because it's not fair,' she blurted out.

'Fair? What does fair mean?' shouted Megwyn. 'When I was only a little older than you, my mother was tied to a chair and ducked in the river. They said that if she lived after the ordeal she must be guilty of being a witch and would be burnt at the stake. And if she drowned then she had been innocent all along and would go to Heaven. Was *that* fair?'

'What happened?' said Joe.

'She drowned, so she was innocent,' said Megwyn bitterly. 'It was only the fact that they had murdered her that kept me safe. They didn't dare do it again. But they knew. They knew,' she yelled, as she got into full swing with her tirade. 'And when their precious little village was suddenly under threat who did they come running to? Megwyn Nashe. Good old Megwyn! She'll save us. And fool that I was, I did. And what thanks did I get for it? Constant complaining, nagging, whining the whole time: all of them wandering round with that sour and sullen expression on their face, bleating to be released again. They make me sick.'

Kerry and Joe stole a quick glance at one another. The eye contact confirmed that they were both thinking exactly the same thing. Yesterday, it had seemed as though Megwyn was determined to keep the people of Cleedale in their underwater village for their own good. She wanted to protect them from the horrors of the late twentieth century. But now she had given herself away. She wasn't interested in their well-being in the slightest; all she wanted to do was avenge her mother's death and her own ill-treatment. It meant that no amount of appealing to the better side of her nature would have any effect. She was so embittered that there probably wasn't one.

'So you're just taking revenge,' said Joe simply, risking a further display of her wrath.

Instead, she smiled and said, 'You're not stupid, are you?'

Joe remained silent.

'Believe me,' she said, 'I really am sorry that I involved you in all this.'

'Well, why did you?' snapped Kerry.

Megwyn sighed and looked up at the ceiling. 'It's impossible,' she said, 'to know how prophecies work. I do not know to this day whether I had some vision of the future when I composed that poem, or whether everything followed as a necessary result of my composing it. Do you understand?'

'Like the chicken and the egg,' said Joe. 'You're saying that you don't know which came first.'

'Precisely,' said Megwyn. 'All I can say is that I couldn't have been more amazed by the sequence of events which led you inexorably to that descent through the waters of the lake, on the four hundredth anniversary of the prophecy.'

'What do you mean?' said Kerry.

'Well, think about it,' said Megwyn. 'If you hadn't been born this couldn't have happened. If your parents hadn't split up there wouldn't have been any need to send you away for the summer. If your aunt, or any of her relatives had moved away from Cleedale Manor, you wouldn't have been anywhere near the lake. *If* she hadn't had a boat . . . *If* it hadn't stopped raining, et cetera, et cetera . . .'

'So many ifs,' said Joe quietly. He wondered vaguely to himself whether the prophecy itself hadn't in some way led to the break-up of his parents. After all, as Megwyn had pointed out, if they had stayed together, he and Kerry wouldn't be here now. But no, surely that couldn't be the case.

'Do you know what I found most fascinating?' Megwyn continued, interrupting his thoughts. 'The way you actually transformed yourselves into the boy of autumn and girl of spring. I'd always wondered what that meant.'

'You mean you didn't know?' said Kerry.

'Of course not,' she said. 'I'd been watching you both a lot of late and I just couldn't imagine what the words meant. Then, when I saw you through the barber's mirror, it all suddenly became clear. I could hardly believe it as I saw the colours of spring being put into your hair, Kerry, and watched as your hair was cropped to an autumnal stubble, Joe. I knew then that even if I had wanted to, there was no way that I could stop the two of you appearing in the village.'

'But what good does it do to keep us here?' said Kerry.

'None whatsoever, my dear,' she said, 'but I can't let you go without releasing the whole of Cleedale. And that,' she added simply, 'I shall never do. NEVER.'

Kerry threatened to burst into tears again. For some reason unknown to her, it was the thought that she would never again see her teddy, Mr Simpkins, which suddenly made her feel completely desperate. Joe watched her lower lip trembling and motioned to her that she shouldn't cry. If Megwyn Nashe was a vindictive old witch, then it was that side of her they would have to appeal to.

'So it's not that you won't change your mind,' said Joe, 'you can't.'

She nodded.

'Can I ask you a favour,' said Joe. 'As we've got to stay here, can we see your Weather Laboratory again?'

Megwyn eyed Joe suspiciously. 'Why?' she said.

'I'd just like to see some of the tricks that you've learnt. And not directed *at* us this time,' he added.

'Well, maybe,' she said, weakening a little.

'You know, I don't think you realize just how powerful you could become with your knowledge,' he said. 'Being able to make it rain, make it sunny, hot and cold, windy or foggy: if you patented some of those things you could become the wealthiest woman in the whole world — or can you only do it down here?'

'Anywhere,' she said proudly.

'Well, there you are, then. Just the money you'd make from them,' he said, pointing to the mock air-conditioning unit on the wall, 'could make you a multi-millionaire.'

'Well, that's as may be,' said Megwyn, clearly flattered by what Joe was saying. 'But as I said, I haven't the slightest intention of leaving.'

'I realize that,' Joe persisted, 'but we really would like to see where it all happens.'

There followed one of those pauses that Megwyn was so good at. Kerry looked at her brother, wondering what on earth

he was up to, but he studiously ignored returning her gaze. Finally Megwyn spoke. She had given in.

'All right,' she said. 'But I give you fair warning: if either of you tries anything, I'll make certain that you won't live to regret it for very long.'

As she led them out of the sitting-room and back down to the hexagonal laboratory Kerry mouthed a question silently at her brother.

But Joe was determined to keep his plan to himself.

'Sh,' he mimed, with his finger over his lips and winked at her.

NINE

So far, so good, thought Joe as they walked back into the hexagon-shaped laboratory. But now what?

'Well, this is it,' said Megwyn. 'The nerve centre, so to speak.'

Both Kerry and Joe looked around the hall with its gleaming walls, innumerable desks and panels, and the 'chrome and glass' extras, which Megwyn had presumably fashioned out of ice in her attempt to reproduce the laboratories she had seen through the mirrors. It had been a totally successful attempt.

'It really is spectacular,' said Kerry.

'Incredible,' said Joe. 'Is there any reason why you made it six-sided?'

'Naturally,' said Megwyn. 'I really couldn't afford to leave anything to chance here. You may, or may not know that, for your ordinary run of the mill witch, the pentagon is of great importance.'

'Five sides,' said Kerry.

'Correct,' said Megwyn. 'Well, as you've gathered, I am the Weather Witch and so for my purposes, the norm had to be adapted a little. The six-sided figure is the basis of all crystalline structures formed by the freezing of water. Have you ever examined a snowflake with a magnifying glass?'

'Yes,' said Joe. 'At school, we looked at them under the microscopes. They're all different but they're all six-sided, right?'

'Precisely,' said Megwyn, looking at him askance.

She couldn't quite get used to the fact that in some areas these two children had a knowledge which was equal to, if not superior to her own. It was quite unnerving.

'Anyway,' she continued, 'to utilize the power of the elements and harness nature to the maximum, I discovered that by reproducing the hexagonal characteristic of the ice units in the laboratory itself, I was able to make my spells a hundred times more effective.'

Kerry watched Megwyn as she continued to talk about the weather. Totally in her element, she gradually seemed to unwind in the presence of the two children. With luck, she would soon start to relax her guard a little, offering them some chink in her defence that they could seize and use to their advantage.

'Let me show you something amusing,' she said, and led them over to a broad table standing against one side of the hall.

Joe looked at Kerry and raised his eyebrows questioningly. All that was on the table was a cup and saucer. There were some pink and green roses painted on the side of the cup, but otherwise there was nothing particularly interesting about either piece of crockery.

'So, ladies and gentlemen,' said Megwyn, as if addressing a whole audience. 'One cup, plain and simple. Nothing in it. Nothing up my sleeve,' she said, shaking her costume theatrically and handing the cup to Kerry for inspection. 'And one saucer, similarly plain, similarly simple. Nothing in it. Nothing up my sleeve,' she repeated, handing Joe the cup. 'However,' she announced, retrieving both cup and saucer from the children, 'with a little bit of elemental magic we shall see what we shall see.'

She carefully placed the cup on the table and laid the saucer down over it. Then, with her eyes closed, she pulled herself up to her full height and began waving her arms around in the air, as if conducting a symphony which only she could hear. Once again, it occurred to Joe and Kerry what a formidable foe she could turn out to be if they weren't extremely cautious. The swinging, darting movements of her arms suddenly came to a halt and she let them hang limply at her sides.

'Now, shall we see whether the weather has been?' she whispered dramatically. Slowly and carefully, she leant forwards and slid the saucer off the top of the cup.

'I knew it. I knew a storm had been brewing!' she cried out, looking down into the cup. 'And, presto! I give you a storm in a teacup!'

Joe was so fascinated by the curious antics of Megwyn, who was prancing around the laboratory and ranting like a deranged magician, that he had completely forgotten about the trick itself. For the first time since they had come into contact with her, she seemed animated. True, her eyes still seemed lifeless – whatever had extinguished their spark could never be rekindled – but there was an energy to her which was remarkable in one so old.

Kerry, on the other hand, was much more interested in the conjuring than the conjuror, and was looking down into the cup with her mouth open in amazement. Joe turned his attention to the teacup as well, and what he saw took his breath away.

'Wow!' he gasped.

In the tiny, confined space of the cup, a severe storm was raging. As they watched, dark, swirling clouds floated around the rim, while beneath them, the minute droplets of rain and hail spun round and were driven against the sides. With their ears down near the top of the cup, they could actually hear the wind howling and whistling about in the cup.

'This is just amazing,' said Joe.

Suddenly, both of them jumped backwards as a blinding flash of lightning zigzagged down from the thick clouds to the bottom of the cup. The thunder, following a couple of seconds later, was deafening.

Kerry burst out laughing. 'I don't believe it,' she said. 'It's wonderful!'

'And if you look very carefully in a few seconds,' said Megwyn, 'I think you'll see something that might interest you.'

Both children leant over the cup and stared intently. It hurt their eyes when the lightning flashed, but they didn't want to miss anything. The period of time between lightning and thunder grew shorter and shorter as the centre of the storm approached. Then, as always happens when a storm is at its peak, there was a sudden lull in the wind and rain, a temporary break in the sequence of thunder and lightning. And as Kerry and Joe looked down into the cup beneath the cloud cover, they saw something that made both of them recoil. For, as they were staring down into the storm, they suddenly realized that the eye of the storm was gazing up at them. And while they were still holding their breath in confusion, it winked at them.

'Did you see it?' asked Megwyn genially. 'A nice touch, I like to think.'

'I just don't know what to say,' said Joe.

'"You're an artist and a genius, Megwyn Nashe", perhaps,' she suggested.

'Well, that goes without saying,' said Joe. 'I really have never seen anything like this before.'

Down in the cup below them, the storm was gradually passing away: the intervals between the lightning and its thunder were increasing on each successive occasion.

'Right, just before it's over completely,' said Megwyn, 'let's try a little something else.' She picked up the saucer and placed it back on top of the cup. 'Now,' she said to Kerry. 'Try and pick them up.'

Kerry went to do as she was told, but to her surprise she found it completely impossible even to budge them a fraction of an inch. She tried again. But no, she wasn't capable of even the slightest movement.

'Come on, you weed,' said Joe. 'Let me have a go.'

'Oh, Mr Macho-Man,' said Kerry. 'Come on, then. Flex those biceps.'

With as much nonchalance as he could muster, Joe leant over and tried to lift the cup and saucer. It immediately became clear, however, that he was going to have to use both hands. And still he had no success. Even with his feet up on the table, and pushing with all his strength, he failed to lever them off the table.

'My hero,' sneered Kerry.

'All right, I give in,' said Joe.

'Well, what can I say?' said Megwyn, 'You certainly made heavy weather of that, didn't you?'

'Heavy weather?' said Joe suspiciously.

'Yes, just an expression nowadays,' said Megwyn, 'but they all have their origins in something more literal. If you make heavy weather of any task, you'll never manage to get it done.' She laughed and picked up the cup and saucer with complete ease. 'You should make light of everything, like me,' she added.

Neither Kerry nor Joe had seen a conjuring act before involving nothing other than a cup and saucer. And what was more, it had been the best bit of magic they'd ever seen. As Megwyn stood there with her cup and saucer held high, doing her little curtsy, they couldn't help it, they just spontaneously burst into a round of applause.

'Bravo!' they shouted. 'More, more!'

'Oh, I think that'll do for the time being,' said Megwyn. 'It's all quite easy, when you know how. The trick is realizing that the influence of the weather on human behaviour isn't a one-way process. If the weather can affect us, then we can affect the weather. It stands to reason.'

'Does it?' said Kerry a little dubiously.

'Of course it does,' said Megwyn, with increasing enthusiasm. 'The weather and the way people feel is all bound up. If you're happy you erupt into gales of laughter. If you're sad, you create your own private cloudburst: you burst into tears. If someone seems friendly we call them warm, and if they're not we say that they're cold, and we probably give them the cold shoulder, just so they won't bother us.'

'I see what you mean,' said Kerry. 'For instance, my mum and dad have got, or rather had,' she added sadly, 'a stormy marriage.'

'And if you eat baked beans, you get wind,' said Joe, and burst out laughing.

'Yes, well, that sort of thing,' said Megwyn. 'We've even given the whole process a name.'

'Have we?' said Kerry seriously, while Joe continued to snigger.

'Indeed, we have,' she said. 'We say that anyone who is influenced, particularly negatively, by the elements is "under the weather." And this is the case with the good people of Cleedale,' she continued. 'They are all under the weather. Literally.'

Joe thought about it. It seemed to describe Cleedale quite well on both counts. Certainly, all the villagers were depressed and, as Thomas and Sarah had explained, the lake which concealed them had been formed by hours of torrential rainfall.

'So, all men, women and children are influenced by the weather, and here in Cleedale,' she said, her voice growing more strident by the second, 'who is it that controls the weather? Eh? Tell me who.'

'You,' said Kerry, and swallowed.

'So who controls the villagers?' she screeched.

'You,' said Joe.

Megwyn erupted into hideous, raucous laughter and turned away from them.

'Yes,' she said more calmly. 'I control them.'

Joe felt his hopes of finding some way out from under the lake retreating. He looked around the hall desperately searching for something, anything, which they could use to their advantage against the Weather Witch, Megwyn Nashe. But there was nothing.

'What seems really unfair,' said Joe, following on from a thought he'd had earlier, 'is that you can trap us here but you can't make us live for ever like all the others.'

'No, I agree that doesn't seem just, does it?' said Megwyn. 'Although I'm sure you'll have a more interesting life down here in your three score and ten years than any of the others, even if they live to be ten thousand.' She took a deep breath and paced across the room. Kerry and Joe watched her. After a dozen or so steps, she spun round. 'How would you describe Sarah Cartwright?' she said. 'In one word.'

'Quite nice,' said Kerry.

'That's two words,' said Megwyn sharply, 'and be honest!'

'Wet,' said Joe and Kerry together.

Megwyn smiled. 'And how would you describe Anne Cartwright?'

'Changeable,' said Kerry, thinking of how she was calm and confident one moment and then frantically worrying about baby John the next.

'Yes, I'd agree there,' said Megwyn. 'Wet and changeable; it's beginning to sound a bit like a weather forecast, isn't it? There is an element of the weather in each and every one of them, dominating their characters. Thomas is tempestuous; Henry is as strong as a force-nine gale; Ebenezer Cudlip gives you the shivers; and Betty Clegg is nothing but an old windbag. As for poor old Dan Boggle, his head is up in the clouds and full of fog!'

'But that's just their character,' said Joe. 'I don't see why it's so important.'

'I think I do,' said Kerry. 'The weather doesn't age, does it? So being under the weather is the reason they're still alive.'

Joe looked at Kerry in amazement.

'I didn't know I had such a genius as a sister,' he said.

'And because our characters are less predictable, less constant,' she continued, ignoring her brother and thinking out loud, 'no individual element can take control.'

'That's it,' said Megwyn. 'Sarah was wet yesterday, she's wet today and she'll be wet tomorrow: but it's that constant wetness keeping her going. On the other hand, there's a continuous battle going on inside you for how you feel, and it's slowly but surely ageing you.'

'But can't *you* do something to help us?' said Joe.

Megwyn shook her head.

'Why not?' said Joe angrily.

'I simply can't,' said Megwyn. 'A spell with that degree of complexity can only be cast once. There's nothing I can do.'

'What's in these?' asked Kerry, trying, perhaps a little too obviously, to change the subject.

'Oh, I forget,' said Megwyn. 'Have a look.'

Kerry pulled open one of the wide drawers and peered down inside. It was full of soft, shimmering objects. They were transparent from above and only became visible when the light caught one of their folds. Then they glinted with all the colours of the rainbow like dragon-fly wings, though infinitely more delicate. Comparing a thick woollen blanket with the wing of an insect would be like comparing the same wing with this silken, gossamer material. It was made of almost nothing at all. Very gently, Kerry lifted one of the objects up on her finger and let it float back down again.

'They're wonderful,' she said. 'Whatever they are.'

Megwyn laughed and came over. 'You remember what I called Betty Clegg?'

'A windbag,' said Kerry.

'Well, here we have a whole drawer full of windbags,' said Megwyn. 'Finest quality.'

'But what are they, exactly?' asked Kerry.

'It's difficult to describe, really,' said Megwyn. 'You know when there is a storm outside the house, and you can hear little blustery bits hurling themselves against the windows?'

'Yes, I know exactly,' said Kerry. She loved it, listening to a storm when she was all tucked up in her warm bed. Each of its different sounds was familiar. There was the wind howling round the chimney, the rain lashing against the windows and, yes, those little buffeting pockets of air that gusted up every now and then.

'Well, those are the windbags,' said Megwyn. 'They travel through the air, bouncing around in the winds of a storm.'

It was while Megwyn and Kerry were discussing the windbags that Joe had his idea. Of course, it could all go hopelessly wrong, but unless something else came up, it looked as though it could be the only solution the Weather Laboratory was going to come up with. But how to distract Megwyn? Being surrounded by the six sides of mirrors it was almost impossible to do anything secretly. He tried to catch Kerry's attention, but he was evidently totally uninteresting in comparison with a windbag, and she didn't even notice him.

Typical, he thought, if you want a thing done . . .

He pulled a second drawer open and looked inside.

'Hey, Kerry, come and have a look at these,' he said.

Both Kerry and Megwyn came over to inspect the contents.

'They look like mini crabs' claws,' said Kerry, smiling.

'I daresay crabs' claws would have the same effect,' said Megwyn.

'What are they used for?' asked Kerry.

The one bit of good luck they had had so far was that Megwyn had neglected to push the drawer full of windbags shut. As Kerry and Megwyn continued talking about the mini crabs' claws, Joe carefully positioned himself next to Kerry, with the open drawer behind him. He slid his hand in, pulled out four of the almost weightless windbags, screwed them up into a tiny ball and stuffed them inside his pocket. His heart was beating so fast, he was sure that Megwyn must be able to hear him. But when he looked over, she was still talking.

'They're not actually *used* for anything,' she was saying. 'But you know when it's a bit chilly sometimes, particularly when the day's been hot and sunny and you're sitting outside with a jumper on. What do you say then? Or what does your mother say?'

It clicked, and Kerry laughed out loud again.

'I don't believe it,' she said.

'Tell me, then,' Megwyn persisted. 'What does she say?'

'She says, "There's a nip in the air!"'

'And here,' said Megwyn, gesturing down into the drawer, 'is the reason for that nip. They tend to get you at the nape of your neck, sending shivers up and down your spine,' she added.

'Funny, eh?' said Kerry to Joe.

'Yeah,' he said, trying at the same time to signal to her that he wanted to leave.

'What?' she mouthed to him.

'Let's go,' he mouthed back.

'Cat got your tongue?' said Megwyn, turning Joe a deep shade of embarrassed crimson as he realized that she was watching him.

'I . . . I just thought, er . . .' he stammered, desperately looking for the right words to say. 'I just thought that we'd taken up enough of your time and ought to be leaving now.'

'Very considerate of you, I'm sure,' said Megwyn, 'but before you leave I've got one question for you.'

This was it, he thought. She was going to ask him what he was doing stealing things from her. And heaven knew what she would do to him if she found the windbags in his pocket. He almost blurted out a confession there and then.

'I was wondering,' continued Megwyn, luckily not giving him enough time to speak first. 'You said that I could be really powerful in your century. How?'

Joe breathed the biggest sigh of relief of his entire life. 'Oh that,' he said, and his mind promptly went blank.

'Easy,' said Kerry, coming to his rescue. 'All you need to have power is money, and with some of the ideas you've got you could become a billionaire overnight.'

'But what sort of ideas?' said Megwyn. 'I never became rich in the sixteenth century. I was too terrified to do anything in case they called me a witch and burned me at the stake.'

'Oh, nobody would be interested now if you said you were into witchcraft,' said Kerry. 'In fact it would probably get you on to chat shows.'

'You mean they wouldn't persecute me?'

'Well, they might,' said Kerry, with a laugh, 'but certainly not for being a witch.'

'So which ideas would make me rich?' Megwyn said, clearly fascinated by the change which had evidently taken place in the real world during the four hundred years she had been concealed under the lake.

'I don't know,' said Kerry. 'The air-conditioning unit, for instance. No electricity bills, no maintenance costs, just constant cool air. Perfect. Or cheap fridges. Everyone's got a fridge.'

'Or the way you've used the miniature suns; you could make sunbeds,' Joe contributed. 'Normally, they cost a packet and every sports centre's got a couple these days.'

'Or even the "storm in a teacup" idea,' said Kerry. 'You could market it as some kind of toy. There's nothing like a useless gimmick for making money. Do you know, just recently a man made a million by selling pet rocks!'

'What, just ordinary rocks?' asked Megwyn, astounded.

'Yep,' said Kerry. 'They were sold as cheap, convenient, house-trained pets. And they outsold everything else on the market that Christmas.'

'How peculiar,' said Megwyn.

'Anyway,' continued Kerry, 'when you've got rich then it's dead easy to get even richer. You could . . .' she thought for a moment. Joe stared at her in amazement wondering just where this flow of money-spinning ideas was coming from.

'You could invest it in vast areas of cheap, arid, desertland, couldn't you?' she continued. 'Then, by making it rain, you could irrigate it all for nothing and end up owning the most fertile area in the world.'

'Or failing that,' said Joe, 'if you *really* wanted to make loads of money for almost no work at all, you could always sell that mirror idea to the highest bidder.'

'Highest bidder?' repeated Megwyn, becoming increasingly alarmed by the acquisitive and cynical nature of the twentieth-century child.

'Yeah,' said Joe. 'Both the Russians and the Americans would give anything to have a device like that. Instant spying, just by looking into a mirror. You could ask the earth!'

Megwyn became quiet. It had occurred to her that no amount of looking into the world of the twentieth century could ever have prepared her for meeting it face to face. Kerry and Joe looked at her eagerly. For a moment, they thought that her deep concentration might mean that she was reconsidering the decision to keep them and the village imprisoned under the lake. But if, for a moment, there had been a trace of life in her eyes it soon disappeared again. Some deep regret, some unsolvable disappointment seemed to be reflected there.

'All that, and no persecution,' she said finally.

'Only the weak are ever persecuted,' said Joe. 'If you're rich and powerful, no one can touch you.'

'You make it all sound so very tempting,' she said, and snorted contemptuously. 'But no.'

'No?' said Kerry.

'No,' repeated Megwyn, 'and now I think it's time you left,' she added briskly.

At last, Joe thought to himself. But don't hurry. Don't make it too obvious.

'Can we come back and see you again?' asked Kerry. 'After all, you are the nearest thing to a relative we've got here.'

'Of course you may,' Megwyn replied, sounding almost genuinely friendly.

'Bye, then,' said Joe and Kerry as they were ushered out.

The moment the door shut behind them, Joe tugged at Kerry's arm and hurried her down over the field.

'What's the rush?' she said, dragging her feet.

'Get a move on,' he insisted, between gritted teeth. 'Before she finds out.'

As they reached the crest of the hill they looked down and could see the two Cartwright children still patiently waiting for them next to the oak tree. Kerry waved.

'Before she finds what out?' she asked.

At that moment the most blood-curdling scream imaginable filled the air. It came from inside the house and roared down the hill. Thomas and Sarah looked round in alarm to see the cause of the noise. There was a lull, almost unnatural in its silence like the calm that descends over an island before a tropical storm begins. And then the scream came again. An echoing howl of rage and anguish.

'I think she just found out,' said Joe. 'Come on. RUN! RUN!'

They hurtled down the hill as fast as they could, in their attempt to get as far away as possible before Megwyn Nashe unleashed the elements she had in her control. Glancing round, Kerry caught a glimpse of a thick blanket of fog just about to descend on them.

'Quicker, quicker!' she urged both of them.

'What's going on?' asked Thomas, as they reached the tree. 'Old Megwyn doesn't sound too happy.'

'No time to explain,' said Joe. 'We've got to get out of here as quickly as possible.'

'This way,' said Thomas, leading them through a shallow stream, round the side of the field and up towards the top of the slope.

'Wouldn't it make more sense to run downhill?' said Joe.

'Watch,' said Thomas, stopping for a second to look down.

The pack of dogs and cats came belting down on the tree, but instead of turning off and following the children, they kept on running down the hill. With their noses to the ground they were obviously following their scent, unaware that they were heading off in the wrong direction.

'We did that,' said Thomas proudly. 'We trailed our coats right down to the river.'

'Brilliant,' said Joe. 'Come on, then.'

They kept running up the slope as fast as they could. Kerry felt herself weakening. She'd never been particularly good at running and she could feel her heart pounding in her ears. 'Must keep going, must keep going,' she urged herself.

Below them, they could hear the dogs and cats going wild in their frustration at having lost their quarry. They were barking and baying, yowling and yelping as they ran round in circles at the river's edge. To make things more difficult, the thick blanket of fog had descended on them, making it almost impossible to smell, let alone see the runaway children. And still Kerry and Joe, Sarah and Thomas, kept on up the hill. By now, they were so out of breath that they were down to a slow trotting walk which was getting harder and harder to keep up.

'Come on,' encouraged Thomas, puffing hard. 'We can make it.'

'I hope . . . I hope,' panted Joe, 'that it works now.'

As no one but Joe knew what he had in mind, his comment went unanswered. The dogs and cats might have lost the trail and ended up chasing one another in the fog, but they weren't all that Megwyn had at her disposal to prevent the children from escaping. Just as they were reaching what they hoped would prove to be the final crest before the top of the hill, a precision volley of icicles landed at their feet. Sticking in the ground like javelins, they formed an instant fence directly in front of them. Sarah screamed out loud, and fell to the ground.

'It's all right,' said Thomas. 'They missed us.'

'But they could have gone right through us,' Sarah whimpered.

'Well, they didn't,' shouted Joe impatiently. 'Quick, let's get round them before we get totally fenced in.'

They ran off again, round the icicles and on up the hill.

'I can see it,' said Thomas.

He was right. About a hundred yards in front of them, the domed wall of the lake arched up and over their heads. They were near, that much was clear, but they certainly weren't there yet. Megwyn was still down in the house screaming out her hot and cold spells, and the results were raining down all around the four children. Keeping a wary eye on the sky, they darted this way and that, still aiming towards the wall of water ahead of them, but frantically trying to dodge the thunderbolts and icicles which would have killed them in an instant.

'We can make it,' said Joe.

'Not far to go,' added Thomas.

Kerry was almost in tears by now; she was so tired. She just wanted to lie down and give up. Thoughts like 'it's all useless', and 'we'll never make it, anyway,' kept running through her head. Suddenly, she became conscious of the sound of snarling and growling approaching from behind at a terrifying rate. Sarah's scream had given the dogs and cats just the lead they needed to get out of the blinding fog and back on their track. And in its turn, the savage sound of the dogs gave Kerry the burst of extra energy *she* needed.

'I know *just* what it must be like to be a fox,' she yelled, as she belted past the other three.

The dogs were undeniably gaining on them. Another couple of seconds and they would have been snapping at their heels. But Megwyn had over-reacted. In her frenzied attempt to ensure that the children would never escape from the village, she had overdone the attack, and it was beginning to show. Already, several of the dogs and cats had been skewered by the thunderbolts. One entire group of them had been enclosed by a volley of icicles which had formed an impenetrable circle around them, penning them in and excluding them from the chase. So frightened had Megwyn been that her dogs had lost the scent, that she had unleashed another weapon from her bag of tricks, a weapon which was now working very much to her disadvantage.

'Come on,' Kerry called to the others, from the wall. 'COME ON!'

'We're *coming*,' yelled Sarah, quite out of character.

As they all made it to the liquid wall which marked the edge of their underwater bubble, they turned round to see what had happened to the pursuing dogs. Although there wasn't a moment to lose, they couldn't help laughing at the spectacle behind them.

Evidently as a last resort, Megwyn had released the crab claw-like nips into the air. Thousands of them. And it was these that were now causing so much havoc. They were pinching the dogs' noses, making them yelp out in pain; they were attaching themselves to the dogs' tails and sending them spinning round and round in a frantic but fruitless attempt to bite them off, until they collapsed in a dizzy heap; they were getting in their ears, nipping their lolling tongues, grasping at their soft underbellies. And the cats weren't faring any better. They hissed and spat impotently as the little claws attached themselves to their whiskers and fur. Worse than this, the nips locked on to the cats' claws as they scratched out, and refused to let them retract again. A cat with its claws out cannot walk, and they lay there, helpless, on the grass as the four children continued their escape.

'I really *do* hope this works,' said Joe, as he carefully pulled the wispy windbags from his pocket and laid them out on the grass.

'What on earth are you going to do with them?' asked Thomas.

'Just a minute,' said Joe. 'I'm thinking of the best way to do this.' He picked up a windbag and, taking hold of the top, he swung it around his head until a little bit of air got in. Then, clamping the opening shut again, he plunged his hand through the wall of water right into the lake, taking care to keep the screwed-up end of the bag out in the open. 'Now,' he said, carefully releasing his grip on the opening of the windbag. As he did so, there was the sound of rushing wind as the pressure of the underwater bubble forced air into the windbag. It inflated totally, forming a large bubble of air in the water. 'Right, who's first?' he said. 'Kerry, you go.'

'What, you expect me to get into that?' she said. 'Are you mad?'

At that moment an icicle spear landed an inch behind her. She felt the wind as it whistled past her shoulder.

'All right, all right,' she said. 'I'm convinced. I'll have a go.'

'Do you think that stuff is strong enough?' said Thomas.

'If it can withstand the buffeting of a gale, it'll manage to float through the water with no problems,' said Joe confidently.

Kerry carefully stepped into the air bubble and sat down at the bottom.

'Make sure you tie it well,' she said to her brother.

'A bit of trust,' he said, knotting it and re-knotting it. 'See you at the top,' he said.

'I hope so,' came Kerry's muffled reply.

Joe let go of the windbag, and the air bubble containing his sister began its wobbling ascent through the water of the lake, away from Cleedale.

'One down, three to go,' said Joe, picking up the second of the windbags. He repeated the process, swinging it round his head, holding the opening to the bag shut and pushing it into the water. He then released his grip slightly and let the air rush into the bag to cause a second bubble of air.

'Magic,' he said. 'Ready, Sarah?'

She was shaking like a leaf, but without saying a word, she stepped forwards and climbed into the inflated balloon.

'One knot, two knots, three knots and chocks away,' shouted Joe, as the second of the windbags began to ascend gracefully through the water.

'You're going to be all right, aren't you?' said Thomas, as he climbed into the third of the stolen windbags that Joe had inflated.

'Of course I am,' he said.

'How are you going to tie it up?' he asked.

'Easy,' said Joe. 'I can do it from the inside. It won't make any difference.'

'Good luck, then,' shouted Thomas, as Joe pushed him away.

There were still thunderbolts and icicles falling sporadically, but fewer now. The dogs and cats seemed to have given up completely and some were already beginning to soak back into the grass like the rain that had created them. Joe looked down the hill to see if Megwyn had any more nasty tricks up her sleeve. No more tricks, but what he did see, to his horror, was the woman herself — in the distance still — but waving her arms around furiously and definitely getting nearer.

'Just give me thirty seconds,' he said to himself, as he swung the bag around his head. 'That's all.'

Joe felt himself becoming increasingly nervous. In a way, it seemed strange that a witch of such awesome power hadn't flown up to him on the wind, or something equally dramatic. And yet, the witch's slow but steady hobbling over the field towards him was somehow even more disturbing.

'Come on, come on,' he urged his fumbling fingers. He pushed his arm into the water, holding on to the end of the windbag, and released it ever so slowly so as to let it fill with air. 'Don't rush it,' he instructed himself. 'Don't mess it up, you won't get a second chance.' The air rushed into the bag. He was shaking so much now that he almost let it slip out of his hand and go rising up to the surface without him. 'Get a grip!' he instructed himself.

Apart from the shaking, another problem was that now the dogs and cats were disappearing, the nips were looking for new targets, and they were buzzing around his head and hands like a swarm of angry wasps. But he didn't dare to swat them away. That was what Megwyn wanted him to do; she wanted him to lose the windbag and be trapped there for ever.

She was only about twenty yards away as he climbed half into the bag. Carefully, he tried to knot the ends together. But everything was so slippery, and his hands were trembling too much. He tried once, twice, but each time, one of the little ears of soft material slipped out of his grasp. He looked up, and through the bubble, he saw Megwyn racing up to him with a big knife. Presumably she intended to puncture his windbag — unless she had more deadly intentions.

'Quickly, quickly,' he muttered, the urgent panic of the moment making his whole head tingle with fear. But his fingers refused to listen.

He was just about to give up when two of the little crab-claw nips lunged at his fingers. He pulled his hands away instinctively and fell back into the windbag. He knew at once that he had been stupid. He should have held on. And with his eyes closed, he waited for the water to come pouring in, and for Megwyn to pull him back into the little village where he would have to remain for the rest of his life.

Seconds passed. And the water hadn't come pouring in. Nor had Megwyn pulled him back on to the grass. What was more, he sensed a gentle rocking, swaying sensation. What had happened?

He cautiously opened his eyes to find out. 'I've made it,' he muttered, in disbelief.

Looking out through the thin skin of transparent material which held the windbag together, he watched what was going on outside. Though blurred by the water and distorted by the

concave surface, he could clearly make out the furious figure of Megwyn jumping up and down on the grass, waving her fists at him in blind rage. But there was nothing she could do. Like the other three, Joe had escaped and he leant back in the air bubble as it rose slowly and gracefully to the surface.

'But I didn't knot it,' he yelled out, in a sudden panic. 'What's holding the top shut?' He looked up at the entrance to the windbag, and there were the two little 'nips in the air', both clutching on as tightly as they could. So Megwyn's last attempt to keep the children there had actually helped him to escape.

Joe burst out laughing, thinking of the old witch stuck at the bottom of the lake and how everything she had attempted at the end had backfired.

'Just you keep your grip on the bag, O K?' he said to the two nips. 'Don't even *think* of letting go!'

TEN

From the dry safety of her ascending air bubble, Kerry looked through into the watery world outside. It was a deep blue colour which, as she rose, gradually grew lighter and lighter. She could see fish of all sizes swimming around in the lake, from tiny sticklebacks darting in and out of the floating weed to enormous carp pulling themselves effortlessly through the water with their tiny fins. Occasionally, one of the braver and more inquisitive of them swam right up to the floating intruder and pressed its snout into the windbag.

'Don't you burst it,' Kerry said and flapped her hand to shoo the fish away.

It was so peaceful under the water. She couldn't hear anything at all except for the sounds of her own body: the deep roaring of the blood coursing through her veins and the high-pitched whistle of her nervous system.

Over to her left, she caught sight of a strange, spherical object turning gently in the water. She looked more closely and saw that it was Sarah who, being lighter than Kerry, was rising to the surface faster in her windbag. As they neared one another Kerry waved and shouted out, 'Hello.' The fish which had been swimming close to the bubble sped off, terrified by the sudden blast of noise. Sarah noticed her and waved back, but in agitation not greeting. She was clearly trying to point something out to Kerry, but the sounds got distorted and the signals lost their clarity as they travelled through the water.

Kerry shrugged and mouthed the words, 'See you soon', while Sarah's bubble rose above hers towards the surface. As she lost sight of her friend she peered into the blue gloom to see what Sarah had been so concerned about. There was nothing there at all, as far as she could make out.

Probably just imagining things, she said to herself, and turned her mind to thinking about how Great-Aunt Eleanor would react to their own story of Cleedale. At least Sarah and Thomas could corroborate what had happened. She certainly wouldn't believe them otherwise.

Deep in thought as to whether or not to tell her friends at school about the whole adventure, she didn't notice that the air bubble had started to revolve. It was only when she realized she could actually hear something from outside the windbag that she looked up.

'Oh no!' she cried out.

Would it never end? As though escaping from Cleedale hadn't been traumatic enough, she now faced the situation of being sucked back down again. The source of her sudden panic and cause of the spinning was the twisting column which sucked in air from outside to provide the villagers underneath the lake with a constant supply of oxygen. It was this tube that had brought both her and Joe down to Cleedale when they had fallen out of the rowing-boat. Now it was threatening her with a repeat performance. And there was absolutely nothing that she could do except hope for the best.

When she had been inside the spinning column of air that first time, she'd imagined that a giant had swallowed her whole and she was on the downward journey to his stomach. Looking at it from the other side was quite different, though. The rapid movement of the water made the outside of the column look solid, and it was only when her tiny bubble of air was dragged right through the opaque wall that its lack of substance became obvious.

The first time the bubble broke through into the column, it was just by a couple of inches. The second time was far more worrying. Almost half of the windbag had already been dragged into the column of air when Kerry looked down. To her horror, she found that she was half-suspended in mid-air and could see through the bottom of the bubble, right down the long tube twisting away below her.

'NO!' she screamed.

Whether it was a case of mind over matter she would never discover, but at the precise moment she yelled out the tiny bubble of air floated away from the column, unharmed. Scarcely able to believe her good fortune, she turned round to see the whirling air chimney twisting off to another part of the lake.

Outside, it continued to get lighter. She looked up. Surely she must be getting near the top now. Yes, she was positive that those were small, white, puffy clouds up in the sky above her head. A moment later, the bubble of air burst through the surface of the lake and out into dazzling sunshine.

I'd forgotten how bright the sun was, she thought happily, gazing up at the sky.

Sarah was bobbing around in her air bubble about twenty yards to her left, and as Kerry was waving to her, the third of the windbags suddenly burst into view. It was Thomas. Kerry watched as he shielded his eyes from the sun. If it was bright for her after only a couple of days in the curious turquoise shades of Cleedale, it must have been almost unbearable for the other two after their four centuries without direct sunlight.

'Have you seen Joe?' she called out to Thomas.

'No,' he called back. 'He left after me.'

Kerry scanned the lake for any sign of her brother. The good news was that not only had they emerged within swimming distance of Great-Aunt Eleanor's jetty but also, to Kerry's extreme surprise, the rowing-boat was back in its moorings. The bad news was that Joe was nowhere to be seen. It was forty-eight hours since she had fallen into the water and now the whole situation was reversed. It was her turn to be anxiously searching around for him.

'It's because he's getting fat,' she told herself, 'he's just coming up to the surface slower than we did.' And yet she remained unconvinced: if anything, Thomas was heavier than her brother.

'Still no sign,' Thomas called out.

'I know that, idiot,' Kerry muttered to herself angrily. 'Nothing like stating the obvious.'

The trouble was that the longer she was being forced to wait, the more anxious and irritable she was becoming. It was almost as if he was doing it on purpose. She simply could not, would not believe that Megwyn had managed to prevent him leaving. It would be too unfair. But *if* she had . . . though Kerry was convinced that she hadn't. But *just supposing* she had . . . even though she knew it couldn't have happened. But just given the eentsiest weentsiest possibility that she might have, then Megwyn would certainly live to regret it. This was the twentieth century, not some backyard sixteenth-century village. They would send down divers and damned well get him back!

Just as Kerry was reaching the peak of her furious indignation, there was a flurry of bubbles and ripples and the fourth windbag popped up right beside her. And there, inside it, was Joe, grinning.

'How do we get out of these things now?' he yelled out.

'Easy!' said Kerry, pinching a little of the material together and then biting a small hole in it. The bubble ripped itself apart and disappeared, letting Kerry slip down into the water.

Joe immediately did the same, and was in the water next to his sister a moment later.

'Come on, you two,' Joe called out to the Cartwrights.

'We can't,' said Thomas.

'Yes, you can,' said Joe, 'the stuff tears really easily.'

'It's not that,' said Thomas.

'Well, what is it?' said Joe.

Sarah mumbled something indistinctly and Thomas looked away.

'What?' shouted Joe. 'Come on, it's not easy treading water in your clothes, you know.'

'WE CAN'T SWIM!' shouted Thomas crossly.

Both Joe and Kerry burst out laughing.

'Well, why didn't you say so before?' said Kerry.

'We thought you wouldn't bring us with you,' said Sarah.

'Good grief,' said Kerry. 'Shall we get the boat?'

'No, I've got a better idea,' said Joe, swimming over towards the two bobbing bubbles of air.

Getting behind them, Kerry and Joe pushed their respective charges towards the bank. It was only when Thomas and Sarah touched the sandy shore of the lake with their feet that they felt confident enough to break free of the windbags.

'Try and keep some of the material,' said Kerry. 'I'm sure it could be useful for something.'

But as they tried to pick some up it simply disappeared into thin air.

'KERRY! JOE!' came a familiar voice from the top of the bank.

'Hello!' they both shouted back.

Even though they'd only known her for such a short time, seeing Great-Aunt Eleanor standing at the top of the hill was like being reunited with a long-lost friend. Kerry rushed up the bank and gave her a big hug.

'I've been so worried,' she said. 'Where on earth have you been?'

'You'll never believe us,' said Joe. 'Not in a million years.'

'Well, come into the house,' she said, 'change out of those wet clothes and – Good Lord, who are they?' she asked, suddenly catching sight of Thomas and Sarah standing dejectedly down by the water's edge.

'Oh, sorry,' said Joe, 'I forgot. Hey, you two,' he called out, 'come up here.'

The two of them clambered up the bank and were formally introduced to Great-Aunt Eleanor.

'We erm . . . met the other day,' said Joe vaguely.

'Well,' said Great-Aunt Eleanor, 'I'm sure there must be some good explanation for all this. Kerry, you'll have to lend Sarah some of your clothes. And, Joe, you can do the same for Thomas. All right, the pair of you?'

'Fine,' said Joe.

'Great,' said Kerry, who just couldn't stop grinning.

As they were walking back up to the house, Thomas turned round and whispered something quietly into Sarah's ear. She nodded. Neither Kerry nor Joe had noticed him saying anything at all, but Great-Aunt Eleanor had exceptionally good ears and what she heard, at least thought she heard, startled her. She spun round on her toes and confronted Thomas.

'*What* did you say?' she demanded.

'Nothing,' he said.

'Yes, you did,' she persisted. 'I distinctly heard you whisper something to your sister. Now, will you please repeat it!'

'I said that you looked like Megwyn Nashe, ma'am,' said Thomas sheepishly.

'Megwyn Nashe?' she repeated. 'Just where have you been?' she asked Joe and Kerry.

'I said you wouldn't believe us,' said Joe.

'So,' said Great-Aunt Eleanor, rubbing her fingers round and round her eyes, 'let me see if I've got this straight.'

Having bathed and changed, they were all relaxing in the sitting-room. Dressed in jeans and T-shirts, both Sarah and Thomas looked much like any other twelve- or thirteen-year-old. It was only when they opened their mouths and spoke that their complete ignorance about anything in the twentieth century gave them away. Great-Aunt Eleanor realized that it was much too consistent to be an act. And even if she could have believed that they'd got all their information about the past from books, there was no mistaking their complete surprise at tasting coffee for the first time. She, Kerry and Joe all burst out laughing when they saw the horror on their faces as they sipped from their mugs.

'You two somehow managed to fall down a watery chute into the village of Cleedale which had remained hidden since 1589?' she said to Kerry and Joe.

'That's right,' said Kerry, 'but it wasn't a coincidence. It had all been foretold.'

'We all knew about the boy of autumn and girl of spring,' Sarah concurred.

'Hold on,' said Great-Aunt Eleanor, closing her eyes again, 'I just want to get all this clear in my own mind. An old witch called Megwyn Nashe, a distant relation of ours, was responsible for hiding the village under the lake, and it was she who you tricked in order to escape. Correct?'

'Spot on,' said Joe, grinning. He, for one, had decided *not* to mention the story to anyone else. They'd lock him up. 'Don't you believe us, then?' he said.

'Of course I believe you,' said Great-Aunt Eleanor. 'Perhaps you'd like me to refresh your memory about *your* reaction when I told you about the Legend of Cleedale. Mr-I'm-so-worldly didn't believe a word of it, did he? Turned his little nose up at my story.'

'All right,' said Joe, turning bright red, 'don't go on.'

'It's funny, you know,' said Great-Aunt Eleanor. 'I very nearly called the police. I probably would have if I'd had a phone, but yesterday afternoon I was sitting in here and suddenly I was absolutely convinced that you were both all right.'

Joe looked at Kerry and grinned.

'You were standing, actually,' he said, 'over by the mirror.'

'Well, standing then,' she said cautiously.

'And then you knocked a vase over with your elbow,' said Kerry.

'How did you know that?' asked Great-Aunt Eleanor quietly. 'How could you possibly have known that?'

'We saw you,' said Kerry.

'Saw me?' said Great-Aunt Eleanor.

'It was Megwyn Nashe,' explained Joe. 'She's got this kind of machine in her laboratory. She can look out through any mirror she chooses.'

Great-Aunt Eleanor looked up at the large mirror above the mantelpiece. 'And you were looking at me through that?' she said.

'That's right,' said Joe, 'you were blaming us for going grey,' he added, and he and Kerry laughed.

'How embarrassing,' said Great-Aunt Eleanor, glancing uneasily over at the mirror again.

'She's probably watching us right now,' said Kerry.

'How extremely perceptive of you,' hissed a hideously unforgettable voice behind them, sending icy shivers down the backs of all those in the room who had heard it before.

They all spun round.

The familiar reflection of the room had disappeared.

Kerry let out a piercing scream and covered her face with her hands. Joe leapt up from his cushion and rushed over to the mirror, terror and fury mixing a potent and venomous cocktail inside him.

'YOU STINKING BAG OF EVIL OLD SLIME!' he roared.

Megwyn's impassive face stared back at him. She had put her hair up, pulling the skin taut, and accentuating the vicious hardness of her face. The thin lips drew back in a cruel mockery of a smile, revealing her blackened teeth. She tapped menacingly on the glass with her yellow nails.

'You thought you'd escaped,' she sneered. 'You won't escape from me. *Ever!* Every time you go to check your pretty-pretty faces, there I'll be!'

No one in the room could help but be affected by the strength of hatred in her voice. Kerry thought guiltily about how she'd suggested that Megwyn should accompany them back to the twentieth century. The thought of so much evil power being unleashed on the world was terrifying. She wouldn't choose to irrigate the deserts but rather the opposite: she'd melt the ice-caps and sit back and watch a thousand coastal cities perish under the rising seas; she'd send hurricanes howling down city streets, toppling skyscrapers like dominoes; she'd scorch the wheat-belt, freeze the tropical rain forests, flood the plains. Just a look into those lifeless eyes confirmed that there were no feelings left inside the sour old woman. She, at least, must never be allowed to leave Cleedale.

While the children had been reacting in their different ways to the witch in the mirror, Great-Aunt Eleanor was carefully watching them. No, it was becoming clear to her that the legend had been kind to Megwyn Nashe. It stressed how she had used all her power to save the village, but that was only half the story. What had not been passed down the generations was the fact that she was cruel, vindictive and possibly deranged.

Great-Aunt Eleanor stood up coolly, smoothed down her Paisley patchwork skirt and walked over to the mirror.

'So you're the great Megwyn Nashe, are you?' she said calmly.

'And you're that vegetable-eating milksop, Eleanor,' Megwyn taunted, from behind the mirror.

Great-Aunt Eleanor remained calm. For some reason that none of the children could quite understand, she was acting as though she was the one who'd got the upper hand.

'This is my proposal,' said Great-Aunt Eleanor.

'Hah!' snorted Megwyn and turned away. 'You think you are in the position to make proposals, do you?'

'Well, *I'm* not sitting underneath a lake,' said Eleanor.

'I choose to be here,' the witch snapped back.

'That brings me on to my proposal,' said Eleanor sweetly.

Joe and Kerry, Thomas and Sarah all exchanged glances a little nervously. None of them knew exactly what she was going to say, but all of them had the feeling that if it came down to a battle, they didn't fancy Great-Aunt Eleanor's chances.

'Spit it out, then,' shouted Megwyn. 'Or shall I just say "no" now?'

'My proposal is that we allow Thomas and Sarah twenty-four hours to have a cursory look around the twentieth century, just to see whether they consider the imprisoned villagers of Cleedale capable of adapting and —'

'"Imprisoned"?' screamed Megwyn. 'I saved them from certain death.'

'Come, now,' said Great-Aunt Eleanor. 'You could have removed the lake any time you wanted after the soldiers had left, but you deliberately kept them under lock and key for your own malicious delight. But that's totally beside the point,' she continued, before Megwyn could interrupt again. 'If they feel that they would like to make a go of this century, then you must release them, of course. If not, then they can return.'

'I'll never release them!' screeched Megwyn, in another furious outburst.

'But, Megwyn,' said Great-Aunt Eleanor patronizingly. 'You have no say in the matter, really. I was merely thinking of what was best for the villagers.'

'No say?' yelled Megwyn.

'Good Lord,' said Great-Aunt Eleanor, 'you do like to repeat things, don't you? Yes; "no say" is what I said.'

Megwyn continued to look angry but perplexed.

'My dear woman,' explained Great-Aunt Eleanor. 'We can drill for oil under the sea; we can build skyscrapers that get lost in the clouds; we have space stations orbiting the earth; and we have landed men on the moon! Do you really think it's going to be too much for us to drain your silly little lake and rescue the people?'

Kerry shuddered, realizing that this particular turn of events would be awful. If they drained the lake *everyone* would be free. Surely, there had to be some way of releasing the villagers while keeping Megwyn incarcerated. She looked at Great-Aunt Eleanor and just prayed that she knew what she was doing.

'The problem with that solution,' continued Great-Aunt Eleanor, 'would be that it would attract too much media attention. You and the villagers would be hounded by TV cameras, magazine editors and newspaper reporters, and I can promise you that some of the gentlemen of the press make *you* seem like a perfectly sane and rational person, Megwyn.'

The face on the screen scowled. For once Megwyn looked totally dumbfounded. It was as though all her arrogant certainty had suddenly drained away. Joe recognized the expression on her face from earlier: she looked as though she was mulling things over, unable to reach a conclusion. After all, Grandma Mary had called her the 'Whether Which'. Perhaps, once again, confronted with a powerful opposition she was being forced into the same indecisive condition.

And while she continued to weigh up whether or not to comply, the five in the sitting-room watched her face as calm reflection contorted into impotent rage. It was the angry side of her nature which slowly began to dominate. They could hear her cursing violently under her breath.

'She doesn't look too happy,' Joe whispered to Kerry.

And indeed she didn't. In her frustration, she was hurling blinding flashes of lightning at the mirror. Time after time they lit up the sitting-room for a dazzling instant.

'Oh do stop being so childish,' said Great-Aunt Eleanor.

'Shan't!' screamed Megwyn petulantly.

'Well, in that case,' said Great-Aunt Eleanor, 'I'm afraid we'll have to leave you until you've calmed down. And do try to make up your mind soon.' And so saying, she took the mirror by its frame and swung it round so that the glass was facing the wall.

'Brilliant,' said Joe.

'Yeah, well done,' said Kerry, and all four of the children congratulated her on her stand against the Weather Witch.

'Oh dear,' said Great-Aunt Eleanor suddenly. 'I think I forgot something.'

'What?' said Kerry in alarm, wondering if there had been some fatal flaw in her bravado.

'The pizza,' said Great-Aunt Eleanor. 'I think I can smell it burning.' And she rushed out of the room and down to the kitchen to inspect it.

'What's pizza?' said Thomas.

'Delicious,' said Kerry.

'Well, it usually is,' said Joe, laughing. 'Let's go and find out.'

Apart from being a bit black around the edges, it *was* delicious and for the two Cartwright children a total assault on the taste-buds. They had never tasted cheese like parmesan before, nor fish like anchovies, nor anything at all like the olives.

'It's superb,' said Thomas, helping himself to another huge slice.

'Did you mean what you said about the twenty-four-hour trial?' said Joe.

'Oh, yes,' said Great-Aunt Eleanor, 'I think it's imperative, don't you? They might hate it here.'

'Well, so far so good,' mumbled Thomas, stuffing more of the pizza into his mouth.

'It's nice to be appreciated,' said Great-Aunt Eleanor. 'Yes, what I suggest,' she said, turning back to Joe, 'is that you and Kerry take Thomas and Sarah up to London for the day. I would have recommended a smaller town, but as you two know London . . . and anyway, if they can cope there, they'll cope anywhere.'

'Fantastic idea,' said Joe.

'We've been to London before,' said Sarah.

'I think you'll find it's changed,' said Great-Aunt Eleanor.

'I can remember it so clearly,' Sarah went on. 'Thousands and thousands of people all rushing around busily. And the noise and dirt. But there was something exciting about it, all the same.'

'Hmm,' said Joe, 'maybe it hasn't changed that much.'

'You'll find it interesting, anyway,' said Great-Aunt Eleanor, 'of that I'm sure. Now, anyone for ice-cream?'

'Ice-cream?' said Sarah, sounding unsure.

'Chocolate and walnut,' said Great-Aunt Eleanor, taking it out of the freezer and dolloping scoops into a bowl.

Kerry and Joe watched in amusement as Thomas prodded it with his spoon. Finally plucking up the courage to taste it, he popped a large spoonful in his mouth. For a second he looked unsure. Then, as the ice-cream began to melt, a look of utter bliss spread over his face and he smiled broadly. He looked up at Great-Aunt Eleanor in wonder.

'That is the most wonderful food I've ever tasted,' he said, and dived back into the bowl for more.

'If he's that enthusiastic about ice-cream, what's he going to be like when he discovers the television and the radio?' said Great-Aunt Eleanor. 'Joe, Kerry, I think you ought to show our guests some of the delights of the twentieth century after dinner.'

'Early twentieth century,' said Joe, teasing.

'All right,' said Great-Aunt Eleanor. 'I will confess that some of the latest ideas might have passed me by.'

'Like a telephone, and a video, and microwave, and a computer, and a . . .' Joe began to rattle off.

'Well, I'm sure that the steam radio will interest him anyway,' said Great-Aunt Eleanor.

'Steam?' said Thomas.

'It's all right, she's joking,' said Joe. 'Aren't you?' he added, suddenly not so sure.

'Go on,' she said, 'look around. Oh, and turn any mirrors you come across to the wall. I think we'll have a few hours without dear old Megwyn poking her nose in, don't you?'

The inspection of the house proved to be an almost unqualified success. Both Thomas and Sarah were, of course, fascinated by the radio and the television. They spent ages fiddling around with the dials, tuning in to different stations and switching channels. But it wasn't the apparatuses in themselves which interested them: they simply accepted that both radios and televisions were able to pick up a transmission, although they didn't really understand why, if the signals were in the air all the time, they couldn't just hear them. But then for that matter, neither Kerry nor Joe understood how they worked, either.

And when watching the television, it wasn't the play, or the war film, or the documentary that happened to be on that interested Thomas and Sarah. It was something far more mundane that both of them noticed.

'Music,' said Sarah.

'Pardon?' said Kerry.

'There's music everywhere,' she said. 'Listen.'

And she flicked from one channel to the other. It was true: as the couple in the play embraced there was a soft piano playing in the background; as the soldiers stormed the beaches they were accompanied by an orchestra.

'It must be lovely always having music around you,' said Sarah wistfully.

Kerry didn't bother to disillusion her.

As they continued on their guided tour of the house it was consistently the small details which fascinated Thomas and Sarah, details which the children born into the twentieth century wouldn't even have noticed: the mixer tap which could produce hot or cold water; the toilet which flushed; the number of books on the bookshelves; the photographs in the magazines; paper money; biros; even the toothpaste! But then, coming from a time when the people used the powder from burnt mouse heads, this was hardly surprising.

But the object which particularly fascinated Thomas was tall, cylindrical and made of metal.

'So how do they get it all inside?' asked Thomas, pressing down on the plastic nozzle. 'It's impossible.'

'Hey, don't do that,' said Kerry. 'You're wasting it.'

'But look,' said Thomas, 'there's already more outside than they could possibly get inside, and it's still coming out.'

Joe sat on the bed, creased up with laughter, as Thomas continued to squirt Kerry's hair mousse all over the dressing-table.

'And listen,' Thomas said, shaking the can next to his ear. 'It sounds liquid. Ugh!' he yelped, as he accidentally shot a large dollop of the foam into his ear. 'But *that's* not liquid, is it?' he said, wiping himself down.

'It's . . . it's pressurized,' said Kerry, trying hard to find some kind of explanation. 'It's liquid in the can, but they add some kind of gas which . . . which . . . Oh, I don't know,' she said.

'Which is destroying the ozone layer,' said Joe, laughing.

'The what layer?' said Thomas.

'I don't think we want to get into that,' said Kerry. 'And put my mousse down!'

'I still think it's odd,' said Thomas sulkily, having one last squirt before doing as he was told.

'Impressed?' said Great-Aunt Eleanor, as they ended up back in the sitting-room.

Sarah simply nodded.

'There are so many new things,' said Thomas.

'Well, I propose . . .' said Great-Aunt Eleanor, and started to laugh. 'It seems to be my day for proposals, doesn't it? Anyway, I propose that you all get an early night, so that you can get the most out of tomorrow. You wouldn't want to make the wrong decision,' she said to Thomas and Sarah.

'No,' said Sarah miserably.

'What is it?' asked Great-Aunt Eleanor.

Joe raised his eyes to the ceiling and mouthed the word 'wet' to Kerry.

'I'm just so frightened about what will happen to Mother and Father, and William and baby John, and Grandma Mary, and all the others if we decide to stay here, but Megwyn Nashe refuses to let the village go.'

It was a serious point and Joe felt unkind at having been so dismissive.

'I mean, she's mad,' said Sarah. 'Even if you could drain the lake and that, it would take time. And she could have . . . have . . .' her lower lip quivered.

'Come on, now,' said Great-Aunt Eleanor, giving her a cuddle.

'She could have killed them all by then,' howled Sarah, and burst into tears.

'There, there,' said Great-Aunt Eleanor, continuing to comfort her by swaying back and forwards and rubbing Sarah's back gently. 'She won't do that. I promise she won't.'

Joe looked at her, wondering whether the promise wasn't a bit rash. But she looked so confident and self-assured that it was difficult to believe that she didn't have something up her sleeve.

'Let's all get a bit of shut-eye,' he said, standing up and yawning theatrically.

'Good idea,' said Kerry. 'Everything will seem much better in the morning.'

'Of course it will,' said Great-Aunt Eleanor.

But despite the general show of optimism, both Thomas and Sarah went up to bed conscious of the weight of responsibility on their shoulders. They couldn't *not* make a decision, but they were terrified of it being the wrong one — a decision which might lead to the death of their whole family, and all the people from Cleedale. Surely, having waited four hundred years this couldn't be what the prophecy had meant by 'freedom from this prison'. Or could it?

Kerry lay there in the dark, listening to the sniffling unhappiness of Sarah as she cried herself to sleep in the next bed.

'It'll all be OK,' she whispered, to herself as much as to comfort Sarah. And then, as she always did when she felt worried, unsure or sad, she cuddled up to Mr Simpkins to feel his soft, velvety head against her cheek.

Tomorrow would be the big day. Tomorrow would be the make-or-break day for so many people, and it all depended on the whims of one crazy old witch, Megwyn Nashe. Whether she would accept Great-Aunt Eleanor's proposal or reject it out of hand, they didn't know. She might even go crazy, destroy the whole of Cleedale and murder all the villagers. The same thoughts were spinning round the heads of all the occupants of Clee Manor that night. But it was pointless trying to speculate. Everything would become clear, but not until tomorrow!

ELEVEN

Inevitably, as it always does in the real world, if not in the tiny village of Cleedale, time passed and the morning arrived. Being used to getting up early, anyway, and having the added incentive of going up to London for the day, it was Thomas and Sarah who woke first. Their excitement ensured that they weren't the only ones awake for long.

'Good grief,' said Great-Aunt Eleanor, from her frying pan, 'I don't think I've been up this early for years.'

'It doesn't get any easier,' said Joe.

'I quite like it,' said Kerry.

'I'll remind you of that when we're back at school,' said Joe.

'That's different,' she said. 'There's nothing to get up for then.'

'More bacon, anyone?' asked Great-Aunt Eleanor.

Everyone said no. In their different ways they were all too excited about the day ahead to eat. Thomas and Sarah were keen to see what London looked like now, and Kerry and Joe were getting all keyed up to show them. It was just as well they *were* going up to London — if they hadn't been, they'd have sat around dwelling on what was happening under the lake.

'I won't make you up a packed lunch,' said Great-Aunt Eleanor, 'you'll easily find something up there to eat. Have you got enough money?'

'Yes, I think so,' said Joe.

'Well, take a bit extra,' she said, rummaging round in her handbag for her purse and pulling out a couple of crisp notes.

'Thanks a lot,' said Joe.

'Yeah, thanks,' said Kerry.

'Right, get all your things together,' she said, 'and I'll run you to the station.'

It was the first time that Thomas or Sarah had been in a moving vehicle not pulled by a horse. They asked questions about what the pedals did and why Great-Aunt Eleanor had to keep moving the stick with her left hand, but it was more out of politeness than interest. And they didn't understand the replies anyway. Like the radio and the television, the car was another unfathomable, twentieth-century box. This one just happened to have wheels.

It was when they overtook a cyclist that both of them became really animated.

'What's that?' exclaimed Sarah.

'A bike,' said Kerry. 'You've got those, haven't you?'

'I've never seen anything like that in my life,' she answered.

'Those things he's turning with his feet make it move, do they?' said Thomas.

'The pedals? Yeah,' said Kerry.

'That's really clever,' said Thomas. 'Why doesn't he just fall off?'

'You keep your balance when you're moving,' said Kerry.

Thomas remained speechless for the rest of the journey. And when he mumbled 'incredible' as Great-Aunt Eleanor was parking in front of the station, it had nothing to do with the fact that the car could also reverse, nothing to do with the Victorian cast-iron splendour of the station, nothing to do with the sight of the railway lines. It was because he had caught sight of another of the miracle bikes, leaning up against a wall.

Kerry and Joe could only smile.

Apart from a few commuters and one old man who was sweeping the ticket-office area, the station was deserted. Great-Aunt Eleanor, surprising even herself by her sudden organizational skills, got everything sorted out. She bought their tickets, checked the times of the trains, and found out which platform to head for.

'We're lucky,' she said, handing all four tickets to Joe. 'It's a through train, so you won't have to change at Reading, and so is the 18.32 this evening. So try and get that one. Your train leaves in four minutes, so I think you ought to get down to the platform. Platform Two. OK?'

They all thanked her once again.

'Have fun,' she said.

'We will,' they assured her, and set off.

Half-way up the steps which took them over the tracks, Sarah turned round.

'Eleanor,' she said nervously, 'I think we've already decided we want to stay. But . . .' She stopped.

'You're still worried about your family and friends,' said Great-Aunt Eleanor. 'Don't worry. I'm going to talk to Megwyn today and, well . . . Let's hope for the best.'

She winked encouragingly at Sarah.

'Come on!' Thomas called out.

'You'd better go,' said Great-Aunt Eleanor, smiling as the girl turned and ran off.

But Great-Aunt Eleanor stood there a moment longer. The smile slowly disappeared from her face and she gazed blankly down at the floor. If Megwyn Nashe was as unpredictable as she had the horrible idea she might be, today was going to test her powers of reasoning and coercion to the very limit.

As she drove away in the car, wondering exactly how she should tackle the volatile Megwyn, the children were just getting on the train.

'And these tracks run all the way to London?' said Thomas.

'Yep,' said Joe, in his element now that the sightseeing day had begun. 'All the way there, and all the way back. There are railway lines running all over the country: right up to the north of Scotland, over to the tip of Cornwall, and they all link up.'

Thomas shook his head in disbelief. 'I didn't know that people could be so clever,' he said.

Joe smiled. He felt all proud and somehow responsible for the fact that men and women in *his* century were so much further advanced than at the time when Thomas and Sarah lived. He was going to do everything he could to make sure that at the end of the day they came away thinking that the twentieth century was just fantastic.

'You're sure that the floor is safe?' said Sarah nervously, as the train began to pick up speed.

'Oh, the odd passenger falls through,' said Joe. 'But they employ special people to scrape them up off the tracks.'

'Joe!' said Kerry sharply. 'Stop it!'

'Well, honestly!' he said. 'Of course it's safe.'

Sarah remained unconvinced and sat with her legs curled up on the chair for the rest of the journey. Just in case.

'Do you know what I remember most about London?' said Thomas. 'The smells.'

'Nice or horrible?' said Joe.

'Both,' said Thomas. 'There was the smell of oranges, which was new. And barrels of fishy oysters. And walking past the ale-houses, there was a strange smell of old beer mixed in with the straw and sawdust. And then perfume,' he continued, re-miniscing. 'All the women had a different perfume on: roses, lavender, and things I'd never even smelled before. But then underneath all those perfumes and fragrances was the smell of human filth.'

'What, you mean the people were dirty?' said Joe.

'Well, they looked all right. But all the streets were narrow and the sewers used to run right down the middle of the road. And I can remember father warning us to keep an eye open for the women emptying their buckets from the windows.'

'What?' said Kerry. 'They'd just throw all the waste out of the window?'

'Yes,' said Thomas and Joe.

'*All* of it?' said Kerry, giggling.

'All of it,' the other two confirmed.

'That's why the Great Plague came,' said Joe matter-of-factly. '1665, it was.'

'Plague?' said Thomas, and shuddered.

'Don't worry,' said Kerry, 'there's no plague in London now!'

They all fell thoughtfully silent and as the landscape sped past, like smeared paint on the windows, they drifted off into their own private daydreams. Gradually, the green and yellow of the fields gave way to the suburban shades of brick-red and grey.

'Not long to go now,' said Joe.

And no sooner had he spoken than the train slowed down and entered the huge, dirty, iron and glass framework covering the station.

'It'll quieten down a little soon,' said Joe, seeing the panic on the faces of Thomas and Sarah at being confronted with so many people. 'They're just commuters off to work.'

Almost like seeing them for the first time, Joe watched the countless thousands of men in suits and women on heels speeding along the platforms.

'What are they all carrying?' said Sarah, pointing at the briefcases that each and every one was swinging along at their side.

'Their sandwiches, probably,' said Kerry and laughed.

'Let's brave it, then,' said Joe, opening the carriage door and stepping down on to the platform. 'Don't wander off!' he instructed Sarah and Thomas strictly, realizing for the first time what a nightmare it must have been for his parents having two young children.

Very soon, they all discovered that it was quite impossible to go any slower than the hurrying crowd of people and abandoned themselves to the pace of the majority. When they emerged on the other side of the ticket barriers into the great hall, however, both Sarah and Thomas automatically stopped and looked around. It was all on such a massive scale. They felt tiny and insignificant standing there in such an excess of space.

'Come on, let's find a bench and wait for it to thin out a bit,' said Joe.

No one objected to his suggestion and, while the Cartwrights soaked up the sheer volume of noise and bustle, Joe went off for refreshments.

'I'll try not to say this too often,' said Thomas, 'but I've never seen anything like this before in my life.'

'What, exactly?' asked Kerry.

'The whole lot. The number of people, that busy rushing sound, the seriousness on everyone's faces. Everything,' he said, with a sweep of his arms that took in the whole station scene.

'Right,' said Great-Aunt Eleanor. 'Let's see what kind of mood you're in today.' She walked across the sitting-room floor to the mantelpiece and turned the mirror round. As she had hoped, the reflection hadn't returned. Instead, she found herself looking down into Megwyn's room. Like the children, she couldn't help being impressed by the modern appearance of the place: the TV in the corner, the bookshelves, the air-conditioning unit. They all *looked* right, but that was as far as it went. Nothing functioned. Nothing could come to life at the press of a switch because it was all a big sham.

'Yes?' came a voice from the settee. Great-Aunt Eleanor looked over and saw, to her horror, that Megwyn was lying there, motionless. Her stillness and deathly pallor merely completed the impression that the room was nothing more than a morgue.

'I didn't see you there,' said Great-Aunt Eleanor.

'Evidently not,' said Megwyn, her voice echoing. 'What do you want?'

'To talk. To ask you what you've decided about my proposal.'

'Decide? What is there to decide?' said Megwyn.

'Stop playing games,' said Great-Aunt Eleanor firmly.

Megwyn pulled herself up off the settee and turned her back to the screen. 'I like games,' she said sulkily.

Great-Aunt Eleanor watched the back of the defiant old

woman. She looked so isolated in the middle of the room she'd created.

'Megwyn, Megwyn,' she said wearily. 'Aren't you lonely down there?'

Megwyn spun round. 'Of course I'm lonely,' she shouted. 'What else could I be?'

'But you've exiled yourself. It was *your* decision to cut yourself off for ever. If you're not even happy now, why did you do it? Why do you continue to do it?'

Thomas and Sarah loved the milkshakes and the hamburgers. They even liked the slimy green gherkin which Kerry and Joe always picked out and threw away. In fact, it was difficult to find anything that didn't interest or excite them. By the time they'd finished the take-away the crowds had dispersed a little and they set off for the centre on the Tube.

'And we go right underground?' said Thomas, as Joe followed the Tube signs.

'Right under. It even goes underneath the river,' he added, knowing, as Thomas and Sarah went totally silent, that he had impressed them again.

This silence continued as they cautiously went down the escalator, gripping the rubber handrail for all they were worth. When they got to the bottom, both of them became mesmerized by the sight of the stairs disappearing under the pavement and had to be dragged off by Kerry and Joe before they fell flat on their faces.

The train soon approached, bringing with it that stale smell. Thomas looked up.

'That's like the London stench I remember,' he said.

They passed through the stations: Edgware Road, Marylebone, Regent's Park, where Joe pointed out that they were below London Zoo, and Oxford Circus, until they arrived at Piccadilly Circus.

'I know that we've just travelled under the city, but somehow

I can't believe it,' said Thomas, as they emerged into the light. 'Does that make any sense?'

'Not really,' said Joe.

'Wow!' said Sarah, the sight of the flashing neon lights all round the Circus wiping out all other thoughts.

'It's spectacular,' said Thomas, gazing round in awe.

'I suppose it is,' said Joe, envying the two for experiencing everything for the first time.

They crossed to the central island where the statue of Eros was blindly pointing its arrow into the middle of nowhere, and sat down on the steps for a breather.

'He's the God of Love,' Kerry was explaining, but neither Thomas nor Sarah were paying attention. They were totally absorbed by the young people sitting all around them.

'Look at him!' whispered Sarah, and started giggling at a skinny punk with a fluorescent-orange Mohican.

'And her over there,' said Thomas, pointing at a girl who'd had all her hair shaved off except for a small cross at the back.

'Don't make it so obvious,' said Joe.

'We thought everyone would look like you two,' explained Sarah, who, like her brother, was unable to take her eyes off the constant parade of different styles wandering past.

There was a sudden screeching of brakes followed by a torrent of abuse and loud barking. A dog on a piece of string had pulled free of its owner and chased a pigeon into the street. The skidding bus had only just managed to stop in time and the driver was screaming at no one in particular about what he would like to do with dogs that ran out into the road.

'It's all so *exciting*!' squealed Sarah, grinning from ear to ear.

Great-Aunt Eleanor returned to the sitting-room with a mug full of strong black coffee. She looked into the mirror.

'Still there, are you? Yes, of course you are. Silly question, really,' she said.

Megwyn scowled back at her. 'Where've you been?'

' I just thought I'd get myself a nice cup of coffee.'

'Coffee?'

'Oh, just a delicious beverage that you'll probably never get to taste,' said Great-Aunt Eleanor.

'Why do you hate me so much?' said Megwyn.

'I don't hate you, I pity you.'

'Why?'

'Because you look so bored,' said Great-Aunt Eleanor.

'I AM bored!' screamed Megwyn. 'I am bored to death!'

'But you're not dead, are you?'

'Do you know,' said Megwyn, ignoring her comment, 'the best thing about Kerry and Joe being here was having someone a bit more interesting to talk to. They weren't quite on my level, of course, but they were infinitely more advanced than the dullards of Cleedale.'

'You stupid woman,' said Great-Aunt Eleanor. 'The only reason Kerry and Joe are interesting is because of their background — and that is precisely what you have deprived everyone else in the village of. If they're boring, it's because *you* have made them boring. You, and you alone, are to blame, Megwyn Nashe.'

'Hey, look, a squirrel,' shouted Sarah.

'Yeah,' said Kerry. 'But it's not like Tag, is it?'

'It's bigger,' said Sarah.

'It's a grey one,' said Kerry.

'I didn't realize that there would still be areas with squirrels in the middle of such a big city,' said Thomas.

'Well, you've got to have somewhere to walk your dog,' said Joe.

They were crossing Green Park down towards Buckingham Palace. The sun was shining bright and hot, and the whole park was littered with men and women lying out on the grass in the shade of the plane trees.

'There are so many people,' said Thomas. 'Everywhere!'

'Yeah,' said Joe, 'some of them work around here, I suppose, but most of them are tourists.'

'From other countries,' said Kerry. 'I should think that you are the only two from a different century!'

'Makes us rather special then, doesn't it?' said Thomas.

'I suppose it does,' Joe agreed, 'but I wouldn't go shouting about it. You're likely to get locked up.'

They stood outside the gates of the Palace and watched the guards in their red jackets and bearskin hats. The flag was flying which, as far as Joe knew, meant that the Queen was at home.

'Can't we go and say hello, then?' said Thomas.

''Fraid not,' said Joe.

'Some things never change,' said Thomas. 'We weren't allowed to say hello to the other one, either.'

From Buckingham Palace they walked along to the Houses of Parliament and Westminster Abbey. Thomas and Sarah continued to be impressed by everything they saw: the intricacy of the stonework on the buildings; the number of people with gaudy Hawaiian shirts and massive-lensed cameras; the little red and green men who told you when, and when not, to cross the dangerous roads; the taste of Cornettos, and cheese and onion crisps.

'The Prime Minister lives down there,' said Joe at the end of Downing Street. 'At number 10.'

'Can we go and see?' said Thomas.

'No,' said Joe. 'The road's nearly always closed off.'

'Why?' said Thomas.

'Oh, I don't know. A lot of people don't like her. I suppose they're frightened someone will lob a bomb through her window or something.'

'Does that sort of thing happen a lot, then?' said Thomas.

Joe thought for a couple of seconds.

'Not in London,' he answered.

Sarah didn't like the wings flapping round her ears at first.

She stood there, with her hands tucked in and her arms wrapped protectively around her head. But gradually, she got used to the pigeons and when Joe bought her a little tub of corn to feed them with, she stuck her hand out, giggling as they came in to land on her arm and shoulder to get to the food.

'And that's Nelson,' Joe said, continuing his potted and extremely idiosyncratic summing-up of the history of London. 'He was an admiral and he lost his arm and his eye and when he was dying, everyone thought he said, "Kiss me, Hardy", but he didn't. He said, "Kismet, Hardy", which means "Fate!"'

Thomas was nodding and making appropriate noises, but he had long since stopped taking in what Joe was rattling on about. It was all too much.

Suddenly, there was a loud bang. Thomas immediately thought that it must be one of those bombs exploding, but it was just a car backfiring. At once, all the pigeons, whether they had been strutting around the square, perching on the surrounding buildings, or feeding from the tourists' outstretched hands, left where they were and flapped noisily into the air. For half a minute they circled round and round in the sky before returning to the exact spot they had left to continue with whatever they had been doing before.

'Why do they always come back?' said Thomas.

'I suppose because they live here,' said Joe.

'But they could go anywhere in the whole world,' said Thomas, looking up at the sky. 'Why here?'

'Probably because they're so well fed,' said Joe, laughing.

'It's funny, though, isn't it?' said Thomas. 'Them all staying here even though they're free. I wonder what we'll all do if . . . when, I mean, when we're free.'

'Why don't you release them?' said Great-Aunt Eleanor.

'I don't want to,' said Megwyn simply.

'Come on,' said Great-Aunt Eleanor. 'I can't believe that it's all malice. Not after four hundred years: you must have got fed up with bearing that grudge ages ago.'

She watched Megwyn carefully for clues as to what she was thinking. But it was difficult to determine what, if anything, was going on behind those lifeless eyes.

'There's some other reason, isn't there?' she persisted.

Megwyn remained silent.

'Isn't there?' she said.

'Yes,' said Megwyn, sounding exasperated. 'Yes, there is another reason. The spell could have gone wrong and they'd all have drowned. I didn't want that: I'm not *all* bad. I do have some feelings.'

'I'm sure you have,' said Great-Aunt Eleanor. 'But that still isn't the real reason.' She narrowed her eyes and looked carefully at the old witch. 'It's something to do with you, isn't it?' she said.

'You're too clever for your own good,' said Megwyn bitterly.

'Bull's-eye,' said Great-Aunt Eleanor. 'So what, exactly is the difficulty?'

Megwyn looked at her great-great-descendant. She was beginning to realize that things were progressing with or without her consent. It was her own fault for making that damned prophecy. If she'd kept her thoughts about the future to herself there wouldn't have been anything to come true! As it was, Megwyn felt she was being pushed further and further into an inescapable corner.

'The difficulty,' she said quietly, 'will be in staying alive if I reverse the spell. It wasn't enough for me merely to mix up the necessary ingredients, I had to breathe life into my creation. If I try it again it could mean farewell Megwyn Nashe.'

Great-Aunt Eleanor continued to look at the old woman impassively. There was so much that she could learn from her if only they could get together. And yet she couldn't allow herself to forget the main aim of their discussion, which was to secure the release of Cleedale from the witch's clutches.

'You're saying that it could kill you,' she said.

'Precisely,' said Megwyn.

'But,' said Great-Aunt Eleanor, slowly and clearly, 'you are not sure.'

'Not a hundred per cent,' Megwyn admitted.

'What's going on in there?' asked Thomas.

'Oh, fruit machines, Space Invaders,' said Joe.

'What?' said Thomas.

'Let's go in and have a go,' said Joe.

Funland was full, wall to wall and row after row, of automatic machines. People of all ages, shapes and sizes were busy pushing coins into the slots as fast as they could and watching the oranges, cherries and bells spin round. Occasionally, the mechanical clink, clink of a winning pay-out would fill the hall.

'What are they doing?' asked Sarah.

'Trying to win some money,' said Kerry. 'You put 10p in here, and if you get three of a kind along here, then you win something. Do you want a go?'

Sarah took the coin, put it in the slot and pressed the START button. The fruit spun round and then, one by one, came to a halt. Orange, bell, lemon.

'Now what?' said Sarah.

'That's it,' said Kerry. 'You lost.'

'Well, I can't see much point in that,' said Sarah.

'Have another go,' said Kerry.

This time when she put the money in, the whole row started flashing.

'Hold that and press START,' Kerry instructed.

As the winning line of lemons rewarded Sarah noisily with a trayful of coins, she suddenly began to see the fun in gambling.

'Another go,' she said.

'Don't you think that after so long it might be time to take a little risk?' said Great-Aunt Eleanor.

'A little risk!' shouted Megwyn. 'My life's at stake.'

'Even better,' Great-Aunt Eleanor replied. 'You'll be able to take a *big* risk.'

Megwyn stared at her, bemused.

'An actual matter of life and death,' she said. 'Isn't that exactly what you need after four hundred years of being bored to death? Just what the doctor ordered, I'd have thought!'

'You're crazy,' said Megwyn.

'I certainly am not crazy,' said Great-Aunt Eleanor. '*I'm* not the one who's spent the last four hundred years cooped up under a lake. *I'm* not the one who's got no one to talk to, nowhere to go to, and nothing to do. I'm not surprised you're going bonkers, quite frankly, Megwyn.'

'Bonkers?' said Megwyn.

'Yes, bonkers: crackers, screwy, nutty, loopy . . . Crazy, my dear Megwyn. Crazy.'

Megwyn looked confused. 'I'm not sure I understand,' she said. 'You think that I ought to go ahead and try the spell even though I might not survive.'

'Well, naturally,' said Great-Aunt Eleanor, as cheerfully and enthusiastically as she could manage. 'What other options are there open to you? You certainly can't continue living the way you are at the moment.'

'I could always come up in a windbag, like the children,' she said. 'I must say I thought that was incredibly inventive of them.'

'But what about the people in the village?' said Great-Aunt Eleanor, suddenly fearing that the old witch might appear in the flesh.

'You're right,' said Megwyn, 'the air bubble under the lake would collapse.'

Great-Aunt Eleanor breathed a sigh of relief.

'And just think what you could achieve if you *were* successful,' she said, continuing with the same jolly optimism and appealing to the witch's greed.

'Yes,' said Megwyn, 'young Kerry and Joe have already given me one or two excellent ideas.'

'Once in a while, everyone has to take a chance, to make a gamble. Otherwise, you might just as well not be alive at all.'

'Have a go on this,' said Joe, introducing Thomas to 'Stakeout'. 'You're a marine, and they're terrorists who've laid a whole load of booby traps. You've got to kill them all before they kill you.'

Joe stuck his 30p in and started frantically thrashing the buttons on either side of the machine in an attempt to blow the terrorists away. Thomas just looked at Sarah and shrugged. When Joe's marine was finally fatally wounded and the action stopped, Thomas decided not to bother with a go.

'Not impressed?' said Joe.

'Seems a bit pointless, really,' said Thomas.

They left Funland with its flashing machines and blank-faced punters still feeding the money in as fast as they could, and headed off for Covent Garden.

'It used to be a fruit and vegetable market,' said Joe.

'Are you sure?' asked Thomas.

''Course I'm sure,' said Joe. Looking round at the rows of tiny shops, cafés and stalls, however, it was difficult to imagine. Out on the piazza, two jugglers were performing. Both were wearing multi-coloured harlequin suits and floppy caps with bells on the end. They were standing in the middle of a huge crowd of people who kept bursting out in appreciative applause. Balls, skittles, hoops; the men tossed them all up, higher and higher, over to one another and back again. The jugglers' hands moved so quickly that it was impossible to follow the path of any of the individual objects as they flew through the air. And as the tricks became increasingly complicated, the clapping grew louder. And in turn, the applause spurred the performers on to still more intricate feats of dexterity. They pulled sticks of wood out of a case, lit them and began tossing the flaming torches back and forth between them. The burning light followed intricate patterns as it sped under the jugglers' legs, behind their backs and round their necks. Thomas and Sarah applauded the act enthusiastically. And the sound of the cheering and whistling brought on a finale which was to top everything that had gone before. Adding three more of the torches, they juggled these, plus the balls, and the skittles, while each kept his balance astride a monocycle.

'More, more,' Thomas shouted, tossing money into the cap which was being passed round.

Great-Aunt Eleanor felt rather sick. She knew that she had almost convinced Megwyn to have a go at reversing the spell she'd cast over Cleedale, and yet the witch still hadn't actually said yes.

'I can see you in the twentieth century,' she said. 'You'd adapt in no time.'

And yet as she sat on watching the curious old woman in her mock-modern sitting-room, Great-Aunt Eleanor couldn't help but feel apprehensive. If the spell went wrong, all the people in the village could die. If the spell went as planned but Megwyn escaped, there was no knowing the power she might release on an unsuspecting world. Great-Aunt Eleanor felt almost like a juggler. She had the lives of so many people in her hands. As long as she didn't make a mistake they would all be OK, but one slip, one moment of doubt, one error of judgement, and the whole lot would come crashing to the ground.

Megwyn looked up and stared into Great-Aunt Eleanor's eyes. Eleanor returned the look: would the balls stay up in the air or not?

'Yes,' said Megwyn simply. 'For better or worse, I've decided to have a try.'

'You mean you're going to attempt to reverse your spell?' said Great-Aunt Eleanor, just to make sure.

'Yes, that's what I'm going to do,' said Megwyn.

'What shall we do now, then?' said Joe.

'You're the guide,' said Thomas.

'Well, what about St Paul's Cathedral?' he suggested.

'I've seen it,' said Thomas.

'Not this one, you haven't,' said Joe. 'Your one was burnt down in the Great Fire. Or we could go to the Science Museum and you could catch up on the last four hundred years of inventions.'

Neither Sarah nor Thomas seemed that keen.

'OK, then,' said Joe. 'We could take a boat down to Hampton Court. I think that was where your Elizabeth used to live. And there's a good maze there. Not there either?' he said, noting their lack of enthusiasm.

'Or . . .'

'I think we're all a bit tired,' said Kerry.

Joe looked at his watch. 'Blimey!' he said, 'I'm not surprised. It's half five. If we're going to get that through train, we ought to be getting back to Paddington.'

Sitting on the Tube again, Thomas and Sarah looked around them, then at one another and smiled. It had already started to become familiar. Without even needing to think about it they knew that this was 'when' they wanted to live.

'We can always come back and see some of the rest,' said Sarah to Kerry.

'You've decided what you want to do, then?' said Kerry.

'There wasn't ever really any doubt, was there?' said Sarah. 'I just thought that your Great-Aunt Eleanor wanted us out of the way for the day.'

'I think you could be right,' said Kerry, smiling.

Sarah was growing on her. Now that she wasn't trapped in the village with her single-word 'wet' character keeping her so anxious and boring, she really was quite nice.

'How do you think she's done?' asked Sarah.

'Well, we haven't known her for long,' said Kerry. 'But I have the feeling that if anyone can convince Megwyn Nashe then Great-Aunt Eleanor is the one.'

'I think you're right,' said Sarah.

'Do you mind if I watch?' said Great-Aunt Eleanor.

'Not at all,' said Megwyn. 'If I am going to go out in a blaze of glory I might as well have an audience.'

Great-Aunt Eleanor didn't know whether to be delighted or appalled that Megwyn had decided to give it a go. She could only keep her fingers crossed and hope that nothing too dreadful occurred. By watching, maybe she could learn something which might help her limit the Weather Witch's power.

Megwyn carried the mock-computer down to her hexagonal laboratory and set it up so that Great-Aunt Eleanor could watch her genius at work. First, she dragged a huge copper cauldron to the very centre of the laboratory, and then proceeded to collect an assortment of items from the many drawers around the room. One by one, she added them to the cauldron, mumbling aloud the name of the ingredient and its quantity. Great-Aunt Eleanor watched intently, making a note of everything the old witch was doing. The longer she watched, the more impressed she became. Megwyn was, indeed, a master of her craft.

> 'One flurry of snowflakes
> One nip in the air
> Three sunny intervals
> One frosty reception
> Two dew drops
> One grain of truth
> Two winds of change
> One heat of the moment
> Three old windbags
> One mare's tale
> One pound of mackerel sky . . .'

And so it went, on and on and on. The list continued, and

Great-Aunt Eleanor knew that the ingredients were so abstract that she would never be able to reproduce the spell.

'And one final ray of sunshine and we're there,' said Megwyn. 'This is it, then,' she said, turning round to face Great-Aunt Eleanor. 'With a little bit of luck, I'll be out and standing next to you before very much longer. If you put the kettle on I'll be able to try this "coffee" you say is so delicious.'

Great-Aunt Eleanor smiled. 'So what is the last thing you have to do?' she asked. 'Have you added everything you need?'

'All the necessary ingredients are ready,' said Megwyn, 'but lifeless. A spell must live if it is to take effect.' She looked down into the heavy cauldron. Thick mists of vapours were coiling out of it. 'What you put in a spell is only half the story,' said Megwyn. 'Useless on its own.'

'What do you have to do, then?'

'I've got to breathe life into them,' said Megwyn. 'And this is the most difficult part, so wish me luck.'

Great-Aunt Eleanor remained silent. She watched motionlessly, scarcely daring to breathe herself as the old witch closed her eyes, took a long, deep breath and bent down over the cauldron. Her long, silvery-grey hair dipped down into the seething elements and as she exhaled, her whole body seemed to empty itself. Thick vapours poured out of the cauldron and the entire room began to shake violently.

Suddenly, the picture in the mirror stopped. Great-Aunt Eleanor stared a little longer, but all she could see was her own face reflected back at her.

'Oh dear,' she said and shuddered.

Hoping that the Weather Laboratory might appear, she continued to look in the mirror. Then, without any warning, there was a blinding, blue flash from the other side of the glass. Great-Aunt Eleanor automatically shielded her eyes, and as she turned away, the mirror came away from the wall and crashed to the floor.

'Good grief,' said Great-Aunt Eleanor, stepping back from the shower of broken glass. 'Now what?'

She was trembling uncontrollably, wishing that there was some way of knowing exactly what had happened.

The train got in as scheduled and Great-Aunt Eleanor, who had taken great pains not to be late by setting three different alarm clocks and writing little notes to herself which she left all over the house, was there waiting for the children on the platform.

'Good day?' she said brightly.

'Fantastic,' said Thomas and Sarah.

'I take it you've decided you'd quite like to stay in the twentieth century, then?' said Great-Aunt Eleanor.

'Oh yes,' said Thomas. 'We just couldn't go back to living in the village now. Not knowing what's here above the lake.'

Great-Aunt Eleanor simply smiled.

They all piled into the car and set off back to the house. At first, everything was fine, but then as they continued along the road it began to get misty. And as they went further, the mist thickened and thickened until they found themselves in the middle of fog so dense that Great-Aunt Eleanor was forced to crawl along at under five miles an hour, with her headlamps full on.

'Well?' said Joe finally, exasperated by his great-aunt's irritating silence.

'Well what, dear?' she said innocently.

'Did you manage to persuade Megwyn or not?' he said.

'Oh dear,' she said, 'I am *so* sorry. I really didn't intend keeping you on tenterhooks. It's just that I was concentrating on driving, what with the fog and everything. Well, let me see,' she said, and proceeded to tell them everything that had happened between her and Megwyn.

They all listened closely to her tale, not letting a single detail slip by without checking it. And when she reached the end, they all groaned out loud.

'So you *still* don't know what's happened?' said Thomas.

'I'm afraid I can only hope,' said Great-Aunt Eleanor. 'As I said, she leant forward over her cauldron, like someone taking an inhalation bath, though she was breathing out, of course, not in. And then suddenly there was a flash and the mirror shattered. Oh, this awful weather! I've never known anything like it.'

After over an hour's painfully slow drive they finally got back to the house. The nearer they had got, the thicker the fog had become and the only conclusion they could come to was that it was coming off the lake. Something was evidently taking place, though it was impossible to say whether or not it had been caused by Megwyn.

'She said that she had to breathe life into her spell,' said Great-Aunt Eleanor. 'Let's just hope that for Cleedale and the villagers, it *was* a breath of life, and not the kiss of death.'

TWELVE

The fog was so thick and pervasive that it even started coming into the house and although no one could smell anything unusual, the effect it had on the occupants of Clee Manor was that of a powerful sleeping potion. All five of them slept more heavily that night than at any other time before or since in their lives. It is difficult to know whether they would ever have woken up at all if they hadn't been roused by an insistent hammering at the door. Joe looked blearily at his watch and was horrified to see that it was almost midday. Great-Aunt Eleanor stirred at the sound of the echoing knock and, pulling on her dressing-gown, went downstairs to see who it was.

'Susan, Mick,' she shouted.

Kerry and Joe heard her from their rooms and raced downstairs to see if the names were just a strange coincidence. They weren't disappointed, though. Standing in the hallway were their parents. Together.

'Mum! Dad!' they both yelled and skidded over to them.

'Hiya, you two,' said Susan.

'You're back, Dad,' said Kerry, hugging him tightly and almost choking with happiness.

'And you're with each other again,' said Joe, grinning.

'That we are,' said Mick. 'Hey, Joe. Crewcut, eh?'

'Yes, what have the pair of you been doing to your hair?' said Susan.

'Don't worry, Joe,' said Mick, 'she never liked my hair short, either.'

'Kerry,' said Susan, 'what are these colours?'

'They'll wash out,' said Kerry quietly.

'I don't think either of them had much choice in the matter,' said Great-Aunt Eleanor cryptically. 'It was something the boy of autumn and girl of spring had to do, wasn't it, children?'

214

Joe and Kerry nodded happily. Their parents looked at each other and decided not to pursue the conversation any further. As far as they were concerned, Great-Aunt Eleanor hadn't changed a bit.

'Anyway, what brings you here?' said Great-Aunt Eleanor.

'Well, we . . . that is, Mick . . .' began Susan.

'I've been an idiot,' said Mick. 'I can't think what I was playing at. I don't want us to split up.' He gave Susan a big hug.

'He turned up last night in the van and said we were all off to Europe for a holiday,' said Susan. 'He didn't know you two were with your great-aunt,' she added to the children.

'So we've driven down to pick you up,' said Mick. 'Nearly didn't find the place either: I've never seen fog so thick.'

'So you're leaving us, are you?' Great-Aunt Eleanor said a little sadly to the children. 'Still, I'm sure you'll have a wonderful time.'

Kerry and Joe looked at her. They couldn't have been more happy to know that their parents were back together, and the prospect of going abroad for the rest of the holiday was fantastic, and yet . . . If only they could have left it till the following day. Just so they'd have known what had happened to the lake, and to Cleedale, and to Megwyn Nashe.

'Couldn't we just stay till tomorrow,' said Joe, 'till the fog clears and everything?'

'We've got masses to show you,' said Kerry, who was just as happy about her parents as she was miserable at the prospect of having to leave with everything unresolved.

'Can't, I'm afraid,' said Mick.

'Oh, go on!' they both said in unison.

'I've got the ferry tickets for later today,' said Mick. 'I can't change them now.'

'Come on, then,' said Susan. 'Go and get your things together.'

Both of them realized that they weren't going to get anywhere by arguing.

'Who is "us"?' asked Mick, as Kerry and Joe went upstairs for their bags.

'I beg your pardon?' said Great-Aunt Eleanor.

'You said that they're leaving "us",' said Mick.

'Ah, yes, I've had a couple of other children staying. They're erm . . . local. I thought it would be nice for Kerry and Joe to have someone their own age to play with.'

'Very thoughtful of you,' said Susan, 'and I'm very grateful that you could take them.'

'It was my pleasure,' said Great-Aunt Eleanor. 'My pleasure entirely.'

It hardly took Kerry and Joe any time at all before they were ready and, having said their happy-sad goodbyes to Sarah and Thomas and promised to visit Great-Aunt Eleanor again soon, they followed their parents out to the Dormobile.

'Just a couple of . . .' Joe started to say as a last attempt to stay and find out what happened.

But Great-Aunt Eleanor motioned him to be silent with a finger over her mouth.

'I'm sure that everything is still happening just the way it's meant to be happening,' she said fatalistically.

Kerry felt a lump in her throat as the old woman leant down to kiss her goodbye.

'It looks as though *everything*'s turned out all right, doesn't it?' Great-Aunt Eleanor whispered, nodding over to Susan and Mick sitting on the front seat. 'And you *will* be back, you know,' she said with a wink. 'That I can guarantee.'

Both Kerry and Joe smiled up at her bravely. They knew exactly what she meant — and it did make them feel a little better. Before the summer, all the events had been conspiring to bring the children down to the lake to fulfil the old prophecy: Mick and Susan had split up; Susan had been worried by the reports in the newspapers; and Kerry and Joe had been sent down to stay with their great-aunt. One event had followed the other with an internal logic completely unknown to the people involved. At the time, they had seemed like a series of random occurrences, but now Kerry, Joe and Great-Aunt Eleanor knew that in some way it had all been planned four hundred years earlier. Now that their parents were together again, however, and Kerry and Joe were able to leave Clee Manor, it could mean only one thing.

Cleedale was free once again!

Kerry and Joe had succeeded in their quest, and as the van was driving off into the thick fog, they whispered the end of the poem they'd come to know so well:

> 'The boy of autumn, girl of spring
> Will freedom from this prison bring.'

*

It wasn't that they hadn't wanted to go back to Cleedale as soon as possible, to find out exactly what had happened, but somehow other things took over and they just didn't get around to it. First, there had been the long camping holiday which took them all over France and Italy, then a new term at school, and Bonfire Night, followed, of course, by Christmas. The time had flown by, and though they could never forget their time in Cleedale, it gradually began to recede into the past – especially as they had both vowed never to tell anyone else of their adventures there.

If Great-Aunt Eleanor had been on the telephone they would have given her a call, but she wasn't and somehow they never got further than *meaning* to write to her. It wasn't until they heard from her the following March that they realized just how much time had passed since their time under the lake. The letter was brief and to the point.

Dear Kerry and Joe,

Do try and come down and stay this Easter. We would very much like you to see everything that we've done in the meantime,

love, G. A. Eleanor

It hadn't proved any problem whatsoever to persuade their

mother to let them go. She and Mick had been getting on so well since their mini-break-up that, if anything, they were glad to get the kids out of the flat for a short break so they could be on their own with each other.

As the train pulled into the station, everything was just the same as on their first arrival. Great-Aunt Eleanor was still wearing a multi-coloured array of clashing clothes and carrying the old, battered basket on her arm. And, as Kerry soon confirmed, she still hadn't learned how to put her make-up on properly. When they stepped down from the train, she welcomed them with the same spontaneous warmth and enthusiasm as before.

'How lovely to see you again,' she said, squeezing them both tightly.

'We're ever so sorry that we haven't written or . . .' Kerry began to say.

'Nonsense, nonsense,' said Great-Aunt Eleanor. 'There's absolutely no point at all in wasting your time putting pen to paper. I've always thought that letters were a very poor medium for communication. You're here now, and that's what counts.'

'Still got the same car, then?' said Joe, looking at the familiar yellow Citroën Diane held together by its display of good-cause stickers.

'Glub Dub?' said Great-Aunt Eleanor. 'But of course. He'll have to give up the ghost completely before I give him up.'

'It's great to be back,' said Kerry, climbing in.

'It's lovely having you,' said Great-Aunt Eleanor.

At first, they had started asking her masses of questions but Great-Aunt Eleanor had refused to answer a single one. And so they drove along to Clee Manor in silence, with both Kerry and Joe trying to guess what would confront them at the other end.

'Just be patient for a few more minutes,' said Great-Aunt Eleanor.

As on that first day when Great-Aunt Eleanor had driven the

two children to her house, she suddenly and without any warning, wrenched the steering-wheel sharply to the left to turn on to the tiny track which led down to the manor. She slammed the brakes on and Glub Dub and its occupants came to a jolting halt.

'Phew! Made it!' said Joe, wiping his brow theatrically.

'A little less of the melodrama, thank you very much,' said Great-Aunt Eleanor.

'Hey,' Kerry yelled out. 'Look who's here!'

Joe looked up to see Thomas and Sarah jumping down off the wall where they'd been sitting waiting. Kerry and Joe leapt out of the car to meet them.

'Hello!' they shouted, and all four of them started swapping their news so loudly and excitedly that no one could hear anyone else speak.

'Right!' shouted Great-Aunt Eleanor, taking control of the situation once again. 'Joe, Kerry, what would you like to do now? Are you hungry? Or would you like a little lie-down? Or perhaps a shower after your journey? Or,' she said, with twinkling eyes, 'would you like to see the village of Cleedale?'

'Cleedale,' they both said without a moment's hesitation.

'As I thought,' she said smiling. 'Excellent.'

She pulled out two velvet blindfolds from her basket and gave them to Sarah and Thomas.

'Right, put these on them,' she said.

'What's going on?' said Joe, as Thomas tied the blindfold tightly over his eyes. He tried to keep it a little bit loose so that he could peek out. But Thomas was thorough, and no light at all got under the material.

'We don't want to spoil the surprise, do we?' said Great-Aunt Eleanor. 'Now, Thomas, Sarah, help them back into the car and we'll drive them down to the house.'

Thomas and Sarah did as they were told.

As they drove down the hill, Kerry remembered the beautiful view across the lake they had suddenly had that first time as they rounded the long bend. She wondered what she would be looking at now if Great-Aunt Eleanor hadn't insisted on the blindfolds.

Having stopped the car in front of the house, Great-Aunt Eleanor, Thomas and Sarah jumped out of the car and carefully helped Kerry and Joe not to knock themselves or trip up as they too climbed out.

'Right,' said Great-Aunt Eleanor. 'All ready? Then follow me.'

Taking them by their arms, Thomas led Joe, and Sarah led Kerry round the side of the house and down a slope. Although they thought they knew where they were going, neither of them was sure. And when they found themselves going down a set of unfamiliar wooden steps they realized they'd both lost their bearings completely. The breeze was warm against their faces, and, with their eyes unable to see, the scent of spring bluebells and hyacinths seemed exceptionally powerful. Having reached the bottom of the steps, they found themselves walking along a series of wooden boards. They could tell from the sound and give under their feet that it was wood, but they still had no idea where they were. At the end, they leant against the wooden railings there and waited.

'Right,' said Great-Aunt Eleanor. 'Remove blindfolds.'

It took a couple of seconds for them to adjust to the brightness of the afternoon sunshine, but when they did and saw what was in front of them, both of them gasped in amazement.

'It's *so* lovely!' said Kerry.

'Perfect,' said Joe, looking down.

They found that the wooden board they had been led along was the old jetty. But now that the lake was empty, the jetty, rather than protruding into the water, formed a platform high above the valley. All around the hillside slopes, forming an unbroken circle, was a dark green carpet of clover, of the four-leafed variety, of course. And there at the bottom, no longer concealed under a lake, was the familiar tiny village of Cleedale.

'So it really did work,' said Joe.

'Indeed it did,' said Great-Aunt Eleanor.

'Look,' said Kerry. 'There's the church next to the duck pond, and the smithy. And over there is your house, right?' she said to Sarah.

'That's right,' said Sarah. 'The one with the smoke coming out of the chimney.'

'Shall we go down and have a closer look?' suggested Great-Aunt Eleanor.

'Yeah, let's,' said Joe excitedly.

The four of them made their way along the winding path to the bottom of the valley. From half-way down, it became apparent that theirs was one of two paths leading into the village. The second snaked its way down from Megwyn's house, and as they looked over, Kerry and Joe could see a constant stream of people walking along it, both up and down.

'Who *are* all those people?' said Kerry.

The closer they got, the more people they could see, milling around the narrow lanes, popping in and out of the buildings, looking round from the top of the church tower.

'I'm sure there are more people now than when we were last here,' said Joe.

'It seemed like the perfect solution,' said Great-Aunt Eleanor.

'What did?' said Joe.

'We've opened the whole place up to tourists,' said Great-Aunt Eleanor. 'Cleedale, an authentic slice of Elizabethan England. "Soak up the atmosphere of the days of Good Queen Bess",' she said, rattling off the blurb from the advertising brochures.

'I don't understand,' said Joe. 'I thought that as everything was so different, the villagers would want to keep themselves hidden.'

'But we simply couldn't,' said Thomas. 'You can't hide a whole village. So we turned our sixteenth-century charm into a twentieth-century marketing point.'

'Everyone assumes it's just a very good reconstruction,' said Great-Aunt Eleanor.

'Brilliant,' said Kerry. 'And is it popular?'

'Business is, as they say, booming,' said Great-Aunt Eleanor, with a big grin on her face.

'Megwyn Nashe would have been proud of us,' said Thomas.

'You mean she isn't here?' said Joe.

'No,' said Great-Aunt Eleanor, her face becoming serious, 'I'm afraid to say that Megwyn's gamble did not pay off, after all. The spell proved a little bit too strong for her.'

'They never found her body,' said Sarah in a hushed and spooky voice. 'It just vanished into thin air.'

'Like the lake,' said Thomas. 'That was what all the fog was: it lasted for nearly a week while the lake was gradually evaporating away.'

Kerry and Joe just stood there, transfixed. It was all too much to take in.

'Do you just want to wander around?' said Great-Aunt Eleanor.

'Yeah, that would be nice,' said Joe.

'I'm just going up to see how the takings are doing,' said Great-Aunt Eleanor, setting off up the path towards Megwyn's old house.

Thomas explained that they had decided to turn her place into the ticket-office and souvenir shop for two reason. Firstly, it was near the top of the hill and so was handy for the visitors' car park they had situated just behind it. Secondly, the peculiar mixture of architectures she had experimented with both inside and out made it a bit of an anomaly in the otherwise perfectly original village.

Walking round, Joe and Kerry found that everything was exactly the same as before except for the fact that tiny wooden plaques had been screwed on to the walls of the various buildings to indicate to the tourists what was inside. The dairy, the bakery, the doctor's surgery, the smithy: they were all labelled with neat signs written in the italic writing of the time.

'It's just so quaint,' Joe heard an American woman saying, as her husband proceeded to take snaps of her posing in front of the forge from every conceivable angle.

'Hello, Father,' said Thomas. 'Look who's come to visit.'

'Kerry and Joe,' said Henry, beaming widely. 'How good of you to come and visit us.'

'Still making horseshoes, then?' said Joe.

'Do you know what, Joe?' he said. 'I'm making more now than I've ever made before in my life. People buy them as good-luck souvenirs, hang them up above their doors. "Genuine, Elizabethan-styled, lucky horseshoes", we sell them as.'

'And, Carlton, will you listen to that accent?' said the excited, eavesdropping American tourist. 'It is just dinky.'

'Dinky,' said Joe, and winced.

'You must go over to the house,' said Henry. 'The others would love to see you again. We all owe you so much.'

'Oh,' said Joe, looking away in embarrassment. 'Rubbish. You don't owe us anything. We just wanted to save our own skins.'

'Stop being so modest,' said Henry. 'If it hadn't been for you two, we'd still be stuck here for ever.'

'But you *are* still here!' said Joe, laughing.

'You know what I mean,' said Henry.

'Yes, I do,' said Joe.

As they left Henry and made their way along the high street to the Cartwrights' house, Thomas turned towards Joe.

'Do you remember the pigeons in Trafalgar Square?' he asked.

Joe nodded, and smiled.

Sitting outside the squire's mansion, just as he had been the first time Joe had walked along the road with Thomas, was the lanky figure of Dan Boggle.

'Afternoon, Dan,' said Joe.

'Afternoon,' he replied, chewing his straw.

'Did you ever see your unicorn?' said Kerry.

223

'No,' said Dan, as though he was talking to an idiot himself. 'A unicorn? There ain't no such thing, is there?'

'No?' said Kerry.

'No,' Dan repeated. 'I don't know why you didn't tell me before. I may be an idiot, but I'm not stupid.'

'How did you find out they were mythological, then?' said Joe.

'I don't know about that,' said Dan, 'but I discovered that they only occur in stories and the like.'

'So you're not going off travelling?' said Kerry.

'Don't need to, do I?' he said. 'I've been looking at some of them animal programmes on the telling-vision of Miss Eleanor's. And I've seen some incredible beasts, I can tell you. Ants that cut up leaves and make their own houses, fish that can fly, frogs that live up trees — all sorts of wonderful creatures. And all in her front room. I've no need to go off travelling anywhere.'

'That's good,' said Joe.

'Are you going to the party this evening?' said Dan.

'What party?' said Joe.

'Oh, Dan,' said Sarah, 'it was meant to be a secret.'

'Sorry,' said Dan miserably.

'Oh, it doesn't matter,' said Thomas. 'Come on, you two, let's be getting back.'

'See you later, then,' said Kerry and Joe.

'Right you are,' said Dan.

And as they turned to go, a whole group of tourists appeared out of nowhere to photograph the village idiot. He played the part perfectly, grinning toothlessly as they clicked their cameras over and over in his face.

'Can I have a hat like that?' said one of the young boys in the group.

'I don't know,' said the mother.

'They're selling village-idiot hats in the shop,' her husband informed her.

'All right, then,' she said to the boy, 'I'll get you one when we leave. Now climb up on the gate next to him and I'll take a photo of the pair of you together.'

'Psst,' came a sound from behind the wall.

'I thought he'd still be here,' said Joe.

'It's me,' said Ebenezer Cudlip, poking his rodent-like head up.

'Why can't you just say hello, like any normal person?' snapped Kerry.

'I like it in this century,' he said, ignoring her. 'The rats are wonderful. All plump and sleek. I've caught hundreds of them, and do you know what?'

'What?' said Joe.

'I've even found a way of making money out of them,' he said. 'I sell them. And do you know who to? To the local laboratories, that's who.'

'Really,' said Kerry, turning away. She simply couldn't stand the creepy little man. The Ebenezer Cudlips of this world were revolting whatever century they happened to find themselves in, she thought to herself.

'See you at the party, then,' he said, as they left him.

'Not if I see you first,' Kerry muttered under her breath.

It almost felt like coming home as they patted the excited Rex on the head and went into the kitchen. Everything looked exactly as they had left it. The Cartwrights were still living without electricity, gas or any of the other amenities of the 1980s in their 'Authentic Elizabethan Cottage', as the sign outside announced.

Anne Cartwright was standing over by the cooking range, holding baby John in one arm while stirring something in a large pot with the other. Grandma Mary was sitting in her rocking-chair talking to Betty Clegg, who'd pulled a stool up next to her.

'Joe! Kerry!' they all exclaimed as the two of them walked into the room.

'Hello, all,' said Joe.

'Hello,' said Kerry, going over to look at the baby. In the eight or so months since they were last there, he had grown considerably.

'He's crawling already,' said Anne, 'whenever he gets the chance.'

'And you've had him christened, at last,' said Kerry.

'"At last" is right,' she said. 'Oh, I was *so* worried. You'll remember that. Still, all's well that ends well,' she said, and gave baby John a great big kiss on the top of his head.

'So, you two,' said Grandma Mary a little grouchily. 'You finally thought about us, did you?'

'Sorry about that,' said Joe. 'We've been meaning to . . .'

'Oh don't mind her,' interrupted Betty Clegg. 'She doesn't mean it.'

'Don't I just?' said the old woman.

'Still taking the spiders?' said Kerry, changing the subject.

'As it happens,' said Grandma Mary, 'I'm not. You might not have found a cure for the ague or the gout in your century, but you certainly know how to conceal the symptoms. I take aspirins now.'

'Better than mice?' said Joe.

'Better *for* the mice, certainly,' said Grandma Mary, chuckling hoarsely.

'So what's happened to the great Dr Beamis Kelly?' asked Joe.

'The old leech?' said Betty Clegg. 'He's never been happier. He's running a small apothecary shop down near the church. Of course, they've had to put severe restraints on the things he can put in his sweets and syrups, but they're really popular. All wrapped up in waxed paper and sold in little tins and bottles.'

'And how about you?' said Kerry. 'What are you doing now?'

'I run the crèche,' said Betty. 'It's lovely. When a big family comes, they can leave the children with me and go and explore the village without the bother of having to keep an eye on their young 'uns the whole time.'

'It sounds as though it's worked out perfectly,' said Kerry.

'There were a couple of teething troubles,' said Betty Clegg. 'Some of the villagers didn't like the idea of being watched by tourists. But they're getting used to it, and it's only for about half of the year anyway.'

'Do you talk to them much?' asked Joe.

'Oh yes,' said Betty. 'I love it. And so do they. They ask all these questions about the sixteenth century, and I ask them a whole load back. It's such an easy way to find everything out, and they think it's all a huge joke with us acting, and all. No, you're right, it couldn't have worked out better.'

'It was sad about Megwyn, though,' said Grandma Mary.

'Oh, I don't know,' said Betty Clegg. 'She wouldn't have fitted in. I can just imagine her turning some poor tourist, who annoyed her with one too many photographs, into a toad. It would have given the place a bad name.'

Outside the window there was some kind of commotion going on. Joe looked out and saw a television camera crew trundling past with their cameras, lights and microphones.

'Hey,' he said, 'they're going to make a film.'

'That'll be for the travel programme,' said Betty Clegg. *'Nice here, innit?* I think it's called. They said they'd be along today.'

' "To put us on the map," they said,' added Grandma Mary scornfully.

Kerry and Joe went out to watch. They followed the TV crew down to the pond where they were already setting their equipment up. Concealing themselves under the swinging branches of a weeping willow tree, they could look out at everything that was going on, without being seen.

'Look,' said Kerry, 'it's whatsisname. You know, the bloke from that programme.'

'Yeah,' said Joe, also recognizing the personality but equally unable to put a name to the face.

The famous, if unnameable, presenter had his face dabbed with powder by the make-up woman and then turned to face the camera. A man shouted, 'Cleedale: Take One', slammed the clapper-board shut and the film started rolling.

'I'm standing here in the middle of Cleedale,' the presenter began, reading from his autocue, 'a small Elizabethan village – no, not Charles's mother, but Elizabeth I. Or Good Queen Bess, as she was called. Around me are buildings, artefacts and villagers apparently straight out of the sixteenth century. Here, you can visit the local forge and watch the blacksmith making his horseshoes in the traditional way. You can pop into the bakery and discuss the merits of using oak chippings as opposed to beech wood in the ovens. And if you're feeling a little under the weather you can go and describe your symptoms to the apothecary who will be only too pleased to mix you up some syrup with tried and tested herbal remedies.'

'If only he knew,' Kerry whispered to her brother.

'Cleedale Village is open from the beginning of March to the end of September and is well worth a visit. It costs £3 for adults to get in, £1 for children and the unwaged. The car-parking facilities are good and there is no charge. And if little Tracey or Trevor are not keen on wandering round the village then you can leave them in the capable hands of the qualified staff in the crèche, again, free of charge. There is a souvenir shop which sells a wide selection of the various products which are made in the village, including potions, lace work, stained-glass decorations, corn dollies, and a hundred and one other high-quality items.

'I think that what impressed me so much about the whole venture is its attention to detail. You won't find anything in the village that you wouldn't have been able to find in a genuine Elizabethan village. Even the people playing the villagers here have obviously been doing their homework. Their knowledge of the methods of agriculture and cottage industry from that period is faultless, and made all the more authentic by their rich yokel accents.'

Kerry couldn't help giggling.

'Sh,' whispered Joe.

'Indeed, such has been their determination that everything should be as realistic as can be, that they have achieved the almost impossible. I was looking round the fields earlier with one of our Elizabethan experts, and he was quite astounded by the display of livestock here. Tell me, Geoffrey,' he said, turning to a second man, 'what was it that surprised you so much?'

'Well, Ken,' he said.

'Kenneth King,' whispered Kerry as she suddenly remembered the name.

'What amazed me was a certain breed of sheep and pig I saw here. In the fields they've got what looks for all the world like a Roscommon. Hornless, long-woolled, white face and legs: the perfect sheep, in fact, for this region. And down in the pens I noticed they're keeping Dorset Blacks. Beautiful pigs they are: short and round with a soft-bluish skin. The thing is, although these were, indeed, common during the time of Elizabeth I, as far as we all thought, both these particular breeds became extinct some time towards the end of the last century. I can't imagine where they got this lot from. Presumably they are some kind of hybrid cross, but I must say I was very impressed by this almost fanatical attempt to reproduce a perfect replica of the past. Very impressed indeed.'

'Thank you, Geoffrey,' said Kenneth King. 'Well, it's difficult *not* to be impressed with Cleedale. The attention to each and every detail, the friendliness of the "villagers", the setting — it all makes for a fascinating excursion for all the family. And if all that isn't enough to tempt you, one more little snippet of information. They say that it never rains here when the gates are open. What more could you ask for?'

The cameras were switched off, and as quickly as they had descended on the village, the TV men and women packed up their equipment and left. And they weren't the only ones to leave. As Joe and Kerry emerged from their hiding-place under the willow, the church bells began to peal, indicating that the village was closing in ten minutes. The tourists obediently began to file up the path, returning to their cars.

'It really was the best possible thing that could have happened,' said Kerry.

'They can get used to the twentieth century if and when they want,' said Joe.

'Sarah said that she and Thomas are going to the school in town,' said Kerry, 'and that when he's finished his A-levels, Thomas is hoping to go to college.'

'There you are!' came a voice from behind them. 'I've been looking for you all over.'

It was Great-Aunt Eleanor.

'We were watching them filming. They were very complimentary about the place,' said Joe.

'So I should hope,' said Great-Aunt Eleanor. 'It is rather wonderful, after all.'

Not for the first time, Joe and Kerry noticed that their great-aunt seemed considerably more decisive, more self-confident than when they had last seen her. She appeared to have everything under control, and loved the role of organizer she had adopted.

'Great,' said Joe.

'Right,' said Great-Aunt Eleanor, in her new self-assured manner, as she watched the last of the tourists disappearing, 'well, as you've no doubt already heard, we're having a party in your honour in the village hall, so perhaps you'd like to come along with me. They've absolutely refused to start without you.'

The sun was sinking fast below the surrounding hills and tingeing the tops of the trees with orange and red as Kerry and Joe followed their Great-Aunt Eleanor along the dusty road.

'It really is lovely here,' said Kelly.

'Isn't it,' Great-Aunt Eleanor agreed.

'I can't imagine that it could have been much more beautiful even if Megwyn had been here using her magic,' said Kerry.

'Oh, Megwyn might have died, but you shouldn't necessarily assume that all her magic died with her,' said Great-Aunt Eleanor mysteriously.

Kerry felt tingles running up and down her spine.

'That TV chap wasn't joking when he said that the weather is always good here. When I want it to be, of course,' she added.

'You mean . . .' said Joe.

'I mean that this evening's lovely sunset is no accident,' said Great-Aunt Eleanor.

'But . . .' said Joe.

'I learnt a fair bit from that old witch,' said Great-Aunt Eleanor quietly.

She raised her arm and pointed towards the old weather vane on top of the village hall. As she narrowed her eyes, a stream of lightning, blue and crackling, came pouring out from her fingertips, sending the arrow on the top spinning round and round.

Both Kerry and Joe looked at their great-aunt in genuine amazement. With Cleedale back in the real world where it belonged, surrounded once again by its ring of lucky, four-leafed clover and being guided by another woman who could

control the very elements, who could say what the future held for the village?

The Weather Witch is dead!

Long live the Weather Witch!